MALORY TOWERS

DARRELL & FRIENDS

Have you read all the

MALORY TOWERS books?

1. First Term at Malory Towers

2. Second Form at Malory Towers

3. Third Year at Malory Towers

4. Upper Fourth at Malory Towers

5. In the Fifth at Malory Towers

6. Last Term at Malory Towers

7. New Term at Malory Towers

8. Summer Term at Malory Towers

9. Winter Term at Malory Towers

10. Fun and Games at Malory Towers

11. Secrets at Malory Towers

12. Goodbye, Malory Towers

13. New Class at Malory Towers (4 short stories)

Enid Blyton

MALORY TOWERS

DARRELL & FRIENDS

Written by Narinder Dhami

HODDER CHILDREN'S BOOKS

First published in Great Britain in 2020 by Hodder & Stoughton

1 3 5 7 9 10 8 6 4 2

Malory Towers®, Enid Blyton® and Enid Blyton's signature are registered trade marks
of Hodder & Stoughton Limited
Text written by Narinder Dhami
Based on the television series produced by King Bert Productions Limited and WildBrain Ltd
and adapted for television by Rachel Flowerday and Sasha Hails.
Text © 2020 Hodder & Stoughton Limited
Cover photograph © 2019 DHX – Malory Productions Inc./Queen Bert Limited

CBBC is a trade mark of the British Broadcasting Corporation and is used under licence.
CBBC logo © BBC 2016

A CIP catalogue record for this book is available from the British Library.

ISBN 978 1 444 95722 8

Typeset in Caslon Twelve by Avon DataSet Ltd, Alcester, Warwickshire

Printed and bound by Clays Ltd, Elcograf S.p.A.

The paper and board used in this book are made from wood from responsible sources.

Hodder Children's Books
An imprint of Hachette Children's Group
Part of Hodder & Stoughton
Carmelite House
50 Victoria Embankment
London EC4Y 0DZ

An Hachette UK Company
www.hachette.co.uk
www.hachettechildrens.co.uk

CHAPTER ONE

AS THE waiting train blasted out a cloud of steam Darrell Rivers raced along the station platform. The platform was packed with people, and so was the train. Girls in the same orange and brown uniform as Darrell were hanging out of the windows, calling goodbye to their families.

Darrell headed towards the far end of the train where she could see a teacher standing beside the end carriage.

'Last call for Malory Towers!' the teacher shouted.

'I'm here!' Darrell panted. 'Darrell Rivers.'

The woman smiled. 'You're just in time! I'm Miss Potts, your form mistress.'

Mr Rivers arrived next, wheeling Darrell's trunk. Mrs Rivers and Darrell's younger sister Felicity followed more slowly, Mrs Rivers leaning on Felicity's arm. Felicity was wearing Darrell's straw boater with its orange and brown ribbon.

'Darling!' Mrs Rivers swept Darrell into a loving embrace. 'You'll get such a lot out of this new school.'

Mr Rivers placed a hand on Darrell's shoulder. 'Make sure you put a lot back.'

Darrell hugged her father, then turned to Felicity. 'Don't forget to write,' she reminded her as a porter hauled the trunk on to the train.

'As if I would!' Felicity replied, desperately wishing she was old enough to go to Malory Towers herself.

The guard blew his whistle, and Miss Potts ushered Darrell aboard the train. It was crammed with Malory Towers girls, and the noise was tremendous.

'Hello, Lottie!'

'Mary, WHAT have you done to your hair?!'

'Hilda, you never wrote to me, you meanie!'

Miss Potts led Darrell, who felt very much the new girl, to another compartment and opened the door to reveal a crowd of first-formers. Darrell blushed under their curious scrutiny.

'Another one for you,' Miss Potts said to the bright-faced girl nearest the door. 'Alicia will show you the ropes, Darrell.'

'Hello!' Alicia grinned at Darrell. 'Budge up, you lot.'

They all shuffled sideways, and Darrell squeezed in.

'Sally's a new girl too,' Alicia told Darrell, indicating the girl opposite them. Darrell smiled eagerly at Sally, but all she received in return was a tight little nod. 'There's a third one somewhere,' Alicia continued, peering through the window. 'Look! There!'

A girl in Malory Towers uniform, a sheet of pale blonde hair rippling down her back, stood on the platform, clinging to her mother. They were both sobbing dramatically.

'Poor thing,' murmured a small, slight girl in the window seat.

Another girl snorted in disgust. 'Bet you half my tuck she's faking it!' she said in a broad Scottish accent.

'Potty will sort them out,' replied a girl with a mass of untidy hair.

Miss Potts was already kindly but firmly separating the two and leading the girl away.

'Introductions!' Alicia announced. She pointed at the Scottish girl. 'Jean. Good egg.' Alicia nodded at the girl with messy hair. 'Irene. Genius at maths and music—'

'Hopeless at everything else,' Irene broke in.

'Girl in the window seat,' Alicia continued, 'Mary-Lou. Too nice for her own good!'

Mary-Lou smiled timidly at Darrell as the door to the compartment opened. 'Are you *terribly* squashed? Would you like this window seat?'

Alicia stifled a giggle as Miss Potts looked in, accompanied by the girl with blonde hair. 'Girls, this is Gwendoline Lacey.'

'Gwendoline MARY Lacey,' Gwendoline said reprovingly. 'And I'm afraid *I'll* need the window seat. I get awfully travel sick.'

She sniffed dramatically, and Miss Potts shot her a keen look before leaving. Mary-Lou kindly made space for Gwendoline, who didn't even say thank you as she sat down.

'Is that someone's sister on the platform?' Sally asked. Darrell looked out and saw Felicity waving madly at her. She was holding Darrell's straw boater.

'Your HAT!' Felicity shrieked. Then a fierce gust of wind ripped it from her hands. Darrell leapt up and headed for the door. Alicia followed, and they both jumped down from the train.

'I'm sorry!' Felicity gasped, pointing upwards.

The hat was wedged in a planter of flowers above them. The porters had piled a stack of trunks underneath, and Darrell made an instant decision. She swung herself on to the bottom trunk and quickly climbed up the others one by one. Standing on the top trunk, Darrell could just reach the hat with her fingertips.

'Hurry!' Felicity pleaded as the train's whistle sounded.

'The ten-thirty to Penzance will be leaving in one minute,' the station master announced.

Darrell launched herself down to the platform from halfway up the stack of trunks. Unfortunately her dress caught on one of them, and there was a loud ripping sound.

'Oh, no!' Felicity groaned when she saw the tear in Darrell's new dress.

Darrell grinned ruefully and dashed back to the train,

Alicia at her heels. 'Don't forget to write!' Darrell yelled, ruffling her sister's hair as she flew past.

The two girls charged back to the compartment and collapsed panting into their seats. The others were wide-eyed with admiration, except Gwendoline. *She* looked extremely disapproving.

'We're going to be great friends, Darrell!' Alicia said, and Darrell beamed at her.

'Darrell's JUST the sort of girl Mother warned me about,' Gwendoline muttered to Sally. 'A *tomboy*. And look how *short* her hair is.'

Sally said nothing and just smiled to herself.

The whistle screamed once more. The train belched out a cloud of steam as it pulled away from the station, the girls cheered and Darrell could hardly contain her excitement. *We're off!* she thought. *Malory Towers, here I come!*

CHAPTER TWO

AS THE train sped towards Cornwall the girls passed the time gossiping and singing songs. Darrell joined in enthusiastically. Sally said nothing. Neither did Gwendoline; she simply sat there looking superior.

'How come you're all changing schools?' Alicia asked, when they'd finished a rousing rendition of 'I Do Like to Be Beside the Seaside'.

'Mother says I need to be *stretched*,' Gwendoline replied solemnly.

Alicia blinked, then looked at Sally.

'I wanted to board,' Sally said shortly. Conversation over.

Alicia's eyebrows almost flew off the top of her head. 'Darrell?'

'Oh, I wanted to go to a school with a pool,' Darrell explained. 'I love swimming, and there wasn't a pool at my old school, St Hilda's—'

'St Hilda's?' Gwendoline's ears pricked up. 'My cousin's there. Apparently they asked a girl to *leave* last year. Did you know her?'

A thrill of horror ran down Darrell's spine. She was

saved from replying when an older girl stuck her head inside the compartment.

'The cliff corner's coming up!' she announced.

There was a cheer and a mad dash to the window.

'Who's *that*?' Darrell asked.

'Pamela.' Alicia grinned. 'Head girl. She's marvellous.'

I can see that, Darrell thought. The head girl looked smart, friendly and confident. Everything Darrell herself wanted to be.

'Look.' Alicia pulled her over to the window.

Darrell craned her neck to catch her first glimpse of her new school. She saw a castle-like building of grey stone with four towers, one at each corner, perched high up on a cliff above the glittering sea. The school looked serene and welcoming.

When the coach pulled up outside the imposing entrance Darrell, Sally and Gwendoline gasped in unison.

'It's HUGE!' Darrell said. 'I'll never know my way about.'

Alicia laughed. 'I'll teach you. Come on!'

Darrell, Sally and Gwendoline followed Alicia off the coach and towards the wide stone steps that led up to the entrance. They were surrounded by a sea of girls flooding in the same direction.

Darrell gazed up at the tall towers. 'It *is* just like a castle!'

'I shall feel a proper lady going up these steps—' Gwendoline said, shaking back her hair.

'You wouldn't say that if you knew what happened to the *real* Lady of Malory Towers,' Alicia interrupted wickedly. 'There's a painting of her hanging in the main corridor.'

'So what happened to her?' Sally asked.

'No one told you?' Alicia raised her eyebrows. 'We've got a GHOST here!'

Gwendoline let out a little shriek as Alicia darted away, laughing. Darrell and the others hurried after her and found themselves in a corridor bustling with girls, but Alicia was nowhere to be seen.

'Are we lost?' Gwendoline asked, peering at the throng of unfamiliar faces around them.

Darrell took charge. 'Alicia said to go to the san first, remember?'

Gwendoline looked blank.

'The sanatorium,' Darrell explained. 'The school hospital.' She pointed along the corridor. 'Let's try that way.'

The three girls hurried along, checking the rooms. Darrell opened a door and shook her head. 'Science lab,' she said.

Gwendoline was horrified. 'We have to do *science*?'

Darrell nodded. 'I like science. Daddy took me to visit his old medical school once. I'd love to be a doctor too.'

'You mean a nurse,' Gwendoline said sharply.

'*Girls* can be doctors,' Darrell said. 'Why not?'

Gwendoline sighed loudly. 'Why would you want to work anyway?'

'Mother says a woman needs a room and money of her own to be truly happy,' Sally added.

'*My* mother says girls only need jobs if they're too plain to catch a husband,' Gwendoline retorted as Darrell opened another door.

'What do you think you're doing?'

The girls spun round guiltily. A large woman with a cross face was striding towards them.

'We're looking for Matron,' Darrell replied.

'*I'm* Matron.' She eyed Darrell up and down with narrowed eyes. 'What in all that's holy happened *here?*' she demanded, pointing at the rip in Darrell's dress.

'It was an accident—' Darrell began.

'An order mark for you.' Matron said, lips pursed. 'Follow me, all of you.' She marched off down the corridor.

Darrell was aghast as they fell in behind Matron. An order mark on her first day? How horribly embarrassing.

'Thank you *so* much for taking us to our dormitory, Matron,' Gwendoline said sweetly.

'We're not going to the dorm,' Matron snapped. 'I'm taking you straight to the headmistress!'

Darrell couldn't believe her ears. Her first day at Malory Towers was turning into a disaster . . .

'It's not fair!' Gwendoline whined as the three girls stood nervously in Miss Grayling's study. 'I didn't do anything.' She directed a bitter look at Darrell. 'It was all *her*—'

'Gwendoline, you're not here because you're in trouble,' Miss Grayling said calmly. The headmistress was a slender, graceful woman with neat grey hair, a warm personality and a natural authority. 'I see all the new girls on their first night.'

'You do?' Darrell exclaimed, relieved. She had liked Miss Grayling and her comfortable study with its air of faded grandeur immediately. Thank goodness they weren't in trouble after all.

The headmistress nodded. 'It's one of my favourite moments, meeting you all on your first day, imagining what you might achieve.' She gazed enquiringly at them. 'What would you like that to be?'

Silence. Darrell glanced at Sally, but she had a frozen rabbit-in-the-headlights look on her face. Gwendoline too was silent.

'Passing our School Certificate?' Darrell blurted out, unable to think of anything else.

Miss Grayling smiled. 'Exams aren't our only measure of success, Darrell. A Malory Towers success is someone who is good-hearted and kind. Loyal and trustable.'

The headmistress caught Gwendoline's eye. Gwendoline squirmed uncomfortably.

'We hope that when you leave here you will be good sound women the world can lean on,' Miss Grayling continued. 'You will all gain tremendously from your time with us. See that you give a lot back.'

Darrell's face lit up. 'That's exactly what my father said!'

'Perhaps one day he and Malory Towers will be equally proud of you,' Miss Grayling replied.

Darrell's heart swelled with emotion. Silently she promised herself she would do her absolute best at Malory Towers. But she didn't notice the look of bitter jealousy on Gwendoline's face.

CHAPTER THREE

THAT EVENING, as the sun set over Malory Towers, Darrell was unpacking in her new dormitory in the North Tower. The dorm was bright and cheerful with rows of beds lined up opposite each other.

Darrell was thrilled to be in the same dorm as Alicia. She knew all the others too – Irene, Mary-Lou, Jean, Gwendoline and Sally. The only two students Darrell hadn't met before were Emily, a quiet, reserved girl, and Katherine, head of the first form.

Darrell stood a photo of her family on her bedside locker and stared fondly at her father, mother and Felicity. She'd have a chance to write to them soon and tell them all about her first day at school.

Sally had just finished unpacking. She also had a family photo in her hands, but to Darrell's intense surprise Sally shoved the photo inside the drawer and closed it.

How odd! Darrell thought, climbing into bed.

Everyone else was in bed now too, except Gwendoline. She was brushing her long blonde hair, counting the strokes.

'Fifty-four, fifty-five, fifty-six—'

'Lights out!' Katherine called.

Gwendoline carried on brushing.

'Hey, new girl!' Katherine said impatiently. 'What's your name – Gwendoline?'

Gwendoline sniffed. 'Gwendoline Mary actually.'

'Get into bed, please,' Katherine ordered.

'I promised Mother I'd do a hundred strokes a night,' Gwendoline protested.

'Katherine's head of form,' Jean said. 'You have to do what she says.'

'Now I've forgotten what number I got to!' Gwendoline wailed.

'Fifty-six,' Irene said helpfully.

'Bed. NOW,' Katherine said, and turned out the lights. The dorm was plunged into darkness, except for pale moonlight shining through the curtains. Gwendoline squealed and jumped underneath the covers.

Darrell snuggled down comfortably as silence fell. Her eyes were just closing when Alicia whispered, 'A long time ago, when this was a private mansion, Lady Jane Malory lived here.'

Darrell's eyes immediately snapped open again.

'Oh, *not* the ghost story!' Mary-Lou groaned.

'One day, when Lady Jane was out riding, she met and fell in love with a highwayman,' Alicia continued.

Darrell was hanging on Alicia's every word when her

attention was distracted by a strange noise. *Scratch. Scratch. Scratch.*

'What's that?' Darrell asked.

'It's Lady Jane's ghost,' Alicia replied, thoroughly enjoying herself. 'She wants to come in.'

Scratch. Scratch. Scratch.

Gwendoline screamed hysterically. 'It's inside the dorm!'

'It can't be her.' Darrell thrust back the blankets. 'Ghosts aren't real, Gwen.'

Katherine switched the lights on, and Darrell quickly identified the source of the scratching. It was coming from the cupboard at the far end of the dorm. The other girls were giggling, except Gwendoline and Mary-Lou who were terrified.

'Stop it, Alicia!' Irene wheezed, snorting with laughter.

'Look, it's *not* me,' Alicia insisted.

Bravely Darrell grasped the door handle and pulled the cupboard open. All she could see inside were piles of clean bed linen.

Then they heard the scratching again, coming from the top shelf of the cupboard. Mary-Lou dived beneath her blankets in terror while Gwendoline scrambled out of bed and fled the dorm.

Grasping the top shelf firmly, Darrell climbed upwards, using the other shelves as precarious footholds. The others watched as she began to fumble through the sheets and pillowcases stacked on the top shelf. To her bemusement she uncovered a small wicker cage behind the piles of bed linen. The door of the cage was ajar, and Darrell came face to face with a little grey mouse.

'It's not a ghost,' Darrell chuckled. 'It's a mouse!'

Footsteps sounded in the corridor, and Gwendoline reappeared, with Matron behind her.

'What's going on?' Matron asked frostily. Her jaw dropped when she saw Darrell clinging to the top shelf of the open cupboard. *'Darrell Rivers!'* she roared angrily, striding towards the cupboard.

The mouse didn't like the sound of Matron's voice. It jumped out of the cupboard down to the floor. Unhurt, it scuttled away, right near to Matron's and Gwendoline's feet.

'Help!' Gwendoline squealed, leaping on to her bed. Shrieking, Matron lifted her long skirt, hopping around in terror. The girls burst into helpless laughter as the frightened mouse vanished down a tiny hole in the floor.

Humiliated and red-faced, Matron turned her iciest glare on the giggling girls as Darrell climbed down from the cupboard. The laughter died away immediately until all that was left was a tense silence 'You, Darrell Rivers, are a troublemaker,' Matron announced furiously. 'I know your type.'

Darrell was stung. 'But, Matron—'

'No pudding for a week.' Matron stalked over to the door. 'Now, everyone, go to sleep.'

A downcast Darrell climbed into bed. She'd really got on the wrong side of Matron, and it was only her first day.

Matron paused in the doorway to nod approvingly at Gwendoline. 'Thank you, Gwendoline. You did the right thing in coming to me.'

Darrell cast a hurt look at Gwendoline. That had been a *really* sneaky thing to do.

Satisfied, Matron clicked off the lights, leaving the dorm in darkness.

CHAPTER FOUR

IT WAS still early, and the dawn was just coming up, flooding the dorm with sunlight, when Darrell woke up. Turning over, she saw Alicia, fully dressed, retrieving the wicker cage from the linen cupboard.

'The mouse was *yours*!' Darrell said.

Alicia grinned. 'He's probably happier roaming free anyway. You were a brick not telling Matron about the cage.' She stuffed it out of sight underneath her bed. 'I'll make it up to you. Come on!'

Darrell was intrigued. 'Where?'

Alicia shook her head, putting her finger to her lips. Darrell jumped eagerly out of bed, and Alicia ushered her over to the door, not even giving her time to dress. They were about to leave when Gwendoline came out of the bathroom. She was brushing her long hair.

'You're going to have to tie that back,' Alicia warned her.

Gwendoline pouted. 'Mother says it's my crowning glory!'

'Don't say I didn't warn you,' Alicia said. 'Oh, and it was pretty mean of you to tell on us last night. That's not the Malory Towers way.'

When Alicia and Darrell left the dorm Gwendoline hesitated, then sneaked out after them. She followed at a distance, curious to find out where they were going.

Alicia led Darrell outside and through the school gardens. 'Don't look!' Alicia was saying, one hand clamped firmly over Darrell's eyes. 'All right – NOW!'

Darrell opened her eyes. There, beside the sea, was the famous Malory Towers swimming-pool. It had been carved out of a stretch of rocks and looked part of the natural landscape with seaweed growing at the sides. Every day when the tide came in the sea swept into the pool and filled it up.

Darrell was transfixed. 'It's amazing!'

'Here.' Alicia pulled a rolled-up swimsuit out of her pocket and tossed it to Darrell. Then she slipped off her dress to reveal her swimming costume underneath. Breathless with anticipation, Darrell quickly wriggled into the swimsuit beneath her nightie.

'Race you!' Alicia yelled.

Leaving their clothes on the rocks, the two of them ran down to the blue-green water and dived in. Darrell yelped with shock because it was so cold, but it was exhilarating to swim in the early-morning sunshine. She loved the way the salty sea water lapped over the rocks, creating waves across the pool.

Neither girl spotted Gwendoline watching them from

the shadow of the cliff, deeply jealous of the fun they were having . . .

'I can't believe we missed breakfast,' Darrell panted when she and Alicia hurried back into school. Girls and teachers were milling around on their way to the first lesson. 'I'm starving!'

'We'll make up for it tonight.' Alicia lowered her voice. 'Midnight feast with the West Tower girls – want to come?'

'You bet!' Darrell didn't need to be asked twice.

Gwendoline came down the stairs as Darrell and Alicia were going up. Her hair was still loose down her back, and Miss Potts, who was hurrying past, put out a hand to stop her.

'Gwendoline!' the teacher exclaimed. 'Your hair!'

Proudly Gwendoline shimmied the blonde waves over her shoulders. 'I always brush it one hun—'

'Tie it back before my class, please,' Miss Potts said sternly.

Gwendoline's mouth fell open, and, blushing, she scuttled back to the dorm. Darrell followed to change into her uniform.

Within five minutes Darrell was ready. She changed and then towel-dried her short hair quickly. Meanwhile, Gwendoline was standing helplessly in front of the mirror, trying to plait her blonde waves.

'Quick, or you'll be late,' Darrell said.

'I knew I'd hate it here,' Gwendoline muttered tearfully. 'I thought we new girls would stick together, but Sally never speaks, and you're off with Alicia the whole time. Why are you friends with *her*?'

'She's fun—' Darrell began.

'You mean she gets you into trouble,' Gwendoline broke in tartly.

'*You* got me into trouble last night,' Darrell reminded her.

'Sorry, I'm just terrified of mice.' Gwendoline stared hopelessly at herself in the mirror. 'I can't plait my hair!'

'Here, let me help.' Darrell grabbed the brush and began plaiting Gwendoline's hair quickly and competently. Gwendoline watched with delight.

'There, you look lovely,' Darrell said, tying the ends of the plaits securely with ribbons.

'Thank you!' Gwendoline held out her little finger. 'Make up?'

Darrell hesitated before hooking her little finger round Gwendoline's. 'Make up,' she agreed.

'Will you be my friend?' Gwendoline demanded.

Without waiting for a reply she tucked her arm possessively into Darrell's and led her out of the dorm.

CHAPTER FIVE

BY THE time Darrell and Gwendoline made it to class they were late, but Miss Potts smiled her approval at Gwendoline's neat plaits.

'*Much* better,' she said. 'But, Darrell, why are *you* late?'

'She was helping me,' Gwendoline said quickly.

Miss Potts nodded, and Darrell flashed a grateful smile at Gwendoline.

'See?' Gwendoline whispered. '*Best* friends.'

Darrell felt uncomfortable as they sat down. She wasn't sure she really *wanted* to be best friends with Gwendoline. They didn't seem to have a lot in common.

Oh, well, maybe I should give her a chance, Darrell decided. Perhaps Gwendoline would enjoy swimming and sports as much as she did . . .

'I'm cold!' Gwendoline wailed, shivering at the side of the lacrosse field, waiting her turn. Her class were practising using their lacrosse sticks, long-handled poles with small nets at the end. They were cradling and running with the ball while Gwendoline watched in disgust. *What a ridiculous game!*

Alicia ran past and overheard Gwendoline complaining. 'That's the spot where Lady Jane met her love,' Alicia yelled, pointing her lacrosse stick at Gwen, 'the night they DIED!'

Gwendoline squealed with fright and shot Alicia a daggers look. *That girl really is the limit*, she thought furiously.

Darrell and Alicia raced on, tossing the ball to each other. Secretly Darrell was disappointed that Gwendoline didn't seem interested in lacrosse. It was so much fun to be racing around outside in the fresh air instead of stuck inside a stuffy old classroom. But then Darrell remembered how Gwendoline had saved her from being in trouble with Miss Potts earlier.

'Alicia,' Darrell said hesitantly, 'could we invite Gwendoline to the midnight feast?'

'G-whining G-wendoline?' Alicia scoffed. 'Not likely!'

Darrell said no more. She didn't want to annoy Alicia.

For the rest of the day Gwendoline insisted on sitting beside Darrell at every lesson. But after classes were over Darrell slipped away on her own. She wanted to write her very first letter home, knowing her parents and Felicity would be waiting eagerly to hear from her.

Darrell settled herself on the grass beneath one of the spreading oak trees and began to write. She described the train journey to Cornwall, her first glimpse of the school, her dormitory and the swimming-pool.

'I've . . . made . . . a . . . wonderful . . . new . . . friend,' Darrell said as she wrote. But when she got to *friend*, she had to stop and think about it. '*Friend?*' Darrell repeated, her forehead creasing into a frown. She wrote '*freind*', then continued. 'She's called . . .'

Darrell finished the page and turned it over.

It was midnight, and the North Tower first-form dormitory was in darkness. Everyone appeared to be asleep.

Darrell had burrowed down under the covers and was sleeping soundly when suddenly her eyes flew open. What was that strange creaking noise?

Nervously Darrell peered into the darkness, but she could hardly see a thing. There was the creaky sound again! Was someone walking around the dorm?

A hand fell on Darrell's shoulder. Darrell almost cried out with shock but managed to stifle her scream when she realised it was Alicia.

'What was that creaking?' Darrell whispered.

Alicia grinned. 'Must have been the ghost. Come on, it's midnight!'

Excited, Darrell tumbled out of bed. She'd read about midnight feasts in stories, and now she was actually going to one herself!

'Don't forget your tuck,' Alicia reminded her.

Darrell retrieved the bag of food she'd stashed

underneath her bed. Then the two girls tiptoed over to the door, completely unaware that someone else was awake too.

Gwendoline was peeping over her blankets. Eyes narrowed, she watched Darrell and Alicia leave the dorm . . .

The midnight feast in the attic room was already well under way when Darrell and Alicia arrived. Darrell was surprised to see so many girls there sprawled around on blankets spread out on the dusty floor.

'At last!' called Betty Hill, one of the West Tower girls. 'Come on, you're missing all the fun!'

Darrell and Alicia quickly added their own tuck to the heaps of cakes, biscuits and sweets. Betty turned on the record player, and some of the girls got up to dance. Darrell beamed and reached for a chocolate biscuit. This was the best fun! Malory Towers was all she'd ever dreamt of and more.

Outside, Gwendoline was peering through the keyhole. A midnight feast? Darrell hadn't even invited her! And they were supposed to be best friends! Gwendoline burned with rage and jealousy as she spied on Darrell munching biscuits and joking with Alicia. How dare her so-called friend treat her like this?

CHAPTER SIX

DARRELL WOKE up, stretched and glanced at the clock. She felt bright-eyed and energetic, despite being awake for several hours during the night. The midnight feast had been glorious fun. Darrell hoped there would be another one soon.

Everyone else was still asleep, or so Darrell thought. It was far too early for breakfast. She had time for a swim.

'Alicia?' Darrell whispered, rummaging for her swimsuit and towel. 'Coming swimming?'

Alicia's eyes remained closed. She waved lazily at Darrell, then snuggled down again.

I suppose that means no! Darrell thought. Slipping her dress over her swimming-costume, she hurried out.

Immediately Gwendoline sat up in bed, checking that none of the other girls were awake. No one stirred. She hopped out of bed and went over to Darrell's bedside locker to examine the photo of Darrell's family. Goodness, was that woman Darrell's *mother*? Mrs Rivers was pale and thin with grey hair. She looked more like Darrell's grandmother! Gwendoline thought complacently of her own pretty mother.

She eased open Darrell's private drawer and saw some untidily written pages on top. *I've made a wonderful new freind called . . .* Gwendoline read. She turned the page eagerly. *Alicia . . .*

Darrell dived neatly into the pool with barely a splash and swam underwater towards the side. She surfaced, pushing her wet hair off her face, and was surprised to find Gwendoline looming over the edge, clutching some sheets of paper in her hand.

'I know where you were last night,' Gwendoline said bitterly. 'Leaving me out isn't a very "best friend" thing to do, is it?'

Darrell hauled herself out of the pool. She felt guilty until she noticed her letter in Gwendoline's hand.

'What are you doing with my letter?' she demanded.

'Oh, it's not very interesting,' Gwendoline sneered. 'Your parents won't miss it. I expect they're glad to be rid of you!'

'Take that back!' Darrell cried. A red mist of anger descended on her. How *dare* Gwendoline read her private letter?

'Poor dowdy Darrell!' Gwendoline jeered. 'With your torn dress and your stupid short hair! Still, your mother's just as bad. I thought the dreary old lady in that photo was your granny!'

Darrell felt rage almost suffocate her. She lunged forward and attempted to pull the letter from Gwen's grasp. But Gwendoline held on tightly, and the pages ripped in two across the middle.

Enraged, Darrell lashed out. But she shoved Gwendoline just a little too hard. Gwendoline staggered backwards, lost her footing on the slippery edge and toppled into the pool with a squeal and a splash.

Shaken out of her fury, Darrell watched in horror as Gwendoline resurfaced. Spluttering, Gwendoline thrashed her way to the side. Ignoring Darrell's outstretched hand, she pulled herself out and stalked off, her clothes soaking wet.

Deeply upset, all anger gone, Darrell raced after her. 'Gwen, I'm *really* sorry! It's this rotten temper of mine. I shouldn't have done that.'

'No, you shouldn't!' Gwendoline spat. 'Miss Grayling needs to know about this. You'll be expelled, Darrell Rivers!'

'I've said I'm sorry.' Darrell was distraught. 'Please don't tell, Gwen!'

Gwendoline hesitated, pushing her dripping hair off her face. 'Well, I *do* need help with my prep,' she said thoughtfully. 'It'll take me an age otherwise . . .'

'We could go to the library after tea,' Darrell suggested.

'Oh, I don't mind when *you* do it.' Gwendoline smiled sweetly. 'As long as it gets done.'

Now Darrell understood the price she had to pay for Gwen's silence. Without saying another word she nodded miserably.

The first lesson of the morning was French with Mam'zelle Rougier. Gwendoline hadn't done her French prep, so Darrell sat in the classroom, bent over Gwen's book, scribbling hard. Gwendoline watched with glee.

'*Allez, allez, allez!*' Mam'zelle Rougier snapped as she swept into the classroom, high heels clacking. The girls sat up straight, apart from Darrell, and Sally, who was next to her, gave her a discreet kick under the desk. Startled, Darrell jerked upright, knocking the book to the floor. Quickly Sally retrieved it, noticing the name on the front.

'Why are *you* doing Gwen's prep?' Sally whispered, handing the book back.

'I have to do it,' Darrell muttered uncomfortably.

Sally shook her head. 'No. You don't. I thought you were smarter than that, Darrell Rivers.'

Darrell knew Sally was right. She *didn't* have to do Gwen's prep. But if she didn't, then she'd have to do something much worse – go to Miss Grayling and confess what had happened at the pool.

CHAPTER SEVEN

'DO YOU think physical violence is ever acceptable, Darrell?' Miss Grayling asked.

Darrell struggled to contain her emotions. What hurt her most was the disappointment in Miss Grayling's voice. For the millionth time in her life Darrell wondered miserably why she couldn't seem to control her temper. 'No. Never,' she muttered. 'Except perhaps in self-defence.'

'And was pushing another pupil into the pool self-defence?'

Darrell shook her head remorsefully. 'I – I was defending my mother,' she murmured. 'You see, Mother was very ill last year, right at the end of the war. That's why her hair's grey. I just –' Darrell gulped – 'I just couldn't bear to hear her called dreary. That's all.'

Too late, a horrified Darrell remembered that Miss Grayling's hair was also grey. But the headmistress didn't seem offended.

'I think of grey hair as a sign of strength,' Miss Grayling said quietly. 'The war brought terrible pain and suffering, even to those of us who survived it.'

Darrell noticed that Miss Grayling was absent-mindedly twisting the simple engagement ring on her left hand. There was no gold wedding band alongside it. For the first time Darrell noticed the photograph of a handsome young man on Miss Grayling's desk. He wore a soldier's uniform, and there was a black ribbon round the photo-frame.

'Would you like to tell me who the other girl is?' the headmistress asked.

Darrell shook her head. 'Please don't ask me to leave,' she begged.

Miss Grayling considered her gravely. 'A temper isn't only a negative trait, Darrell. It shows spirit and fire. But you must learn to harness it for good. Are you willing to attempt that?'

'Oh, yes!' Darrell replied honestly.

'Then let's put this behind us.'

Darrell blinked back tears of relief. 'Thank you, Miss Grayling,' she said with heartfelt gratitude. She left the study, encouraged by the headmistress's belief in her. She'd strive not to let Miss Grayling down again.

Darrell avoided Gwendoline for the rest of the morning. She didn't intend to do another word of Gwen's prep for her. Let her do her own work!

At lunchtime some of the first-form girls were playing stuck-in-the-mud on the lacrosse field. Darrell joined in enthusiastically while Gwendoline stood on the sidelines.

Alicia, who was 'it', managed to tag Darrell. 'Got you!' she yelled. 'You're stuck-in-the-mud!'

Darrell froze, legs planted apart. 'Quick, someone rescue me!' she hollered. 'Gwen?'

'I'm not playing, and you shouldn't be either!' Gwendoline hissed. 'My prep's late! I'm going to Miss Grayling.'

'I've already been.' Darrell stared Gwendoline straight in the eye. 'You can't threaten me now, Gwen.'

Gwendoline glared at her as Sally raced over to Darrell and dived through her legs.

'SAVED!' Sally called.

'Hurrah!' Darrell yelled. 'I'm free!' Away she ran, confident in the knowledge that Gwendoline couldn't blackmail her any more.

Later that evening, after fuming all day, Gwendoline caught up with Darrell outside the common room.

'I don't want to be friends with you after all,' Gwendoline said spitefully. 'Miss Grayling will see what you're really like soon enough, Darrell Rivers. I bet your last school was glad to be rid of you!'

Darrell couldn't help flinching. Gwendoline noticed this and pounced eagerly.

'Your last school was St Hilda's, wasn't it?'

Gwendoline's eyes gleamed with suspicious malice. 'Are *you* the girl who was asked to leave?' She smirked. 'I bet you are! I'm going to write to my cousin and ask.'

'W-why would you do that?' Darrell stammered.

'Because I think everyone should hear what sort of a girl you really are,' Gwendoline replied triumphantly. 'Don't you?'

CHAPTER EIGHT

ONE MORNING, a week later, Darrell and Alicia were washing at the bathroom sinks. Steam rose from the hot water, misting up the mirrors.

'Team trials today!' Alicia said. 'Nervous?'

'A bit!' Darrell sighed. 'I wish there was more than one place up for grabs.'

Gwendoline watched grumpily from the basins opposite. She hated seeing the other two girls so friendly.

'You're good,' Alicia said. 'It'd be *cracking* to be on the team together.'

Turning back to her mirror, Gwendoline immediately let out a piercing scream. A message had mysteriously appeared on the glass. *I'M WATCHING YOU!*

'*Who's* watching me?' Gwendoline wailed.

'It's a message from Lady Jane herself, Gwen,' Alicia replied solemnly. 'Beware!' Smiling, she walked out.

'Aren't you scared?' Gwendoline asked Darrell shakily.

Darrell shrugged. 'I don't believe in ghosts.'

'Is this a trick?' Gwendoline scowled. 'Did *you* do this?'

'Honestly, Gwen, it wasn't me.'

'You know, it's been a while since I wrote to my cousin,' Gwendoline snapped. 'She'll write back any day now. Maybe even *today*.'

Darrell's face fell.

'So if it *was* you who was asked to leave St Hilda's,' Gwendoline continued, 'I'll soon know why.'

The bell sounded, and Darrell went down for breakfast, but she was too anxious about Gwen's threats to eat much.

'So how hard is this English assessment going to be?' Sally asked.

'Brutal,' Jean said. 'Potty likes to put new girls through their paces.'

Darrell gulped. She'd forgotten about the test with Miss Potts this morning. Something else to worry about . . .

'Darrell Rivers!' Matron marched over to the table, noting that Darrell was wearing her lacrosse kit. 'Is your dress mended? No team trials if it isn't!'

'Do you think I'd be sitting here if it was still torn, Matron?' Darrell asked brightly.

'I'll inspect it later then,' Matron said, looking slightly disappointed.

Darrell nodded, but pulled a face after Matron had left.

'Not fixed it?' Alicia enquired.

Darrell sighed. 'No.'

'I can do it,' said Emily, much to Darrell's surprise. Usually she hardly said a word. 'I'm not trialling, and I love to sew.'

'I'd be really grateful.' Darrell beamed at her, wondering why Emily looked so tired. She kept yawning, and her eyes were pink-rimmed.

'Ooh, here's the mail!' Alicia announced as Katherine arrived with the post.

Gwendoline smiled sweetly at Darrell. 'Is there one for me, Katherine?'

Katherine flicked through the letters. 'Yes, Gwen.'

Darrell couldn't eat another mouthful of porridge. She watched with dread as Gwendoline took the letter, smiling expectantly. But when Gwendoline studied the envelope, her face fell. 'But this is MY letter to my cousin!' she complained. 'Surely I didn't get the address wrong?'

Darrell saw that the envelope had been addressed to *Joan Lacey, St Hilda's School, Cromley, Glos*. Someone had crossed out the address and written *Return to Sender* in red pen. Darrell breathed a sigh of relief. She was off the hook – for now.

'I'll just have to send it again then, won't I?' Gwendoline said crossly.

'One for you too, Darrell.' Katherine handed her a letter.

Eagerly Darrell ripped open the envelope. A

colourful drawing of their family home by Felicity fell out, and also a long letter from Mrs Rivers. Darrell scanned it quickly. 'Hey, Sally!' she exclaimed. 'My mother says she bumped into yours and saw your baby sister. Mother says the baby's adorable!'

'I don't have a baby sister,' Sally replied coldly.

Confused, Darrell glanced back at her letter. 'But Mother says . . .' she began. It was too late, however. Sally had gone.

Back in the dorm, Darrell slipped into the bathroom and stood thoughtfully in front of Gwendoline's mirror. She rubbed the glass with her forefinger. It felt sticky.

Darrell grabbed a bar of soap and scribbled an invisible word on a clean mirror. Then she turned on the hot tap. Steam rose up, and the word *Boo!* appeared in the mirror.

'So you figured it out,' said Alicia from behind her. 'Well done. My brothers showed me that trick.'

'Gwendoline thought *I'd* done it,' Darrell muttered.

Alicia laughed. 'You're not scared of darling Gwendoline, are you?'

Darrell tried to smile. If only Alicia knew . . .

'Come on.' Alicia grabbed her arm. 'You can't be late for trials!'

* * *

'I can't find my boots!' Darrell groaned despairingly.

'My boots are missing too,' Gwendoline said, although she didn't look at all concerned. '*Such* a shame.'

The lacrosse trials were about to start. Pamela, the head girl, was already out on the field with the lacrosse team and the new girls.

Darrell and Gwendoline were last out of the changing rooms, minus their boots. Darrell sprinted towards the others, knowing she was late, but the grass was muddy, and she slipped over, landing on her bottom. Blushing, she hauled herself to her feet.

'Where are your boots?' Pamela asked.

'We couldn't find them,' Gwendoline replied.

'I can play like this,' Darrell said hopefully.

'Sorry, no.' Pamela's tone was kind but firm. 'It's too dangerous. Go and look again.'

Disappointed, Darrell rushed back to the changing room and turned it upside down, searching for her boots. Gwendoline had also returned and was brushing her hair at the mirror.

'Oh, blast!' Darrell groaned after twenty minutes, slumping on to the bench. 'I give up!'

'I don't know why you're so upset,' Gwendoline remarked casually. 'It's just sport. The English assessment is far more important.'

'I'm no good at stuff like that.' Darrell sounded despondent.

'Poor you,' Gwendoline cooed patronisingly. 'Pamela's fabulous, isn't she? I'd love to be her monitor.'

'What's a monitor?'

Gwendoline looked superior. 'Don't you know *anything*? Each sixth-form girl has a first-former to help her. I've told Pamela I'd be perfect.'

Darrell's low spirits fell even further. She'd have given anything to be Pamela's monitor.

'Pamela said she'd announce it today,' Gwendoline added cheerfully and left.

Darrell changed out of her lacrosse kit, telling herself to buck up. But remembering the English assessment, her spirits dipped again. Darrell always tried hard, but she knew her handwriting and spelling weren't the best.

When Darrell left the changing room she ran into the girls coming in after the trials, Katherine carrying the lacrosse sticks. Sally was red-faced and smiling.

'You were utterly brilliant,' Jean was telling her.

Sally beamed. 'I played centre at my old school.'

'Sally was good then?' Darrell murmured to Alicia.

'Phenomenal!' Alicia exclaimed.

Katherine had gone to put the lacrosse sticks away. Now she came out of the changing room holding two pairs of boots.

'Hey, Darrell!' Katherine called. 'Yours and Gwen's boots were in the games cupboard. Why ever did you put them in there?'

'I didn't!' Darrell exclaimed, taking her boots from Katherine.

'No,' Alicia said grimly. 'Gwen did.'

Darrell was shocked. 'She wouldn't have! Would she?'

At that moment Pamela came along to pin the team sheet for the next lacrosse match on the noticeboard. The girls crowded around her, buzzing with anticipation.

'Sally! You're in!' Alicia called, and Sally glowed with pride.

'Congratulations, Sally,' Darrell said, but secretly she was bitterly disappointed. *That could have been me*, she thought unhappily, *if it hadn't been for Gwen* . . .

CHAPTER NINE

DARRELL WAS scribbling frantically. The English test was nearly over, and she hadn't finished.

Darrell glanced over at Sally and Gwendoline. Sally had put her pen down, and Gwendoline was doodling a flower at the bottom of her paper. Miserably Darrell stared at her work. It was a mess – scrawly handwriting, crossings-out and big ink blots.

'Right, time's up,' Miss Potts said. 'Pens down.'

Gloomily Darrell threw her pen down on the desk and stretched her aching muscles. But her elbow caught the open inkpot, and, to Darrell's horror, it overturned. Black ink flooded across her test paper, obliterating everything she'd written.

'Oh, no!' Darrell groaned. She whipped out her handkerchief and began dabbing at the streams of ink while Miss Potts grabbed some sheets of blotting paper and rushed over.

'Darrell, how clumsy!' The teacher blotted Darrell's test paper, then held it up. 'Oh dear, you'll have to redo this.'

'Now?' Darrell asked wearily.

Miss Potts nodded and gave her a new sheet of paper as Gwendoline and Sally left. Darrell was exhausted, but still determined to do her best. She bent over her new paper and started scribbling . . .

Teatime had finished, but the girls had saved some food for Darrell. Gwendoline leant across the table and sneaked a piece of cucumber from the plate.

'Don't,' Irene said sternly. 'That's Darrell's.'

Gwendoline snorted in disgust. 'Huh! She knocked that ink over on *purpose*, you know!'

A weary, ink-stained and hungry Darrell arrived just in time to hear this. 'Why would I do that?' she asked as Irene passed her the plate of food.

'It was as good as cheating!' Gwendoline declared.

'Take that back, Gwen,' Katherine ordered.

'Fine!' Gwendoline sniffed. 'When Darrell knocked ink over her paper and got the chance to do it again it WASN'T cheating!'

Darrell was downcast. It *did* sound bad.

'Eat up, Darrell, and let's get some fresh air,' Alicia said briskly. 'Bit of a stink around here!'

Gwendoline was outraged, but Darrell felt a little better. No one believed Gwen, thank goodness. As if she'd ever cheat like that!

Darrell soon cheered up when Alicia insisted they went to the lacrosse field to practise catching. It was marvellous to run around and stretch her legs in the cool evening air.

'You're easily as good as Sally,' Alicia said, hurling the ball to Darrell. But her pass was far too high, and the ball sailed over Darrell's head. 'I could kill Gwen! Why has she got it in for you?'

Pretending not to hear, Darrell scooped up the ball and tossed it neatly back to Alicia.

'Good pass!' Alicia exclaimed. She spotted Pamela walking by and called, 'Pamela! Watch this!'

Alicia hurled the ball high into the air again, but this time it was just about within Darrell's reach. She leapt like a gazelle and skilfully netted it.

'Super, Darrell!' Pamela called, impressed.

'You *have* to let her on the team, Pamela,' Alicia pleaded. 'Can't you?'

'Well, I can't magic up a place,' Pamela said, 'but I *could* make you first reserve, if you like, Darrell?'

Darrell gasped ecstatically. 'Yes, please!' Maybe her luck was finally changing . . .

As the girls went back into school with Pamela Gwendoline saw them, and her jaw dropped. Darrell Rivers chatting with the head girl!

'You might not get a game, you know, Darrell,' Pamela was saying.

'I know, but I'll work hard,' Darrell assured her.

'Hello, Pamela,' Gwendoline said eagerly. 'Do you need me for anything?'

'Oh, Gwen, I've decided to make Sally my monitor,' Pamela said apologetically. 'Now she's on the lacrosse team, we'll see a lot of each other.'

Gwendoline flushed with rage.

Just then Miss Potts bustled up to the girls. 'Darrell, here you are. I just read your essay.'

'Oh.' Darrell felt instantly deflated.

Miss Potts smiled. 'You need to work on your spelling and presentation, but you write very well.'

'I do?' Darrell exclaimed, beaming with pride.

'Have you read mine?' Gwendoline demanded.

'Yes.' Miss Potts frowned. 'We'll talk about that another time, Gwendoline. You have several areas you need to work on.'

Alicia slapped Darrell on the back. 'Come on, let's go and put your boots under lock and key!'

Gwendoline watched them go, hating Darrell more than ever. Her gaze fell on the payphone near the entrance, and she made an instant decision. Fishing a coin from her pocket, she hurried over and dialled. 'Operator, can you put me through to St Hilda's in Cromley? Thank you.'

As Gwendoline waited impatiently Jean tapped her on the shoulder. 'You can't make calls now,' she said sternly. 'It's the seniors' turn.'

Sure enough, there was a group of older girls heading towards them. Reluctantly Gwendoline replaced the receiver and picked up her coin.

'I want to ring my cousin at St Hilda's,' she grumbled. 'There's a phone in the village, isn't there?'

'Yes, but you're not allowed to go alone,' Jean replied.

Gwendoline waited until Jean had left. Then she slipped outside and hurried down the drive towards the school gates.

Up in the dorm Darrell pinned Felicity's drawing next to her bed. She was fizzing with energy now. Her day had improved no end!

'Darrell Rivers!' Matron called from the doorway. 'I'm waiting!'

Darrell spun round, confused. Then she remembered – her torn dress . . .

'Here it is, Darrell.' Emily hurried across the dorm, holding out the dress. 'You left it on my bed.' She winked, and Darrell shot her a grateful look. She handed the tunic to Matron, who examined it closely. The tear had been beautifully mended and was now invisible.

Matron seemed disappointed. 'You're full of surprises, Darrell Rivers,' she remarked.

'Thank you, Matron,' Darrell said politely.

'I'll still be keeping a close eye on you,' Matron snapped. 'Katherine, is everyone here?'

'Yes, Matron,' Katherine replied a little doubtfully.

'Then you may have an hour for quiet reading.

I'll be back for lights out.'

After Matron left Katherine rushed to check the bathroom. 'Where's Gwen?' she asked, coming back into the dorm. 'She knows she should be here by now.'

Gwendoline had sneaked out of the school gates and was walking down the country lane towards the village. However, it was much further away than she'd thought.

'Another mile?' Gwendoline groaned to herself, pausing to read a road sign. She sighed and almost turned back there and then. But she was determined to make that call to her cousin at St Hilda's and find out the truth about Darrell Rivers.

CHAPTER TEN

IN THE dorm the other girls were discussing where Gwendoline might have gone.

'She could have run away,' Mary-Lou suggested.

'Why?' Emily asked, puzzled.

'Maybe because she's scared of the ghost, like me?' Mary-Lou pulled a face. 'But I'm scared of running away as well!'

'If Gwen's not back by lights out, Matron will have our guts for garters,' Alicia pointed out.

'I think Gwen's gone to the village,' Jean said suddenly.

'By *herself*?' Sally was incredulous.

'She's been trying to make a phone call,' Jean explained. 'To St Hilda's, I think.'

Darrell's heart plummeted. 'I'll go down there and bring her back,' she burst out recklessly.

The other girls stared at her in shock.

'But it's getting dark!' Katherine pointed out. 'And there isn't time. Matron will be back—'

'I'll run.' Darrell grabbed her sweater and a torch. 'I'll be back before you – or Matron – know it.'

The others watched, impressed by her daring, as Darrell raced out of the dorm. *She had to catch up with Gwendoline before she made that phone call.* But first she had to make it out of school without being spotted by Matron . . .

Music was blaring out from the san as Darrell crept towards it. Inside Matron was singing along loudly, *'My old man said follow the van, and don't dilly-dally on the way!'*

Under cover of the noise Darrell raced swiftly past the door and out of school. Then she headed down the drive towards the school gates.

It could be a long way to the village, Darrell thought with a sinking heart as she started off along the country lane. Maybe Gwendoline had spoken to her cousin already . . .

Darrell speeded up. She darted round a sharp bend in the lane and almost collided with a teenage boy on a bicycle. The boy braked so hard, he almost flew over the handlebars.

'Watch it!' he yelled.

'Sorry,' Darrell panted. 'Are you from round here?'

The boy looked amused. 'Where else would I be from?'

'How far is the village?' Darrell wanted to know.

'You're *not* from round here then!' The boy grinned at her. 'It'll take you ages.' He held out his hand. 'Ron Gilson.'

Darrell shook hands despondently. How would she ever catch up with Gwen? 'Darrell Rivers. I'm from Malory—'

'Towers,' Ron broke in. 'I know. I run errands up there sometimes.'

Darrell was staring at Ron's bicycle. 'Could I borrow your bike?' she blurted out.

Ron gaped at her in amazement. 'It's not mine; it's my brother's.'

'It's an emergency!' Darrell pleaded. 'How about I rent it? A shilling?'

Ron grinned. He jumped off the bike and held his hand out for the money. But Darrell had already climbed on and was pedalling away at top speed.

'Sorry, I don't have any money on me!' she called over her shoulder. 'Come and find me up at the school, and I'll pay you then. Promise!' And she shot off down the lane, leaving Ron open-mouthed behind her.

When Darrell reached the village she turned into the high street and cycled like a mad thing towards the phone box. There it was, next to the greengrocer's – and Gwendoline was inside! But maybe she hadn't made the call yet? Darrell braked and skidded to a halt. Jumping off the bike, she banged on the glass. Startled, Gwendoline turned round.

'Don't do it, Gwen,' Darrell panted, flinging open

the door of the phone box. '*Please.*'

Slowly Gwendoline replaced the receiver. 'Too late. My cousin's told me *everything*.'

Darrell groaned. All her effort had been wasted.

'Not a pretty tale, is it?' Gwendoline remarked, shaking her head.

'Please don't tell the others,' Darrell begged.

'I can't keep a secret like that,' Gwendoline said loftily. 'What you did was *dreadful*.'

'Miss Grayling said this would be a fresh start.' Darrell fought to hold back tears. 'She said no one needed to know why I had to leave St Hilda's.'

'I knew it!' Gwendoline gasped triumphantly. 'It WAS you!'

Darrell stared at her in horror. 'You tricked me!'

'I couldn't get through to St Hilda's.' Gwendoline was smirking now, thoroughly pleased with herself. 'But turns out it didn't matter! Not so clever now, are you?'

'She's coming!' Emily had been standing at the door, watching out for Matron. Now she flew across the dorm and dived under her blankets.

'What are we going to do?' Mary-Lou whispered, gazing with concern at Darrell's and Gwen's empty beds.

Alicia turned to Jean. 'Just keep Matron talking,' she said urgently. 'Say whatever you have to.'

'Good evening, girls.' Matron marched into the dorm. 'Put your books down. It's time for lights out.'

'Matron! Your hair!' Jean exclaimed loudly. 'It looks *lovely*!'

Matron paused, looking slightly suspicious at Jean's over-the-top enthusiasm. Behind her, Alicia started stuffing her own bed with a pile of her clothes. Then she scooted silently over to Darrell's bed and jumped in, pulling the blankets right up.

'You look like Rita Hayworth, Matron,' Jean said admiringly. 'You know she got electric shocks to change her hairline?'

'That sounds uncomfortable,' Matron remarked, patting her hair complacently. She was flattered to be compared with a famous film star.

'Apparently they stick a needle in at the base of every single hair, then – ZAP!' Jean struggled not to laugh. 'Goodnight, Matron.'

Matron moved on to Darrell's bed, and Alicia let out a small but dramatic snore. Satisfied, Matron passed by. She was now heading towards where Gwendoline slept. Then, right on cue, there was a shriek from Mary-Lou.

'Matron, my leg!' Mary-Lou groaned. 'I think it's cramp!'

Tutting loudly, Matron hurried over to Mary-Lou. Immediately Jean rolled out of bed and stuffed her pillows under the covers to form a human-shaped lump.

Then she jumped into Gwen's bed and pulled the blankets over her head.

Matron, meanwhile, was rubbing Mary-Lou's leg fiercely. 'Ow!' Mary-Lou winced. Matron hurt more than having cramp! 'That's better, thank you.'

Matron headed for the door. She was slightly suspicious, but she'd had enough for one night. 'Goodnight, girls,' she said and switched off the lights. Irene immediately snorted with laughter but was shushed by the others. After a moment, Katherine tiptoed over to the door and listened. 'She's gone,' she whispered.

Everyone started giggling, apart from Mary-Lou.

'That snore, Alicia!' Irene spluttered.

Alicia grinned at Jean. 'Rita Hayworth? Really?'

'What if Darrell and Gwendoline don't come back?' Mary-Lou asked anxiously, and all the laughter immediately stopped.

CHAPTER ELEVEN

MISERABLY DARRELL pushed Ron's bike along the country lane. She was heading back to school, a very smug Gwendoline walking alongside her.

'So why were you asked to leave St Hilda's?' Gwendoline asked again.

Darrell glanced round. It was getting dark, and everything looked different. 'I thought we had to turn off somewhere here. Can you remember?'

'Stop changing the subject and just tell me!' Gwendoline snapped.

'I can't.' Darrell chewed at her lip. 'I promised.'

'Who?'

'Miss Grayling.'

Gwendoline's eyes almost popped out of her head. Darrell's secret must be HUGE!

'Can't you just trust me?' Darrell asked wearily. 'I know we haven't exactly hit it off, but—'

'And whose fault is that?' Gwendoline interrupted. 'You're always with Alicia!'

'I'm trying to make friends, Gwen.'

'I offered to be your friend, remember?' Gwendoline

said bitterly.

'We still can be,' Darrell promised. 'Please don't tell, Gwen. It's been awful, and I couldn't bear it if everything went wrong again . . .'

Gwendoline was silent, considering this. Then a loud screeching noise high above them made both girls clutch at each other in a panic.

'I think it's just an owl,' Darrell said. She directed her torch at the road ahead of them. To her concern it didn't look familiar at all. She was beginning to think they'd taken a wrong turn somewhere.

'Are we lost?' Gwendoline asked in a trembling voice.

No one in the dorm was asleep.

'It's awfully late,' Jean fretted.

'We might have to tell Matron after all,' Katherine said.

'No,' said Alicia, 'Let's wait a bit longer . . .'

Out on the dark country roads Darrell and Gwendoline were well and truly lost. They'd reached a crossroads, but there were no signposts. Darrell was utterly dismayed. She had no idea which direction to take now.

'This is all your fault!' Gwendoline yelled at her. A fox barked in the distance, and Gwendoline let out a hysterical scream.

'Shhh!' Darrell said. She'd just had an idea. 'Listen

for a moment.'

'We'll never find our way back!' Gwendoline wailed. 'We're going to die out here of exposure!'

'Quiet!' Darrell pleaded. 'Here, have my sweater if you're cold.' She thrust it at Gwendoline who pulled it on, shivering, while Darrell listened, head cocked to one side. There it was – a familiar soft, swishing sound.

'The sea!' Darrell exclaimed. 'It's behind us. That means Malory Towers is *that* way.' She climbed on to the bike. 'Jump on the back, Gwen.'

'I most certainly will NOT!' Gwendoline said, outraged.

'Stay here then,' Darrell retorted.

Gwendoline didn't protest any further. She did as Darrell said, clinging on to her tightly.

'We'll get back safely, Gwen,' Darrell said as she pedalled off down the lane. 'Just you wait and see.'

Twenty minutes later Darrell and Gwendoline tumbled thankfully through the door into school. The others had been watching out for them, and Alicia, Katherine, Irene and Sally had dashed downstairs to let them in.

'What took you so long?' Alicia whispered urgently.

'We got lost,' Darrell replied.

'Goodness, you look a fright!' Sally said, noting how pale and distressed Darrell was. 'Did something happen?'

'Did you meet the ghost?' Irene chuckled.

'No, it's far worse than that,' Gwendoline said smugly. 'Isn't it, Darrell?'

Darrell was filled with dread. Gwendoline was going to tell after all. How could she stop her?

'Quick, upstairs!' Katherine murmured. 'Before someone catches us. You can tell us everything then.'

Darrell followed the others back to the dorm. Somehow she had to prevent Gwendoline from revealing her secret . . .

Everyone else was wide awake when they arrived. Darrell stared at their curious faces, and her heart pounded nervously. 'Gwen was so brave!' she blurted out. Everyone, including Gwendoline, looked surprised, but she recovered fast.

'Well, of course I was,' Gwendoline boasted.

'There were some jolly awful noises out there in the dark, and we were lost, but she kept us both going,' Darrell said desperately.

Gwendoline preened herself. 'Yes, I did, didn't I?'

Darrell directed a pleading look at her. *Please don't tell.* Gwendoline looked thoughtful, and Darrell's heart leapt. She was sure she'd managed to persuade Gwendoline to keep quiet.

'Ha!' Alicia said scornfully. 'Gwen should be singing *your* praises, not the other way round. Darrell saved your useless neck!' She stared contemptuously at

Gwendoline, then turned to the others. 'You know she hid Darrell's boots?' There was a murmur of disapproval. 'You really are too vile for words, Gwendoline Mary!'

Gwendoline was enraged. 'Darrell's really taken you all in, hasn't she?' she spat.

'Please, Gwen,' Darrell said faintly. 'Don't.'

Confused, Alicia and the others gazed at Darrell.

'Gwen, that's enough,' Katherine said firmly.

Gwendoline ignored her. 'You need to know the truth,' she announced. '*Darrell Rivers* was the girl who was asked to leave St Hilda's! So, who's vile *now*?'

Gwendoline glanced triumphantly at the shocked girls. Darrell could barely breathe.

'You're lying, you beastly thing,' Alicia said, disgusted.

'She isn't.' Darrell could hardly get the words out. 'I *was* asked to leave.'

'Aha!' Gwendoline squealed, utterly delighted. 'SEE?'

'I'm sorry I kept it a secret,' Darrell said quietly. 'But Malory Towers was supposed to be my second chance.'

'Miss Grayling knows?' Katherine asked.

Darrell nodded.

'First thing tomorrow, we must go to Miss Grayling and *demand* that Darrell's removed,' Gwendoline said gleefully.

'We'll do no such thing.' Katherine's tone was frosty.

'If Miss Grayling thinks Darrell should be at Malory Towers,' said Jean, 'then that's good enough for me.'

'Agreed.' Alicia nodded. 'I don't give a fig about what happened at stupid St Hilda's. What matters is what happens here.'

Darrell's whole body sagged with relief. Her secret was out, but everything seemed to be all right. She could hardly believe it. Neither could Gwendoline. Her mouth had dropped open in shock, and she shot Darrell a furious look. This was far from over!

'Time for bed,' said Katherine.

'Lacrosse practice tomorrow before breakfast.' Alicia turned to Darrell. 'You'll pair with me, won't you?'

Darrell beamed. Alicia still wanted to be her friend!

'Goodnight, Darrell.' Alicia smiled at her. 'Sleep well.'

Exhausted now, Darrell changed into her nightie and snuggled down under the covers. Sleepily she smiled at the photo of her family at her bedside. Maybe she was going to fit in at Malory Towers after all . . .

CHAPTER TWELVE

MARY-LOU, KATHERINE, Jean and Gwendoline were sprawled on the grass in the early-evening sun. Gwendoline was examining her nails while Mary-Lou, Katherine and Jean worked on their history projects.

'It says here that the Malory Towers servants aired the laundry in these very gardens,' said Mary-Lou. 'Fascinating, isn't it?'

'Not really!' Jean sighed. 'A history project about Malory Towers isn't as interesting as it sounds.'

Darrell rushed over, wrapped in a towelling robe. 'Anyone seen Alicia? We're going swimming.'

'I say, you two have become rather chummy,' Mary-Lou remarked.

'I hope Betty Hill doesn't mind,' remarked Gwendoline sweetly. 'After all, *she* is Alicia's best friend.'

'It's possible to have more than one friend, Gwen,' Darrell said, annoyed.

'Should you be swimming with our history projects due?' Katherine asked.

'I've almost finished,' Darrell replied. 'I'm doing mine on Lady Jane Malory herself.'

Alicia and Betty appeared, arm in arm and heading into school. Darrell waved. 'Hey, Alicia! The pool's the *other* way!'

'Betty's not feeling well,' Alicia said. 'We're going to the san.'

Darrell was disappointed, but she could see Betty was pale and shivering. 'Maybe afterwards then?' Darrell said hopefully.

'No, I'll stay and keep Betty company,' replied Alicia.

'I could come too?'

Alicia laughed. 'What are you, my shadow? Go swim!' She rolled her eyes at Betty as they walked off. 'Honestly, new girls . . .'

Humiliated, Darrell turned away, only to meet Gwendoline's mocking gaze. Darrell's cheeks burned. Was Alicia going to be a friend or not?

Later that evening, Darrell was curled up on her bed working on her history project. The others were already in their nighties, and Gwendoline was brushing her hair. Only Alicia wasn't there. But then she rushed in, tearing open a brown-paper parcel.

'Look what my brothers sent me!' Alicia exclaimed. She lifted the lid off a colourful box to reveal a mixed array of delicious-looking sweets. A handwritten card lay on top. *Enjoy! But don't be greedy.*

'Who'd like one?' Alicia said innocently, offering

the box round.

Immediately Katherine, Irene, Jean and Mary-Lou clapped their hands firmly over their mouths.

'They'll be trick sweets,' Jean said. 'Like last term.'

Irene shuddered. 'I could taste soap for a week!'

'Oh, don't be such babies!' Alicia scoffed. 'Shame Betty's in the san. She'd be game.'

Seeing her moment, Darrell stepped up. 'I'll try one.'

Ignoring the large cherry candies, Darrell selected a small boiled sweet. Everyone watched as she popped it into her mouth and sucked. Darrell gasped, grabbed her throat and started gagging. The girls were horrified.

'Only joking!' Darrell confessed. 'It's delicious.'

The others burst into relieved giggles.

'Who's next?' Alicia asked, offering the box with a flourish.

Mary-Lou was about to choose one of the large cherry candies when Gwendoline leant over and swiped it from under her nose. She popped it into her mouth. *Yummy!* Gwendoline smiled happily. But the others stared at her in amazement.

'Oh, Gwen!' Irene gasped. 'Your teeth!' She snorted with helpless laughter, and the other girls joined in.

Puzzled, Gwendoline ran to the mirror. There she stared at herself in utter horror – her teeth were bright blue!

'I'm sure it'll brush out,' Darrell consoled her.

'No need to look so . . . blue.'

This sent the girls into hysterics, and Gwendoline stormed off into the bathroom.

'What's all this noise?' Matron appeared in the doorway, her hawk-eyed gaze sweeping around the room. She spotted the box on Alicia's bed immediately 'Sweets? I'll be confiscating *those*!'

'But, Matron!' the girls protested in unison.

'You'll get them back at the end of term,' Matron said grimly. 'Now, into bed, please.'

Back in the san Matron couldn't resist taking a peep inside the box. They *did* look delicious. She placed the box high up on the shelf with everything else that had been confiscated – comics, records and make-up.

In the dorm, as the girls climbed into bed, Alicia noticed a book on Darrell's bedside locker. '*A Record of the Life and Death of Lady Jane Malory*,' Alicia read. 'What a stuffy old book!' She smiled. 'I can tell you how she *really* died, and why her ghost haunts Malory Towers to this very day . . .'

So, after lights out, Alicia perched cross-legged at the bottom of Mary-Lou's bed, holding a torch. Darrell and Irene sat either side of a terrified Mary-Lou who had the covers pulled up to her chin.

'On a dark, misty night,' Alicia said solemnly, 'Lady Jane crept out of Malory Towers to elope with her love.'

'Fast Jack the highwayman?' Irene asked.

'Don't interrupt!' Alicia warned. 'From his window her father saw Jack help Jane on to her horse. And he followed.'

'Did he catch them?' Mary-Lou whispered, then nearly jumped out of her skin as Irene began drumming the rhythmic beat of the galloping horses' hooves on the bed.

'WORSE!' Alicia said solemnly. 'He chased them into a fog, and their horse lost its way. Then Jane's father heard the sound of their horses' hooves stop.' Irene stopped drumming. 'Next he heard a blood-curdling scream as they plummeted over the cliff to their watery grave . . .'

'How awful!' Irene gasped.

'At least they died together,' Alicia pointed out.

'I meant for the horse!' Irene replied.

Darrell laughed, but Mary-Lou was round-eyed with horror.

'Now Lady Jane's tragic ghost wanders the hall of Malory Towers,' Alicia announced dramatically. 'Some girls say they've felt her frozen hands clutching at their shoulders, desperate to be saved from the icy depths . . .'

'Stop whispering and get back to your own beds,' Katherine warned, 'or I'll fetch Matron.'

'All that ghost stuff is just nonsense,' Darrell whispered to Alicia as they headed across the dorm.

'Don't be so sure,' Alicia murmured. 'Strange things happen at Malory Towers. You'll see . . .'

When the bell rang the following morning Gwendoline rushed straight into the bathroom to scrub her still blue teeth, while the other girls rolled out of bed to get ready for the day. Suddenly a scream rang out.

'Look!' Trembling uncontrollably, Mary-Lou pointed across the dorm. There, on the wall beside the door, was a dripping red hand-print.

'This is all our fault!' Mary-Lou whimpered. 'We made fun of the ghost, and now she's sent us a sign! What do you think she wants?'

CHAPTER THIRTEEN

THERE WAS a stunned silence for a few moments.

'What does she want?' Sally repeated, staring dubiously at the wall. 'To wash her hands maybe?'

Darrell went over and rubbed a finger across the red hand-print.

'Don't touch it!' Mary-Lou gasped. When Darrell popped her finger into her mouth and licked it, Mary-Lou screamed again, bolting from the dorm.

'It's just strawberry jam!' Darrell called after her.

'Don't you know scaring people is *my* job?' Alicia asked with mock severity.

'Your handiwork, I presume?' Darrell indicated the hand-print.

'Not guilty,' Alicia replied. 'I told you, strange things happen at Malory Towers . . .'

The first lesson of the day was French. As Darrell and Alicia dawdled along the corridor Mam'zelle Rougier swept past them.

'Come, girls, *allez*!' Mam'zelle Rougier said sharply. 'You will be late.'

Alicia sighed. 'Mam'zelle Rougier's class is *boring* without Betty to liven it up! She thinks up the best pranks.'

Darrell was determined to rise to the challenge. 'I know something we could do,' she whispered as they entered the classroom. 'But I'll need your help . . .'

The two girls found seats together at the back, sharing a mischievous glance as Mam'zelle Rougier cleaned the blackboard.

'Gwendoline, you are late!' The teacher glared at Gwendoline as she hurried in.

'Sorry, Mam'zelle,' Gwendoline murmured. She shot a pointed look at Alicia. 'I was cleaning my teeth.' Darrell suppressed a giggle. Gwendoline's teeth were now white again.

'Today we are going to learn something exciting,' Mam'zelle Rougier announced. 'Reflexive pronouns!'

The girls groaned.

'Open your books to Chapter Four,' Mam'zelle Rougier instructed.

Immediately Darrell threw her book to the floor with a thud.

'Darrell Rivers!' Mam'zelle Rougier gasped. 'What are you *doing*?'

'You said to throw our books on the floor,' Darrell replied.

Mam'zelle Rougier was outraged. 'I most certainly did not!'

'Darrell has an ear infection, Mam'zelle Rougier,' Alicia explained. 'You'll have to speak up.'

'If I speak like *this*, can you hear me, Darrell?' Mam'zelle Rougier asked loudly.

'No, I'm not allowed to drink beer!' Darrell said, shocked. The other girls had already caught on to what was happening, and Irene snorted with laughter. The teacher shot her a stern look.

Jean was pinching her nose to stop herself howling hysterically, and Mam'zelle Rougier bore down on her angrily. 'Jean, you think this is funny?'

Jean shook her head as a giggle escaped Mary-Lou.

'Mary-Lou, please!' Mam'zelle Rougier snapped.

'Hairy blue cheese?' Darrell said, straight-faced. This was too much. The class collapsed into uncontrollable giggles.

'Silence!' Mam'zelle Rougier shouted.

The door opened, and Miss Potts looked in. 'Is there a reason for all this noise?' she asked.

The girls quietened immediately.

'Darrell Rivers says she can't hear,' Gwendoline piped up.

Miss Potts eyed Darrell closely. 'Perhaps if you sat near the front of the class, Darrell, it wouldn't be such a problem?' she suggested.

Darrell didn't even pretend not to hear. Red-faced, she grabbed her books and quickly moved to an empty seat near the blackboard.

'I think she's cured,' Miss Potts told Mam'zelle Rougier with just a hint of sarcasm and left.

The French teacher scowled at Darrell. 'Now – reflexive pronouns!' she said sourly.

When the class ended the girls crowded around Darrell while Gwendoline watched jealously.

'Oh, I nearly *died* when you said you couldn't drink beer!' Mary-Lou sighed.

'I thought I was going to burst!' Jean chuckled.

Alicia threw her arm round Darrell's shoulders. 'It's great to have another fun girl in North Tower,' she said. Darrell beamed proudly at her.

The girls scattered to their next lessons, leaving Darrell packing up her books. Only Gwendoline remained behind.

'Little Miss Popular,' Gwendoline jeered. 'But do you *really* believe Alicia is going to hang around with you once Betty's out of the san?'

'I hope you're not jealous, Gwen,' Darrell replied, 'because the last thing you need is green eyes to go with those blue teeth!' And she headed for the art room, leaving Gwendoline seething.

Darrell squinted at her sketch. The subject wasn't very inspiring, she thought with a sigh. Their usual art model was ill, and Miss Grayling had asked Matron to take her place. Matron was dressed as a Valkyrie maiden with a long blonde wig and a silver shield and sword. She looked extremely grumpy and hadn't smiled once.

The hour-long lesson was almost up, and Matron was tired. Rubbing her arms, she stretched and yawned. Darrell's eyes almost fell out of her head with shock. *Matron's teeth were bright blue!*

The other girls also noticed, and they began to point and laugh. Realising her error, Matron closed her mouth with a snap. Miss Potts, who was busy marking books, glanced up, but too late to notice anything. Quickly Darrell took one of her coloured pencils and amended her sketch.

'Lesson over, girls,' Miss Potts said. 'Let's show our appreciation for our stand-in model.'

The girls applauded as a tight-lipped Matron hurried out.

'Oh, that was too funny,' Alicia laughed. 'Matron's been secretly scoffing my sweets!'

'Looks like Gwendoline isn't the only greedy one around here,' Darrell said, showing Alicia her sketch of Matron.

Alicia giggled when she saw the blue teeth in Darrell's drawing. 'We have to tell the others right away,' she said, then groaned. 'Oh, gosh, I just remembered I promised to visit Betty in the san.'

Disappointment flashed across Darrell's face. She

sighed. 'I'd better check my history project anyway.'

Alicia shrugged. 'Actually, Betty and your project can wait! This gossip is just too juicy to keep to ourselves. Come on!' She linked arms with Darrell and marched off with her in tow.

Meanwhile, Matron was back in the san, desperately scrubbing away at her blue teeth. There was a knock at the door, and Matron hurriedly inspected herself in the mirror. Her teeth were still blue. Sighing, she went to the door. Gwendoline stood outside.

'Yes?' Matron grunted, careful to keep her mouth half closed.

'I brought you this.' Gwendoline held out a tin. 'It's bicarbonate of soda. To get the blue stain off your teeth.' Crocodile tears welled in Gwendoline's eyes. 'Those horrid girls played the same trick on me.'

'You poor child.' Gratefully Matron took the tin and patted Gwen's arm. 'What girls?'

Gwendoline sniffed. 'Well, I'm not one to tell tales, but . . .'

CHAPTER FOURTEEN

IT WAS the middle of the night, and the North Tower first-form dorm was silent. A window rattled in the breeze, then swung open with a creak.

The noise woke Sally, and yawning, she sat up. Everyone else seemed to be asleep. It had been a busy evening. Darrell had been working on her history project, *The Ghost of Lady Jane Malory*, until lights out, scribbling away and then rubbing out what she'd written, looking frustrated. And Gwendoline was up to something. She'd skipped into the dorm and directed a smug look at Darrell, who hadn't noticed. Sally wondered what was going on.

She slid out of bed and closed the window. Almost immediately another sound caught her attention. It was the slap-slap-slap of bare feet running along the corridor outside the dorm.

Sally didn't hesitate. She raced for the door just in time to hear the footsteps heading downstairs. Bravely Sally followed.

At the bottom of the stairs Sally saw a door swing closed further along the corridor. Heart fluttering, she tiptoed in that direction. Then the door handle rattled sharply, stopping Sally in her tracks. Nervously she backed away. As she did so Sally glanced up at the painting on the wall. Lady Jane Malory, pale and beautiful in her jewels, lace dress and black-velvet cloak, stared down at her. Her eyes seemed to bore right into Sally's.

Sally gulped. Then the door began to creak open, and she froze where she stood. Was she about to meet Lady Jane Malory in person?

As the door opened a frightening shadow spilled out from inside the room. Then a figure emerged. Sally could hardly breathe, until she realised the eerie figure looked very familiar.

'*Irene!*' Sally murmured.

Irene ignored Sally. She was scooping handfuls of strawberry jam from a jar and eating it hungrily. Sally moved a little closer, but still Irene didn't look at her. She appeared to be in some sort of trance.

'Irene?' Sally said again, confused.

'Oh, Sally, you're so brave to go after the ghost yourself!' Mary-Lou said admiringly. The girls were hurrying to their next lesson, carrying their books.

'But it wasn't a ghost,' Sally pointed out. 'It was Irene sleepwalking.'

Alicia laughed. 'Sleep-*eating*, you mean!'

'That explains why I'm never hungry in the mornings.' Irene grinned. 'And why I sometimes find jam in my hair!'

Gwendoline pulled a face. *Yuck!*

'You should tell Matron, Irene,' said Darrell. 'My father's a doctor, and he says sleepwalking is serious.'

'Darrell's right,' Katherine said gently. 'Come on, let's go to Matron.'

Gwendoline caught up with Darrell as Irene and Katherine headed towards the san. 'Have *you* seen Matron yet, Darrell?'

Darrell raised her eyebrows. 'No. Why?'

'Oh, no reason,' Gwendoline said airily, hiding a smile.

'Why on earth did you tell Irene to go to the san, Darrell?' Alicia grumbled. 'We could have got up to all sorts of mischief and blamed it on Irene's sleepwalking!'

'You don't really mean that, do you?' Darrell was taken aback by Alicia's callousness.

'Of course I do,' Alicia said carelessly. 'Now, shall we swim at break?'

Darrell sighed. 'I have to work on my history project for Miss Potts. I keep finding mistakes.'

'Come on, I owe you a swim,' Alicia urged.

'All right,' Darrell agreed. She and Alicia had such fun together. Darrell couldn't think of anyone at Malory Towers she'd rather have as a friend . . .

After a quick dip in the pool, the two girls rushed back into school, towelling themselves dry. They only had a few minutes to get to their next lesson when Darrell stopped suddenly, shaking her wet hair.

'Hurry, we'll be late!' Alicia warned her.

'What?' Darrell gasped. 'I can't hear you. My ears are blocked with water!'

Alicia doubled up laughing.

'It's not funny!' Darrell groaned.

'Oh, it's *definitely* funny,' Alicia said, grinning. 'Guess who we have next lesson?'

'*Bonjour!*' Mam'zelle Rougier marched into the classroom. Darrell, seated at the back with Alicia, kept her eyes down. Cautiously she shook her head, trying to unblock her ears.

Mam'zelle Rougier glowered at her. 'Darrell Rivers, did I not tell you to sit at the front?' she snapped.

Darrell didn't reply because she didn't hear. Instead, she kept shaking her head and poking at her ears. Highly amused, Alicia nudged her, and finally Darrell looked up. 'Sorry, Mam'zelle. Did you say something? I can't hear because my ears are blocked with water.'

The class erupted into giggles.

'Silence!' Mam'zelle Rougier stalked across the classroom towards Darrell. 'You shall not fool me twice!'

'But, Mam'zelle, it's true!' Darrell pleaded, red-faced.

'Oh, poor Darrell Rivers!' Mam'zelle said scathingly. 'If there is something wrong with your ears, we must call Matron.'

Darrell was horrified. 'No, Mam'zelle!'

'Are you sure?' Mam'zelle asked coldly. 'Because I can summon Matron just like this!' She clicked her fingers.

Someone knocked at the door, and Matron walked in. Everyone, including Mam'zelle Rougier, stared at her in stunned silence.

'Sorry, can I borrow Darrell Rivers and Alicia Johns?' Matron asked sternly. Darrell and Alicia exchanged nervous glances, and Mam'zelle Rougier smiled.

'They are all yours, Matron,' she said.

CHAPTER FIFTEEN

'stop playing with your ears, girl!' Matron ordered, escorting Darrell and Alicia down the corridor. 'Do you hear me?'

Finally Darrell's ears unblocked themselves, and she gasped with relief. 'Yes, I can hear you, Matron!'

'Then hear this,' Matron said grimly, 'I know you two were behind those trick sweets.'

'Whoever told you that?' Alicia asked, feigning innocence.

'Never you mind,' Matron replied. 'But we'll see how funny it is Gwen – I mean –' she attempted to cover up her slip of the tongue – '*when* you see Miss Grayling.'

Matron marched on. Behind her, Darrell and Alicia mouthed '*Gwen!*' at each other.

'Sorry, Matron.' Darrell was thinking fast. 'We hope you don't get into too much trouble.'

'*Me?*' Matron spun round.

'Well, Miss Grayling will know you ate one of the sweets,' Darrell pointed out. 'How else would you know they were *trick* sweets?'

'Darrell!' Alicia pretended to be shocked. 'You can't

be serious! Matron would *never* steal a sweet. All confiscated property has to be returned at the end of term. That's the rule.'

Matron shifted uncomfortably.

'Besides, do her teeth look blue to you?' Alicia continued.

'No,' Darrell admitted. 'Although . . .' She and Alicia peered closely at Matron's teeth. Self-consciously Matron clapped her hand to her mouth.

'Well, I've made my point,' she said in a muffled voice. 'I'll let you off with a warning this time.'

Smothering their grins, the two girls headed off down the corridor.

Darrell and Alicia went to lunch in high spirits. They were giggling together in the dining hall when suddenly Alicia jumped to her feet.

'Betty!' She waved madly at Betty Hill, who'd just come in. 'When did you get out of the san?'

Without a thought for Darrell Alicia sprinted over and linked arms with her best friend.

Darrell sighed. She'd lost her appetite. She was about to leave when Miss Potts appeared.

'Darrell, I've marked your history project,' Miss Potts said quietly. 'You and I need to have a long chat.'

'I imagine you're as disappointed as I am?' Miss Potts said.

Darrell nodded, staring miserably at her project. It was covered in corrections.

'I really tried,' she muttered.

'Did you?' Miss Potts sounded sceptical. 'From what I hear you're more interested in making mischief with Alicia Johns.'

Darrell flushed.

'For some, like Alicia, success comes easily in life,' Miss Potts continued. 'Others have to work at it. Didn't you say you wanted to be a doctor like your father?'

'Yes,' Darrell whispered.

'Life is hard enough for girls with ambition, Darrell, without sabotaging your own chances. What would your father think about how you've been behaving?'

Tears filled Darrell's eyes. 'I try hard with my work, but it doesn't seem to make any difference.'

'Then you need to try harder.' Miss Potts picked up Darrell's project. 'Your writing shows lots of potential, Darrell. You have a strong voice. But you *must* put in the work.'

Darrell fought back her tears. After everything that had happened at St Hilda's she simply *couldn't* let her parents down again . . .

Later that evening, Irene, Mary-Lou and Sally were up in the dorm before the others arrived for bed. Irene was cleaning the jam off the wall, Mary-Lou holding a bowl of soapy water for her. Sally sat on her bed, reading.

'I'll sleep well tonight now I know you're the ghost, Irene,' Mary-Lou said with relief.

Irene shrugged, wiping the wall with a cloth. 'There could still be a ghost, you know.'

Mary-Lou was aghast. 'Oh, I hadn't thought of that!'

'There's no such thing as ghosts.' Sally put her book down. 'Watch this.' She called out, 'Lady Jane Malory, if you are here, make yourself known!'

Silence. Sally smiled – until they all heard the unearthly sound of screeching and scraping, like someone rattling metal chains, heading towards the dorm. Sally's smile vanished, and Irene and Mary-Lou huddled together, petrified.

Matron appeared in the doorway, dragging a metal camp bed along the floor. 'I shall be sleeping in here until Irene's sleepwalking is under control,' she said bitterly. This had been Miss Grayling's idea, not hers. She hauled the bed across the room as Sally, Irene and Mary-Lou exchanged glances.

'Well, at least it wasn't the ghost,' Mary-Lou said, sighing.

'No, it's worse!' Sally whispered.

None of the other girls were pleased to see Matron in their dorm, except Gwendoline. Sally was even more annoyed when she woke with a start in the middle of the night and realised it was Matron's loud snoring that had disturbed her. She was about to bury her head under the pillow, when suddenly the snoring stopped. Sally sighed with relief – until seconds later she once again heard a very familiar sound. The slap of bare feet running along the corridor.

Sally sat up. Everyone else appeared to be asleep, but Irene's bed was empty. Sally tiptoed into the corridor and saw the figure disappearing down the stairs. 'Irene!' she called. No answer.

Sally hurried downstairs herself. She caught a glimpse of the figure again, right at the end of the corridor, and called, '*Irene!*'

'All right, I'm here now!' said a sleepy voice behind her. Irene was stumbling down the stairs, yawning. 'What are we looking at?'

Sally couldn't speak. Unnerved, she stared first at Irene, and then along the corridor where the figure had vanished into the shadows. Lady Jane Malory gazed down at both girls from the portrait on the wall, her expression unreadable.

CHAPTER SIXTEEN

IT WAS a glorious Cornish day. The sun was beating down from a sapphire-blue sky, and the Malory Towers girls were enjoying themselves playing tennis or diving into the pool to cool off.

Darrell was deeply envious. She was stuck inside, trying to thread a tiny needle with sweaty fingers. The Domestic Science class was working together on embroidering a tablecloth with a picture of Malory Towers.

'Done!' Darrell muttered, threading the needle at last. But when she pulled it through the cloth too hard the thread snapped.

'Patience, Darrell.' Miss Potts sighed. 'Irene, could you please stop tapping out a tune with your needle and *concentrate*? All your stitches are different sizes! Alicia, your stitches are too big, and, Mary-Lou, yours are too small.'

Gwendoline coughed loudly.

'Your embroidery is excellent, Gwendoline,' Miss Potts began, then stopped. 'But the stonework is NOT pink!'

Gwendoline pouted. 'I *like* pink.'

Miss Potts sighed again.

'Can we swim for the second half of the lesson, Miss Potts?' Alicia asked eagerly.

Miss Potts considered this. 'Yes, you may swim. *If* you finish this section.'

'I'd rather carry on sewing.' Gwendoline sniffed. 'Needlework is an essential skill for a *lady*.'

'I don't want to be a lady,' Darrell declared, stitching faster. 'I want a career.'

'Having boys' hair doesn't mean you actually have to *be* a boy!' Gwendoline giggled.

'Be quiet,' Darrell muttered. 'You don't know anything about my hair.'

'Oh, no!' Irene groaned, standing up and pulling the tablecloth with her. 'I've stitched it to myself!'

Miss Potts rolled her eyes. 'I *told* you to concentrate, Irene!'

'I'll help you, Irene.' Gwendoline grabbed her scissors, flipped the cloth over and began snipping at the threads underneath.

'I'm free!' Irene exclaimed as Gwendoline pulled the tablecloth away.

'Look how much you've cut, Gwen!' Alicia said accusingly. 'This whole section's going to unravel now.'

'I was helping Irene,' Gwendoline protested.

Miss Potts inspected the damage. 'Take a short

break, girls. But I'm afraid it *will* be sewing next lesson after all.'

Darrell noticed Gwendoline smirking. *Gwendoline cut those threads on purpose to get out of swimming!* Darrell guessed. *How could she?*

Annoyed, Darrell stayed behind when the others left to see if she could repair the damage herself. But it was hopeless. All the stitching was now unravelling, and Darrell gave up just as Emily came in. She took in the situation at a glance.

'Let me have a go,' Emily said.

'Do you think you can fix it?' Darrell asked eagerly.

'I'll see what I can do,' Emily promised, rubbing her tired eyes.

When Miss Potts returned she gazed with admiration at the neatly tied knots and tidy threads on the back of the tablecloth. 'This is astonishing work, Emily!' she said. 'Looks like you can have your swim after all.'

Gwendoline's face fell, and Darrell grinned.

'Apart from *you*, Darrell,' Miss Potts continued. 'I'm sorry, but your English prep is late. No swimming until it's done.'

Darrell's own face fell. She immediately raced up to the dorm and, grabbing her exercise book, she read quickly through the story she'd written. A few moments later Mary-Lou hurried in to get her swimming kit. As she rummaged through her locker, the window flew open with a bang.

'The GHOST!' Mary-Lou shrieked.

Darrell didn't even lift her head. 'It's just the window,' she said, scribbling away. 'Someone probably didn't close it properly.'

Mary-Lou didn't look convinced. 'Do you need help with your English prep?' she offered shyly.

'I'm nearly done,' Darrell muttered. Mary-Lou scurried out, looking deflated, but Darrell didn't notice.

Darrell began checking her spellings. 'Whisper. Is it w-i-s-p-e-r?' She opened her dictionary and was surprised. 'No, it's got an *h* in it!' She corrected it and moved on to the next word. 'Witches.' She'd written *whitches*. Darrell consulted the dictionary again and laughed. 'No *h* this time! *W-i-t-c-h-e-s.*'

Closing her book with relief, Darrell grabbed her swimming kit and rushed downstairs to deliver her prep to Miss Potts. Then, anxious not to miss another minute of swimming, she tore along the corridor. Careering recklessly round the corner, Darrell bumped into Gwendoline, who was coming the other way.

'Sorry!' Darrell gasped. Gwendoline was with Mary-Lou and Margaret, a pleasant, motherly woman who was Matron's assistant. 'Hang on, aren't you going swimming?'

'We're going to the san to see Matron,' Gwendoline

said solemnly. 'Poor Mary-Lou has sunstroke.'

'We don't know that for sure until Matron has seen her, Gwendoline,' said Margaret.

Darrell frowned. 'Sunstroke?'

Mary-Lou opened her mouth to speak, but Gwendoline got in first. 'Actually, I'm feeling a bit iffy myself,' Gwendoline said, sighing.

'But neither of you like sitting in the sun!' Darrell pointed out, puzzled.

'That's true,' Mary-Lou murmured. 'We always sit in the shade.'

'Do you have a headache?' Darrell asked.

Mary-Lou shook her head.

'Are you feeling sick or dizzy?' Darrell continued.

Again, Mary-Lou shook her head.

'Then it's not sunstroke,' Darrell said confidently.

Margaret smiled. 'I'm impressed.'

'My father's a doctor,' Darrell explained. 'Going to the san will just waste Matron's time.'

'And no one wants to do *that*,' Margaret said wryly. 'Off you go to the pool, girls.'

A furious Gwendoline turned on Darrell. 'Being a doctor's daughter doesn't make *you* a doctor!' she hissed.

'It's not fair to use Mary-Lou like that so *you* can miss swimming, Gwen,' Darrell said.

Gwendoline flushed. 'I wasn't – and you're a nasty piece of work to think otherwise, Darrell Rivers!' She flounced off, nose in the air. Mary-Lou remained behind, looking extremely awkward.

'Come ON, Mary-Lou!' Gwendoline ordered her.

An agonised expression on her face, Mary-Lou trotted obediently after her. Darrell shook her head. She felt sorry for the timid Mary-Lou, but she had to learn to fight her own battles.

CHAPTER SEVENTEEN

THE POOL glittered in the sunshine, white-tipped waves rolling across its surface. Girls were swimming, while some batted a beach ball around and others sat on the edge of the pool, kicking their legs in the water. Darrell hurried across the rocks. She could hardly wait to plunge into the blue-green waves and feel their coolness against her hot skin.

Alicia, Irene, Jean and Katherine were already in the pool. So was Mary-Lou, but she was clinging nervously to the edge, while Gwendoline stood shivering on the side. Alicia waved at Darrell. 'Come on, you're missing out!'

Darrell threw off her towelling robe and dived in, surfacing right next to Alicia. Alicia laughed and, leaping on Darrell's back, gave her a playful ducking. Darrell came up spluttering and ducked Alicia right back. Gwendoline watched them having fun with barely concealed jealousy.

Darrell scooped up water with both hands and tossed it upwards like a fountain. Gwendoline got splashed and, scowling, moved hastily out of the way.

'Jump in!' Darrell called wickedly. 'I dare you!'

Gwendoline shuddered. 'I prefer the ladylike way, thank you.' She braced herself and dipped her toe in the water before slowly climbing in.

'Are you all right?' Mary-Lou asked.

'Of course – I love swimming!' Gwendoline lied. 'It's just that first cold plunge . . .' She shivered.

Mary-Lou stared longingly at Darrell and Alicia. They were swimming underwater like fishes, without any fear at all. 'I wish I could swim like them,' she said with a sigh.

'Show-offs!' muttered Gwendoline sourly. 'Darrell thinks she's *so* marvellous!'

'But she *is* marvellous, isn't she?' Mary-Lou said wistfully. 'She's isn't scared of anything. That looks such fun.'

Darrell and Alicia were dunking each other again with shrieks of laughter.

'Anyone can do *that*!' Gwendoline sniffed. 'I'll dunk you, if that's what you want!'

'Oh, no!' Mary-Lou sounded frightened, but Gwendoline grabbed her anyway. She pushed Mary-Lou under the water, holding her down.

Darrell had clambered out of the pool to use the diving board. She was poised to dive into the deep end when she noticed Gwendoline dunking Mary-Lou very roughly. 'Gwen!' Darrell shouted.

Gwendoline didn't hear her. She released Mary-Lou who struggled to the surface, gasping and spluttering. Gwendoline laughed. 'This is how Darrell Rivers plays!' she said spitefully. 'Do you *really* think it's fun?' And once again she pushed Mary-Lou underwater. This time she held her there just a little too long. Mary-Lou's arms and legs flailed as she fought to free herself.

'Gwen!' Darrell yelled. 'Stop that!'

No one else had noticed what was happening. Darrell dived into the water and swam directly towards Gwen. She shoved her away, and Mary-Lou bobbed to the surface. She was shivering and coughing up salty water. 'Thank you, Darrell,' she whispered.

Utterly furious, Darrell turned on Gwendoline. 'You BEAST!' she shouted.

Everyone turned, just as Darrell slapped Gwen's cheek hard. Gwendoline cried out, staggering backwards, and Mary-Lou whimpered in distress.

The whole pool fell silent.

'Darrell Rivers!' Katherine called sternly.

Shaking with rage, Darrell pointed at Gwen. 'She attacked Mary-Lou!'

'The only one I saw attacking was YOU!' Katherine retorted as Alicia, Sally, Jean and Irene watched in disbelief. 'I'm ashamed of you.'

'Well, I'm ashamed of YOU!' Darrell yelled. 'If I was

head of form, I'd jolly well see that Gwendoline left Mary-Lou alone!'

Sally put out a hand. 'Darrell, stop—'

'Get out of the pool, Darrell! Now!' Katherine had had enough. 'Good thing the lifeguard didn't see you do that. Or a teacher!'

Darrell's temper was still blazing. Hoping for some support, she glanced at Alicia, but her friend turned away. Hurt, Darrell hauled herself out of the pool and ran off.

'What the devil was all that about?' Alicia said.

'Are you all right, Mary-Lou?' asked Irene.

Still coughing, Mary-Lou burst into tears, and Katherine turned to Gwendoline. 'What happened?'

Tears were streaming down Gwendoline's face too. She climbed out of the pool and hurried away without replying.

'Right, go and get dressed, girls, and then come to the common room.' Katherine took charge of the situation. 'I'm calling a form meeting.'

Alicia, Irene and Jean glanced at each other. A meeting was only ever called by the head of form in very serious circumstances . . .

'What's a form meeting?' Sally asked as they hurried towards the common room twenty minutes later.

'It's like a council meeting,' Jean explained. 'We talk

about what's happened and decide what to do.'

'Who'd have thought Darrell could be such a spitfire!' Alicia marvelled.

'Do you think . . . ?' Jean hesitated. 'The reason Darrell had to leave St Hilda's . . . Do you think it was—'

'Because she walloped someone?' Irene said bluntly.

'Irene!' Jean exclaimed.

'What?' Irene shrugged. 'It's what we're all thinking!'

'We don't know what happened at Darrell's old school,' Sally pointed out. 'And we don't actually know what happened just now. I don't think we should judge anyone until we do.'

It was the longest speech anyone had ever heard Sally make.

'Wow!' Alicia said, impressed. 'Do you just save up all your words until you really need them?'

'You should try it,' Sally said tartly, and walked on, leaving Alicia open-mouthed.

Led by Katherine, the girls hurried towards the common room. As they dashed along the corridor they came across Miss Grayling and Miss Potts deep in conversation.

'Slow down, girls,' Miss Grayling said calmly. 'No need to rush.'

'Sorry, Miss Grayling,' everyone muttered, moderating their pace.

The headmistress gazed closely at them. 'Is everything

quite all right, Katherine?'

'Fine, thank you, Miss Grayling,' Katherine replied firmly. 'If there's anything we can't manage, I'll let you know.'

The girls moved on down the corridor, and Miss Grayling raised her eyebrows at Miss Potts. 'Something's afoot!' she said.

Miss Potts nodded. 'Don't worry. I'll keep an eye out.'

CHAPTER EIGHTEEN

SPLASH!

Darrell stood on a lonely stretch of beach, flinging stones into the sea with all her might. She was still bitterly angry, not just with Gwendoline but with herself for losing her temper so spectacularly. She picked up another stone and tossed it into the foamy waves. And after she'd promised Miss Grayling to behave better too . . .

'What did them stones ever do to you?' said a teasing voice.

'Hello, Ron,' Darrell said gloomily.

Ron sauntered across the wet sand to join her. He was collecting samphire and had a bucket full of the edible green plants. 'All right?'

Darrell sighed. 'Not really.'

Ron pulled a paper bag out of his pocket and offered it to her. 'A humbug makes everything seem better,' he remarked, eyes twinkling. Darrell hesitated. Sweets were still being rationed after the war, and she didn't want to dip into Ron's allowance.

'Go on,' Ron urged, 'I got extra this week. Swapped

'em for my butter ration, didn't I?'

Darrell stared at him dispiritedly. 'I did something awful,' she confessed. 'I hit someone. A girl in my class.'

Ron's eyes widened. 'She must have done something pretty bad.'

'She did. But so did I.' Darrell sighed again. 'And now I have to apologise.'

'Here, take them.' Ron thrust the paper bag of sweets at Darrell. 'One humbug for now, and one for later. You'll need them!'

Darrell managed to smile at Ron as she accepted the bag, but she knew she had to go and apologise to Gwendoline, Katherine and the others right away. She wasn't looking forward to it at all . . .

Feeling thoroughly sorry for herself, Gwendoline sat on her bed, brushing her hair. Darrell hurried into the dorm and moved towards her.

'Gwendoline, I—'

Gwendoline let loose a melodramatic shriek and retreated to the top of her bed, clutching at the bedpost.

'I'm so sorry for what I did,' Darrell said earnestly. 'Please accept my apology.' She held out her hand, but Gwendoline flinched and cowered as if terrified Darrell would hit her again.

'I was so awfully angry, I couldn't stop myself. But I was utterly wrong, and I'm so sorry.' Darrell stood waiting, hand still out, hoping Gwendoline would accept her apology.

Gwendoline crossed her arms firmly, refusing to shake hands with Darrell and make up. 'I should hope you are!' she said coldly, obviously enjoying being the injured party. 'If my mother knew girls at Malory Towers behaved like you do, she'd never have sent me here.'

Scrambling off her bed, Gwendoline flounced past Darrell. She paused in the doorway to fling a contemptuous look at her. 'And you called *me* a beast!'

Darrell sighed. She'd done the right thing, but Gwendoline hadn't accepted her apology. How could she fix things *now*?

Meanwhile, the North Tower first-form girls were in the common room, deep in discussion about Darrell. Mary-Lou was wrapped in a blanket, still pale and upset.

'There must be a reason Darrell exploded like that,' Sally said for the third time.

'Reason or not, she cheeked Katherine!' Jean rubbed Mary-Lou's back gently. 'That was jolly rude. And that was on top of her being . . . you know . . .'

'Violent?' Irene suggested.

'Irene!' Jean gasped.

'All right, that's enough,' Katherine broke in. 'We all

like Darrell, but we can't let that sort of thing pass—'

'Katherine, please don't punish her,' Mary-Lou broke in. 'She saved me from drowning!'

'Mary-Lou, *please*.' Katherine sighed. 'I'm quite sure Gwen wasn't trying to drown you.' She glanced around at the others. 'Did anyone actually see what happened?'

They all shook their heads.

'We should hear both Gwen's *and* Darrell's sides of the story,' said Sally firmly.

Alicia shrugged impatiently. 'Either way, it's obvious Darrell should apologise. To Katherine and to Gwen. We can send her to Coventry until she does.'

Sally looked blank.

'Sending someone to Coventry means none of us will speak to Darrell or even look at her,' Irene explained helpfully. 'We'll just pretend she's not in the room.'

'That's horrible!' Sally was appalled. 'Isn't that just as awful as slapping someone?'

The common room door opened, and everyone froze.

'Sorry to interrupt.' Miss Potts walked in, observing the girls closely without seeming to. 'Don't mind me.' She walked over to the shelves and selected a book. 'You all look very serious. Anything I can help with?'

'Just finishing up a meeting, Miss Potts,' Katherine replied.

Miss Potts nodded and left. She was on her way downstairs when she noticed Darrell sitting alone on the bottom step.

'Everything all right, Darrell?' asked Miss Potts kindly.

'Yes, Miss Potts,' Darrell murmured, head down.

'If you're looking for the others, they're in the common room,' Miss Potts told her.

Darrell drew in a deep breath and stood up. 'Thank you, Miss Potts.'

'Congratulations on your story, by the way.' The teacher smiled. 'Excellent imagination and much better spelling.'

Darrell forced a smile.

'Do come and talk to me if there's anything worrying you, won't you?' Miss Potts added as Darrell turned to leave. 'I know it's not easy being new.'

'Thank you,' Darrell said again. She went upstairs with dragging footsteps, unaware that Miss Potts was watching her.

In the common room the other girls were still arguing.

'I won't send Darrell to Coventry,' Sally was saying as the door opened. 'What good is an apology if it's forced out of someone?'

Darrell walked in, and a strained silence immediately fell.

'Hello, Darrell,' Sally said loudly and deliberately.

Darrell headed straight for Katherine and held out

her hand. 'Sorry to interrupt, but I *must* apologise, Katherine. I'm most awfully sorry I spoke to you like that. I was in a rage, but that's no excuse.'

'Oh!' Katherine was flustered for a moment. Then she took Darrell's hand and shook it. 'Apology accepted.'

Darrell turned to the others. 'When I came to Malory Towers I promised that I wouldn't lose my temper any more. And I have.' She looked distressed. 'It's an awful fault of mine. I'm utterly ashamed of it.'

Darrell was so emotional all the other girls softened towards her.

'Darrell, if Gwendoline did something wrong, it's not up to *you* to punish her,' Katherine said gravely. 'That's my job, or Pamela's, or a teacher's. Not yours.'

Darrell nodded. She knew Katherine was right.

'And that means there's something else you have to do,' continued Katherine, 'Something you're not going to like at all ...'

Darrell looked apprehensive. What did Katherine mean?

Outside the common room stood Gwen, a damp flannel in her hand. She had her ear pressed to the door, listening avidly to what was being said.

'Gwendoline?'

Gwendoline jumped.

'What on earth are you doing listening at keyholes?' Miss Potts remarked as she passed by. 'If you want to hear what's going on, then go inside!'

Reluctantly Gwendoline opened the door and went in. She held the flannel against her cheek, whimpering with pretend pain.

'Gwen, that's good timing,' Katherine said. She nodded at a worried-looking Darrell. 'Would you please apologise to Gwendoline?'

Darrell laughed with relief. 'Oh, I did that already!'

The tense atmosphere eased, and the girls looked at Darrell with admiration. Gwendoline scowled. 'You fibber, Darrell Rivers!' she snapped. 'You never did!'

Darrell's jaw dropped. 'You know I did, Gwen.'

'You're lying!' Gwendoline glanced triumphantly at the others 'See what kind of girl Darrell Rivers is? A liar!'

Darrell's temper flared hotly. How could everyone, even Alicia, believe Gwendoline and her lies? Darrell couldn't bear to stay in the room a moment longer. She stumbled over to the door, flung it open and slammed it behind her.

CHAPTER NINETEEN

THE GIRLS stared at each other in shock. Only Gwendoline was smiling, pleased that everyone was now on her side.

Before anyone could say a word, however, the door opened again, and Darrell came in quietly. The girls watched in nervous silence. What on earth would Darrell do?

Darrell breathed deeply. Despite Gwen's lies, she was determined to keep a lid on her anger. 'I apologise for what happened, Gwen.' Darrell stared her straight in the eye. 'Again. And I truly am sorry.'

'Easy to say.' Gwendoline sniffed. 'But how do we know you won't do it again?'

'What I did was wrong, Gwen, but so was what you did to Mary-Lou.' Darrell glanced at Mary-Lou, huddled in her blanket.

'We were just playing a dunking game like you and Alicia,' Gwendoline defended herself. 'Isn't that right, Mary-Lou?'

Mary-Lou stared warily at Gwendoline and gave a tiny little nod. Gwendoline shot Katherine a triumphant look.

'You held her under too long!' Darrell pointed out.

'She was struggling to breathe. Weren't you, Mary-Lou?'

Everyone turned to stare at Mary-Lou who shrank back into the blanket.

'I don't – I don't want to get anyone into trouble,' Mary-Lou said, gulping and began to cry.

'I see.' Katherine eyed Gwendoline sternly. 'I think you owe Mary-Lou an apology, Gwen.'

Gwendoline shrugged. '*Sorry!*' she said, but plainly she didn't mean it, unlike Darrell.

'Thank you,' Katherine said calmly. 'The matter's now closed. We'll give both of you a second chance.'

The bell rang, and the girls left the common room. Gwendoline hung back, feeling quite hard done by. After all, *she* was the one who'd been slapped by that awful Darrell Rivers! And as for Mary-Lou, she was just a silly crybaby . . .

Gwendoline hurried upstairs and into the dorm bathroom where Jean was washing her hands. There she examined her cheek in the mirror.

'Just look at the horrid mark Darrell left!' Gwendoline complained, although there was actually nothing there at all.

'Yes, it's huge.' Jean's tone was dry. 'However will you cope?'

'I think she's bruised the bone.' Gwendoline pretended to wince as she touched her cheek. 'I'll *have* to go to Matron.'

Jean's eyebrows rose. 'If you're really worried, then of course you should. But if there's nothing wrong, then it's just telling tales, isn't it?' She went out, leaving Gwendoline scowling at her reflection.

After the meeting, Darrell had gone down to the changing room. She was digging mud out of the soles of her lacrosse boots, giving them a good clean. Having something practical to do helped her to calm down.

Mary-Lou peeked round the door, her expression a mixture of guilt and gratitude. 'Thank you for saving my life this afternoon, Darrell,' she said nervously.

'Don't exaggerate,' Darrell muttered, scrubbing at her boots.

'I'm not!' Mary-Lou bit her lip. 'I'm sorry I didn't explain it properly to the others. I wanted to, but Gwen was there, and—'

'Oh, Mary-Lou!' Darrell groaned, frustrated. 'If you don't pull yourself together, people are going to walk all over you for your whole life.'

'I'm sorry...' Mary-Lou said miserably. 'I just couldn't say anything.'

Darrell softened a little. 'Look, if I try not to lose my temper, could you be a little braver?'

Mary-Lou looked worried. 'How much braver?' she asked, and Darrell couldn't help smiling.

* * *

'Did you get to the bottom of the first-form mystery?' Miss Grayling asked that evening, moving a pawn across the chessboard.

'Not really.' Miss Potts contemplated her next move. 'But I'm sure Katherine has it in hand. It was something to do with Darrell Rivers. Do the girls know about her last school, St Hilda's?'

Miss Grayling shook her head. 'I promised her a fresh start.'

'Well, she's full of goodwill and enthusiasm,' Miss Potts said thoughtfully.

'She has great potential,' Miss Grayling replied. 'In fact, she reminds me of one of our best girls . . .' She smiled as Miss Potts moved her queen. '*You* were quite hotheaded once upon a time!'

'Let's be clear, though.' Miss Potts's expression was serious. 'Unlike Darrell Rivers, *I* was never expelled for pushing a teacher down the stairs.'

'I'm not certain we know the full story there.' Miss Grayling made her final move. 'Checkmate.'

Darrell was feeling much calmer. Her lacrosse boots were now spotless, so she headed for the dorm. No one was there except Sally, who was lying on her bed reading and eating ginger biscuits.

Darrell went to her own bed and was surprised to see a daisy-chain draped round her family photograph.

Where had that come from, she wondered.

'Mary-Lou made it for you,' Sally explained.

'You're still speaking to me then?' Darrell was only half joking.

'Very, very politely and from a safe distance,' Sally replied solemnly.

Darrell smiled. 'Is everyone scared of me?'

'Maybe a little.' Sally was forthright. 'But Mary-Lou isn't – and she's scared of *everything*.'

Darrell sat on her bed and thought for a moment. Then she took a tin of talcum powder and scattered a thin layer on the white windowsill, where it was almost invisible. Next she pulled a hair from her brush, opened the window and stuck the hair between the frame and the side of the window.

Sally watched, fascinated. 'What are you doing?' she asked.

'Setting a ghost trap!' Darrell replied. 'I'm going to prove to Mary-Lou that nothing's coming in or out. And try to help her to be a bit braver . . .'

'Mary-Lou's brave all right,' Sally said thoughtfully. 'She sleeps here every night, even though she's convinced the ghost is real.'

Darrell nodded. 'You're right. She's such a contradiction!'

'All the best people are,' Sally said wisely.

The two girls smiled at each other. Sally snapped her

last ginger biscuit in two and offered Darrell half. Darrell took it, then retrieved the humbugs Ron had given her from her bedside drawer. She kept one herself and gave the other to Sally. The two girls sat side by side on Sally's bed, enjoying their tuck.

Somehow today ended up being all right after all, Darrell thought with satisfaction.

CHAPTER TWENTY

LACROSSE BALLS whizzed across the pitch as the under-fourteens team raced up and down, practising their passing. Pamela, who was in charge, blew her whistle.

'Good work!' she exclaimed. 'Now go and rest. I want you on top form tomorrow!'

Panting and muddy, the girls headed back to school.

'Your last throw was brilliant, Alicia,' said Jean.

Alicia grinned. 'Didn't go in, though, did it? You and your amazing saves!'

'Between you two Harpton Hall won't know what's hit them!' Darrell said encouragingly. 'I wish I was playing too, but Sally's a wizard centre.' She glanced around. Where *was* Sally anyway?

Sally was lagging behind the others, grey-faced and holding her stomach. Pamela, looking concerned, was beside her.

Darrell fell back to join them. 'What's up?' she asked.

'Just a tummy-ache,' Pamela said.

Sally winced and attempted a smile. 'I blame the liver and onions we had last night.'

Darrell pulled a face. It *had* been disgusting! Just

then Ron passed them, also going towards the school, a wooden crate in his arms. Curious, Darrell peeped inside the crate and gasped with delight. 'Ron! *Oranges?*' Because oranges were imported from overseas, it had been difficult to get them during the war, and they were still scarce.

'For the match tomorrow,' Ron explained. 'I ain't never tried one.'

'I'll sneak you one,' Darrell whispered. 'You're coming to the match, right?'

Ron grinned. 'Nah, my grandpa says girls' sport is boring! He says they ain't bold or daring enough . . .' His voice faltered as he noticed the expression on Darrell's face.

'Your grandpa's obviously never met Darrell!' Sally joked.

They all laughed, and Sally winced again.

'See you tomorrow at the match!' Darrell told Ron firmly.

Looking abashed, Ron turned in the direction of the kitchens.

While the girls were getting changed Pamela came in. 'Darrell, will you take Sally to Matron?' she asked.

'I'm fine to go by myself,' Sally said firmly and stumbled out of the changing room. Darrell was about to go after her when Alicia turned to Pamela. 'What happens if Sally's not better by tomorrow?' she said.

'The first reserve will play,' Pamela replied.

'But – *I'm* first reserve!' Darrell gasped. Eyes shining, she raced after Sally. This could be her big chance to make the team!

Sally and Darrell were relieved that Matron wasn't in the san when they arrived. They both preferred Matron's assistant Margaret, who was much kinder and less sharp-tongued. Margaret took Sally's temperature and laid a cool hand against her forehead. 'You're a little feverish,' Margaret said, checking the thermometer. 'And you say your tummy hurts?'

Sally nodded.

'It's probably nothing to worry about, but I'll keep you here for a while, just to be certain,' Margaret said with a comforting smile.

'Lucky you, getting Margaret and not Matron!' Darrell murmured as Margaret went to make up a bed for Sally. 'I wish Margaret was in charge instead. Matron bosses her around so – it'd be great to see Margaret telling *her* what to do for a change!'

Sally managed a smile.

'Should I ask the secretary to call your parents?' asked Darrell, trying to be helpful.

'No!' Sally's pale face flushed with anger. 'Keep your nose out of my business, Darrell Rivers!'

Darrell was taken aback. Leaving Sally in the san, she went to look for Alicia. Darrell found her in the common room, oiling the net of her lacrosse stick ready for the match tomorrow. The other girls were there too, Irene playing the piano.

'I can't work Sally out,' Darrell complained to Alicia, sitting down next to her. 'One minute she's great. Then the next, she's biting your head off or saying nothing at all!'

'Better that than someone who never stops talking about themselves,' Alicia said airily. 'Oh, and speaking of Gwen . . .'

Gwendoline had just entered the common room. She was looking around for a seat, but the only one vacant was between Darrell and Mary-Lou.

'Could you move up, Mary-Lou?' Gwendoline said pointedly.

Irene stopped playing with a crash of discordant chords, and the atmosphere grew tense.

'I thought we were putting all that swimming-pool stuff behind us,' said Alicia equally pointedly.

'Easy for *you* to say.' Gwendoline touched her cheek, wincing dramatically.

Alicia shook her head in disgust.

'It's all right,' Mary-Lou said hurriedly, and moved up so Gwendoline could sit the other side of her.

Time to change the subject, Alicia decided. 'Irene, put that new record of mine on, will you?'

Irene rushed over to the record player, and moments

later an energetic, foot-tapping track blared out. 'Come on, you lot,' Irene said, grabbing Katherine's hand. 'My cousin taught me this new dance.'

The girls grinned as Irene launched into some intricate footwork. Katherine copied her, and Darrell and Alicia jumped up to join in. They were spinning around when Darrell got dizzy and crashed into Pamela who'd just walked in.

'Is that dancing or do you just have a stone in your shoe?' Pamela joked, raising her eyebrows. Darrell grinned, out of breath. 'I've been to the san to check on Sally, and it looks like we'll need you tomorrow, Darrell.'

Darrell was thrilled beyond anything, but, with a huge effort, she managed to control herself. Her gain was poor Sally's loss, and she didn't want to celebrate *too* much. 'I shan't let you down!' Darrell promised.

CHAPTER TWENTY-ONE

DARRELL COULDN'T sleep. She was wide awake, still grinning from ear to ear whenever she thought about the lacrosse match tomorrow. She was playing! She was *actually* playing!

All the other girls appeared to be asleep, but Darrell's attention was suddenly caught by a soft, whimpering sound. She slid out from under the covers and crept over to Mary-Lou's bed.

'Mary-Lou, what's wrong?' Darrell's tone was kind but a little exasperated.

'I'm sorry,' Mary-Lou murmured, distressed. 'But the window keeps creaking. I think it's the – you know.'

Darrell sighed. 'You're worried about the ghost?'

'A little bit,' Mary-Lou said. But Darrell could tell she was petrified.

Darrell grabbed her hand and pulled her out of bed. 'Look.' She led Mary-Lou to the window. 'Last night I set a ghost trap. Talcum powder and a hair. They're still there! Because there's no ghost . . .' She squeezed May-Lou's hand.

'How come you're not scared of anything, Darrell?'

whispered Mary-Lou.

'Because there's nothing to be scared of at Malory Towers,' Darrell replied confidently.

Alicia half sat up in bed, a stern expression on her face. 'Pipe down, you two!' she said. 'I need to be rested for the match. St Hilda's won't beat themselves!'

'St Hilda's?' Darrell repeated, puzzled. Alicia must be half asleep! 'But we're playing Harpton Hall tomorrow.'

'No, we're not.' Alicia's eyes were already closing as she snuggled back down under the covers. 'They cancelled. St Hilda's stepped in, last minute.'

Darrell couldn't believe what she was hearing. All her excitement at making the team instantly disintegrated into nothing. The St Hilda's lacrosse team coming to Malory Towers? This was a *disaster*. Devastated, Darrell fought back tears.

Gwendoline was awake too and had heard what Alicia said. 'How *interesting!*' she remarked gleefully. 'That's your old school, isn't it, Darrell? I can't WAIT to catch up with my cousin Joan tomorrow!'

Darrell was too stunned to reply.

'You must be looking forward to seeing all your old chums!' Gwendoline continued with poisonous friendliness. 'Oh! But maybe not! After all, I imagine they all know why you were asked to leave.' She smiled a sweetly malicious smile and slid down under the covers, very pleased with herself.

Darrell's knees were trembling so much, she collapsed on to her bed.

'Darrell, are you all right?' Mary-Lou asked, gazing at her with concern.

Darrell couldn't answer. She was panic-stricken, a feeling of enormous dread engulfing her. She couldn't play tomorrow now. She just couldn't . . .

Darrell hesitated in the doorway of the san. It was the following morning, and she'd hardly slept at all following Alicia's revelation. Desperate and stressed, Darrell glanced around. No Matron. The coast was clear.

Darrell hurried over to Sally's bed. She was lying very still, and looked rather washed out, Darrell thought with a rising sense of panic. 'Morning, Sally, are you feeling better?' she asked hopefully.

'Not much, worse luck,' Sally replied in a weak voice.

'You'll be well enough for this afternoon, though, won't you?' Darrell said bracingly. 'The team needs you.'

'The team have got YOU!' Sally said. 'And you'll be great.'

Darrell looked wretched.

'Don't feel guilty, you silly,' Sally murmured. '*You* didn't make me have a tummy-ache.'

'It's not that.' Darrell hesitated. She'd never told anyone the whole story before, not even her parents or

Miss Grayling. 'It's the St Hilda's games mistress. Miss Gale. She . . .' Darrell's voice tailed away miserably.

'She what?' Sally prompted, curious.

Emotion welled up inside Darrell. But then Margaret arrived and bustled over, cup of tea in hand, putting a stop to their conversation.

'Darrell! You shouldn't be in here,' Margaret said kindly. 'You'll wear Sally out.'

An idea flashed into Darrell's head. 'Actually, I don't feel well either, Margaret,' she fibbed.

Sally looked surprised as Margaret led Darrell to a chair and sat her down.

'Oh, poor you.' Margaret was sympathetic. 'It must be going round. Let's see now . . .' She put her cup down and felt Darrell's forehead. 'You don't *seem* hot. Open up.' She popped a thermometer into Darrell's mouth, then left her for a few moments and returned to her desk.

Darrell knew she was about to be caught out. She didn't really have a temperature, of course. Glancing around for inspiration, she noticed Margaret's steaming cup of tea on the table next to her.

Carefully, so that Sally and Margaret didn't see, Darrell dipped the thermometer into the hot tea and then whisked it straight out again, back into her mouth.

Margaret returned to check the thermometer, and Darrell waited tensely. What would Margaret say?

* * *

Miss Grayling looked troubled as she walked down the main school corridor alongside Miss Potts. 'If only I'd realised the replacement team was St Hilda's,' she murmured.

'Still time to call it off,' Miss Potts said, looking every bit as worried.

Miss Grayling considered this. 'No,' she said finally. 'It's for the best. An opportunity to face up to her past.'

'Miss Potts!' Jean tore up to them, eyes round with shock. 'Have you heard? Darrell's in the san. She can't play!'

Miss Grayling caught Miss Potts's eye. 'When did this happen, Jean?'

'First thing!' Jean replied breathlessly.

Miss Grayling and Miss Potts stared meaningfully at each other, but at that moment the St Hilda's coach approached the school. A crowd of Malory Towers girls poured out to meet them. Gwendoline was among them, looking for her cousin.

'There she is!' Gwendoline exclaimed to Mary-Lou. '*Joan!*' She waved madly at the coach.

Joan glanced over but didn't wave back.

'I'm sure she just didn't see you,' Mary-Lou began kindly.

'Shut up, Mary-Lou!' Gwendoline snapped.

A long crocodile of St Hilda's girls marched off

the coach, unsmiling and subdued. The team had brought some of their supporters, both girls and teachers, with them.

'Goodness, they're serious!' Alicia remarked. 'There's the captain, Penelope.'

Gwendoline stared at Penelope in disgust. 'Yuck, she's got the same ghastly haircut as Darrell – short as a boy,' she said with a disapproving sniff. 'St Hilda's – patron saint of bad taste!'

Last off the coach was the St Hilda's games mistress, Miss Gale. She smiled in a very friendly way as Miss Grayling stepped forward to greet her.

'Miss Gale? Welcome to Malory Towers.'

'Thank you.' Miss Gale was equally gracious. 'Penelope –' she turned to the short-haired captain – 'do you have our team sheet?'

Alicia took the team sheet and handed over the Malory Towers one. Penelope scanned it and froze. 'Darrell Rivers is here,' she murmured to Miss Gale.

The games mistress smiled even more widely. 'Is she now? Always fun to see where a St Hilda's girl ends up.'

'Darrell's ill today,' Alicia explained. 'She can't play.'

'Shame,' Miss Gale commented. 'Isn't it, Penelope?'

But the only emotion Miss Grayling could detect on Penelope's face was relief. The headmistress frowned. Leaving Miss Potts to show the St Hilda's team to the changing room, Miss Grayling went back into school.

Darrell was in the bed next to Sally, who seemed to be asleep. But Darrell was wide awake, tossing and turning. The match would be starting soon . . . Had she done the right thing?

'How's that fever?' said Miss Grayling softly, appearing at Darrell's bedside.

Darrell blushed miserably as the headmistress placed a cool hand on her forehead. She knew instantly that Miss Grayling had guessed she wasn't really ill.

'I know it must be hard seeing your old schoolmates again, Darrell,' Miss Grayling said. 'But the team needs you.'

Sally's eyes were closed, but she wasn't asleep. She was silently listening to everything Miss Grayling said.

'Sorry, Miss Grayling.' Darrell struggled to force the words out. 'I *do* feel sick . . .'

'Sick with worry perhaps.' Miss Grayling stared steadily at her. 'But, Darrell, we have to face our fears. That's how we find the courage to overcome them.'

Sally wondered what Darrell would do. Would she find the courage to go out and play?

CHAPTER TWENTY-TWO

ALICIA LED the St Hilda's team towards the lacrosse pitch. They were quite stand-offish and didn't say much to the Malory Towers girls, or even to each other. Alicia noticed a couple of them shivering in the cool breeze blowing in off the sea and smiled wickedly.

'This is the path Lady Jane Malory took to her death many years ago,' Alicia announced. 'So if you feel an icy breeze . . .'

The St Hilda's girls looked nervous.

'Really?' Penelope asked sarcastically. 'Trying to put us off with ghost stories, are you? That kind of trick is just the lowest of the low—'

Penelope broke off, staring wild-eyed over Alicia's shoulder. Curious, Alicia turned and saw Darrell, pale but determined, waiting on the pitch with her lacrosse stick. Alicia's face lit up with delight, but Darrell didn't even notice her. She was focused on Penelope, her horrified gaze fixed on her former schoolmate's cropped hair.

'Pen!' Darrell murmured. 'Your hair . . .' She put up a trembling hand and touched her own shorn locks.

Penelope stared coldly at Darrell. 'I had it cut.' She shrugged. 'You started a craze!'

Miss Gale strode on to the pitch to join them. 'Well, Darrell, I see you're feeling better,' she said cheerfully.

Darrell shrank back as the games mistress set about organising the St Hilda's team. Mary-Lou, who was standing on the sidelines, noticed Darrell was shaking with nerves.

'Darrell, are you scared?' Mary-Lou asked sympathetically.

'No!' Darrell said, then hung her head. 'Maybe a little bit.'

'You said there was nothing to be scared of at Malory Towers,' Mary-Lou reminded her.

'But this isn't Malory Towers,' Darrell replied in a small voice. 'This is my *old* school.'

Mary-Lou squeezed her hand. 'You'll be great!' she said.

Further up the pitch the St Hilda's girls were huddled together for Penelope's team talk.

'New plan,' Penelope said in a low voice. 'Darrell's playing, so all we have to do to win is make her lose her temper. Foul her if you can do it without being spotted by the referees – empty stick checks, tripping, hitting. Anything goes. You know what she's like. She'll be sent off, Malory Towers will be a player down, and we'll be on the up!' The St Hilda's girls cheered and clacked their sticks together.

Sally, wrapped in a blanket, had been allowed out of the san to watch the game. She was sitting on a bench at the side of the pitch with Mary-Lou, Irene and Katherine. The older Malory Towers girls, including Pamela, had also come to watch.

'Look.' Sally nudged Mary-Lou. 'Even Miss Grayling's here.' The headmistress was standing on the sidelines with some of the teachers.

'Hello, you lot.' Ron sidled towards the bench, looking rather sheepish. 'Any chance you can explain this whole shebang?'

'Budge up, Irene!' said Sally, making room for Ron. 'The St Hilda's teacher is a referee, and so is our form mistress, Miss Potts.' She pointed both women out to Ron as Darrell and Penelope moved to the middle of the pitch.

'The two centres begin,' Sally explained as Miss Potts blew her whistle. 'Look, now they both try to get the ball, and that starts the game off.'

The play quickly became fast and furious. Darrell was first surprised, then enraged by how many of the St Hilda's girls kept tackling her and committing sneaky fouls when the referees weren't looking. She warned herself to keep calm, but it was tricky with girls continually trying to stop her running and passing by fair means or foul.

Meanwhile, Sally tried to keep Ron up to date with what was happening, but it was difficult when the action was so fierce.

'St Hilda's are good, but we're better!' Sally told him, 'Even though the St Hilda's girls are trying to needle Darrell.' The ball flew through the air and landed on the ground. Darrell and Penelope dashed towards it, and both tried to scoop it up.

'Covering!' Penelope shouted, looking towards Miss Gale. The games mistress blew her whistle and strode towards them.

Ron glanced at Sally, bemused.

'When the ball's on the ground you're not allowed to cover it with your net to stop your opponent picking it up,' Sally said.

Ron looked even more confused. 'Darrell didn't. Did she?'

'No,' Sally said thoughtfully.

Red with frustration, Darrell turned to Miss Gale. 'I *wasn't—*' she began.

Miss Gale shook her head sadly. 'Same old Darrell. Never admit when you're wrong.' She waved her hand. 'You know the rules. Move four yards back.'

Fuming, Darrell backed away. Penelope had *lied*. It was so unfair.

Penelope passed to another of the St Hilda's team,

who returned the ball to her captain. Penelope raced for the goal, and, although Jean made a valiant attempt to stop the ball, it flew straight as an arrow into the net. Darrell groaned as the girl at the scoreboard flipped it to 0–1.

'They're CHEATING!' Ron said furiously as the St Hilda's team celebrated.

'And now they're ahead.' Sally's face was grim.

As the teams ran back to restart the game Darrell confronted Penelope. 'Will you stop messing me around?' she muttered.

'What do *you* think?' Penelope replied airily.

Heroically Darrell swallowed down her temper, although it took a massive effort. When play resumed she collected a magnificent pass from Alicia five minutes later and raced for goal. The St Hilda's goalie loomed up in front of Darrell, but she flung the ball with all her might towards the net.

'GOAL!' roared Sally, Ron, Irene, Mary-Lou and all the Malory Towers girls. Beaming, the girl at the scoreboard adjusted the score to 1–1.

'Good show, Darrell!' Irene applauded wildly.

'Hang on,' Ron said suddenly as Miss Gale headed over to Darrell. 'What's this all about?'

'Foot fault!' Miss Gale was saying. 'I'm terribly sorry, Darrell, but that goal is disqualified.'

'*Foot fault?*' Ron spluttered.

'She's saying Darrell had her foot in the goal circle when she scored,' Sally explained miserably. 'That's not allowed.'

'But Darrell didn't!' Ron said helplessly.

Miss Potts was frowning. 'It didn't look like that to me,' she said.

Miss Gale eyed Penelope. 'You saw it too, didn't you?'

Penelope nodded.

'I trust my captain,' Miss Gale declared.

Miss Potts raised her eyebrows but said no more.

The scoreboard flipped back to 0–1, and there was almost a riot in the Malory Towers ranks. Darrell, white with anger, was only stopping herself from losing her cool by digging her nails into her palms so hard it hurt. The game restarted, but after only a few minutes Miss Potts blew the whistle for half-time. The St Hilda's team bounced delightedly off the pitch, while the Malory Towers girls followed, downcast.

'My foot never TOUCHED the line!' Darrell burst out as she stomped past the bench where the others were sitting. 'She's got a problem with me, and she's taking it out on our whole team!'

'Yes,' Sally said calmly. 'Because she *wants* you to react like this.'

That brought Darrell up short. She skidded to a halt on the muddy grass and turned to face Sally. 'Sally, you have to help me,' she pleaded. 'I can't think I'm so angry.'

'You've got half the St Hilda's team on your back all the time,' Sally replied. 'That means *our* team have players unmarked.'

Darrell grinned. 'So I *pass?* Yes, because they're expecting me to hang on to the ball and try to score myself.'

Sally smiled. 'Go on, surprise them!'

CHAPTER TWENTY-THREE

FEELING VERY frustrated, Gwendoline was searching for Joan. She'd *seen* her cousin arrive on the St Hilda's coach, but Joan hadn't acknowledged Gwendoline's friendly wave. Nor had Joan come to find Gwendoline during half-time, and now the break was nearly over. Joan had simply vanished.

Annoyed, Gwendoline went to check the St Hilda's coach. She stopped short to see Joan sitting on the coach steps eating sandwiches. 'Joan! There you are!' Gwendoline exclaimed, trying not to sound as irritated as she felt. 'Why didn't you say hello?'

Joan's mouth was full of cheese sandwich, and she couldn't reply. But Gwendoline could tell her cousin wasn't particularly pleased to see her. 'I've been trying to call you, AND I wrote!' Gwendoline continued. 'I have to know about Darrell Rivers. I saw her with your captain, Penelope. Did Darrell attack *her*? Is that why she was expelled?'

Joan swallowed down her sandwich. 'Hello, Gwen. I got your letter.'

'Then why didn't you reply?' Gwendoline demanded.

'Because you're mean,' Joan replied calmly.

'I am NOT!' gasped Gwendoline.

Joan stared at her scornfully. 'It isn't up to you to dig into what Darrell did or didn't do,' she said. 'She has a right to a fresh start, just like you!'

'What do you mean by that?' Gwendoline was taken aback.

'Why do you think your father sent you to boarding school?' Joan asked.

'Because I'm gifted!' Gwendoline retorted haughtily.

'No, it was because you need some sense knocked into you! And soon, by the look of things.' Joan popped the last bit of sandwich in her mouth and walked away, leaving Gwendoline seething.

The lacrosse game had restarted, and Sally, Ron and the others were watching tensely from the sidelines. Darrell received the ball, and, as usual, a group of St Hilda's players rushed to surround her. Darrell reacted quickly and passed to Alicia who had acres of space. Alicia raced for goal.

'Great pass, Darrell!' Sally yelled. 'Go, Alicia!'

Alicia tossed the ball neatly past the St Hilda's keeper and into the net. The Malory Towers girls erupted with excitement, screaming, 'GOAL!' Even Ron jumped to his feet, applauding. The scoreboard had just flipped to 1–1 when Penelope raised her hand.

'Covering!' she yelled. 'Darrell Rivers – again!'

Miss Gale immediately blew her whistle. 'Darrell Rivers, repeat offence! The goal is disallowed.'

Darrell couldn't believe what she was hearing. She bit down hard on her lip to stop the furious words erupting out of her, but she longed to rush over to Miss Gale and argue her case. Darrell didn't need to, however. Miss Potts was already jogging over to the St Hilda's captain. 'I was watching Darrell, and I didn't see anything.' Miss Potts stared hard at Penelope. 'I think you might have been mistaken, Penelope.'

Penelope blushed under Miss Potts's suspicious gaze. 'Maybe I was,' she said falteringly.

'Goal stands!' Miss Gale said, her face like thunder.

Potty's on to them! Darrell sighed with relief, and this helped her keep her temper under control. She grinned at Sally and Ron. A plate of quartered oranges was being passed along the bench, and Ron looked like all his Christmases had come at once as he bit into a juicy piece.

Before the game restarted Jean raced out of goal to speak to Darrell and Alicia. 'We just need one more goal!' Jean said urgently.

Alicia glanced at the clock on the scoreboard. 'But there's only a few minutes left!'

Nearby, Penelope grabbed another St Hilda's girl. 'Darrell keeps passing to the right attack,' she said urgently. 'Mark her too, or we're done for!'

All three Malory Towers girls heard what Penelope said. 'They're scared!' Darrell whispered, suddenly full of confidence. 'We can win this. Come on!'

The game began once more. This time it was Alicia who was swamped by St Hilda's girls every time Darrell passed to her. The St Hilda's girls were running around at top speed, trying to stop Darrell and Alicia tossing the ball between them, and they were tiring fast. When Darrell threw the ball to Alicia the St Hilda's girls rushed towards her. But when Alicia neatly passed the ball back to an unmarked Darrell the St Hilda's girls, with their aching legs, couldn't get back fast enough to stop Darrell charging towards the goal.

'Focus!' Darrell told herself, eyes on the prize. Breathing hard, she flung the ball past the St Hilda's keeper.

The Malory Towers supporters went wild as the scoreboard changed to 2–1. They jumped up and down, cheering and chanting Darrell's name as the game finished. When the jubilant Malory Towers team left the pitch, followed by the dispirited St Hilda's and a furious Miss Gale, no one noticed that the captain, Penelope, looked very afraid . . .

'I'm an idiot!' Ron said, catching Darrell's arm. 'Lacrosse is great. It was savage out there!'

Darrell laughed as they headed to the tables of refreshments that had been set out in front of the school. There Sally handed out more orange quarters.

'You saved our bacon!' Mary-Lou told Darrell. 'I'm awfully glad you came to Malory Towers.'

'And I'm glad we got *you* and not that dreadful Penelope!' Jean added.

'Why did she pick on you, Darrell?' Alicia asked curiously.

'I don't know,' Darrell fibbed. She glanced around, a cold feeling of dread suddenly clutching at the pit of her stomach. 'Where *is* Penelope?'

Behind the St Hilda's coach, out of sight, Miss Gale was standing over Penelope. The games mistress was no longer all smiles. There was a cruel expression on her face as she watched an exhausted Penelope doing press-ups in the mud. 'Stupid girl!' Miss Gale muttered. 'You lost us the match.'

Tears sprang to Penelope's eyes. 'I did everything you said!' she panted.

Darrell appeared round the side of the coach, unseen by both of them. She stopped, appalled, unaware that a curious Gwendoline had followed her and was watching from a safe distance.

'If you had, we'd have won,' Miss Gale snapped back. 'So what was wrong with you today? Couldn't see the ball? Hair in your eyes, was that it?'

Darrell flinched.

'No!' Penelope whispered.

'Leave her alone!' Darrell shouted.

CHAPTER TWENTY-FOUR

MISS GALE spun round incredulously.

'Nothing's wrong with Penelope!' Darrell could hardly force the words out she was so unimaginably angry. 'But something's very wrong with YOU!'

Gwendoline goggled in disbelief, eyes out on stalks, as Miss Gale marched over to Darrell. 'How dare you, Darrell Rivers!' the games teacher roared, jabbing her finger in Darrell's face.

Furiously Darrell reached out to swipe her hand away, but Penelope cried out a warning from where she lay in the mud. 'Don't, Darrell! It's not worth it!'

Darrell's hand fell as she struggled to compose herself.

'Miss Potts! Miss Potts!' Gwendoline squealed. 'Darrell Rivers is attacking a teacher!'

Teachers and students from both schools heard Gwendoline shouting and ran to the scene. Darrell, fists clenched, was still staring down Miss Gale. 'I won't let you do that to her!' Darrell said as Sally, Alicia, Mary-Lou and the others joined the silent crowd.

'Or what?' Miss Gale asked scornfully. 'You'll attack

me? You'll push me down the stairs again?'

Gwendoline gasped. So that's what Darrell had done! She cast a triumphant look at the other girls. Meanwhile, Miss Grayling and Miss Potts exchanged concerned glances. Darrell's secret was out now.

'I didn't push you!' Darrell cried, stung by this injustice. 'You fell! But you can't go around cutting people's hair to punish them. It's not right! You're appalling!'

Gwendoline glanced around at the crowd. Everyone, even Miss Grayling, was silent. Gwendoline could hardly believe her luck. She was utterly delighted to see how spectacularly Darrell Rivers had messed up. She'd definitely be expelled from Malory Towers now, and it served her right!

Darrell bent down and helped Penelope up. Another St Hilda's teacher hurried forward and put an arm round Penelope's shoulders.

'I'm not going to stand for this!' Miss Gale blustered. 'Girls – on to the coach at once!'

Penelope did as Miss Gale said, but not before flashing a grateful smile at Darrell.

As Miss Gale swept up the last stragglers on to the coach, she turned and directed a bitter look at Miss Grayling. 'If *this* is how you let Malory Towers girls behave, Miss Grayling, then I don't think we'll be back.' She turned to board the coach herself and promptly tripped over the bottom step. The Malory Towers girls exploded with laughter as Miss Gale struggled to stay upright. Darrell joined in, but quickly sobered up when Miss Grayling stepped forward with quiet authority.

'Darrell, my study, please.'

Darrell nodded, her face distraught.

The girls could talk about nothing else as Darrell silently accompanied the headmistress inside. Even the stunning victory at the lacrosse match was forgotten now. The confrontation between Darrell and Miss Gale was the sole topic of conversation. The girls met up in the common room, Sally holding a hot-water bottle on her tummy, to discuss what had happened.

'So that Miss Gale cut Darrell's hair as a punishment?' Irene mused. She was at the piano playing a sombre, funereal dirge that seemed to fit their mood. 'That's evil. I can't believe it.'

'I can't believe Darrell Rivers pushed her down the stairs,' Gwendoline said gleefully. She paused. 'Actually, I completely, totally CAN.'

'I *don't* believe it,' Mary-Lou said loyally.

'Why would St Hilda's ask Darrell to leave if it wasn't true?' asked Gwendoline triumphantly as Emily walked in.

'Emily, where've you been?' demanded Gwen.

Emily looked wary. 'Catching up on some sewing. Why?'

'You've missed the biggest, most shocking scandal!' Gwendoline said self-importantly. 'A big secret about someone in our dorm is out!'

Emily appeared slightly panicked. 'Who?' she asked.

Sally sighed. 'Irene, can't you play something happy?'

Irene launched into a jolly, upbeat tune that just seemed to make everything worse. She stopped playing and closed the piano.

'Darrell Rivers!' Gwendoline said with relish. 'We know why she was asked to leave St Hilda's.'

'Oh, is that all?' Emily's worried expression vanished. 'I thought we all decided it didn't matter.'

'Exactly,' said Katherine.

'Darrell won't be expelled, will she?' Mary-Lou whispered.

Gwendoline smiled smugly. 'Miss Grayling will do *something*. She knows how a lady should behave.'

'Darrell?'

Trembling, Darrell raised her eyes to meet Miss Grayling's gaze.

'It's extremely important that my girls behave impeccably to our guests,' Miss Grayling continued quietly, 'which is why—'

'You're going to expel me.' Darrell was shaking from head to toe with emotion.

'Which is why I was so proud of you just now.'

Darrell thought she'd misheard. '*What?*'

'This is the positive use of your temper that we talked about in your first week.' Miss Grayling smiled at her. 'You stood up for someone in the face of injustice, no matter the cost.'

Tears of gratitude welled in Darrell's eyes.

'Why didn't you tell your parents that Miss Gale was a bully who picked on her pupils?' Miss Grayling probed gently.

'I – don't know.' Darrell couldn't find the right words to explain. 'She made me think I was stupid . . . And that I deserved to be punished.'

'It's always wrong when a more powerful person enjoys making a weaker one feel small.' Miss Grayling paused to allow Darrell to think this over. 'However, it would have been better to explain things to your team captain or to Miss Potts. So I *will* have to give you a punishment.'

Darrell squared her shoulders and nodded. She was ready . . .

Five minutes later Darrell left the headmistress's study to find Alicia, Jean and the rest of the lacrosse team waiting for her, along with Sally and the others.

'What happened?' Alicia asked.

'Did she . . . ?' Irene looked concerned.

'No.' Darrell sighed. 'But I have to clear up outside.

And then I have to clean all the boots and lacrosse sticks.'

'Not expelled is good,' Irene said encouragingly.

'I can help you clean up—' Sally began, but Darrell shook her head. 'No, you're not well,' she said. 'Leave it to me. I deserve it!' And Darrell walked off, still churning with emotion.

'So unfair!' Jean said indignantly. 'It's that horrid Miss Gale who should be punished!'

Inside her study Miss Grayling was talking on the telephone. 'I'm so glad you agree, Headmistress. Miss Gale doesn't belong with you at St Hilda's, or any other school for that matter. It's a relief to know she'll never be able to do this again . . .'

Miss Potts entered as Miss Grayling hung up with a satisfied expression. Miss Potts, on the other hand, looked worried.

'The cat's out of the bag then,' said Miss Potts. 'What have you said to Darrell? She's staying, isn't she?'

'She is,' Miss Grayling assured her.

'So how do we convince the other girls to ignore the gossip and make their own judgements about her?'

'We can't,' Miss Grayling said wisely. 'We have to trust that we – and Darrell – have already done enough for them to make the right decision.'

* * *

Outside, Darrell had finished clearing away the remains of the refreshments. Next, she collected some boot-cleaning kit and headed for the changing room. The lacrosse team's boots and their sticks were lined up ready to be cleaned, but Darrell stared at them in confusion. *They were already spotless!* 'But how...' Darrell murmured to herself.

Suddenly the whole lacrosse team, along with Pamela, Sally, Irene and the others jumped out from behind the cupboards, cheering their heads off.

'Woman of the match!' Alicia exclaimed, slapping Darrell on the back.

'Terrific performance in your first game,' Jean said approvingly.

'Topping goal!' Pamela added.

'And you didn't see red either,' Sally pointed out. 'Not *on* the pitch anyway!'

'You've cleaned *all* the boots?' Darrell felt quite choked with emotion.

'I saved you one.' Irene held up a muddy boot by its laces. 'Just in case you felt left out.'

'And now – ginger cake!' Jean said. 'Miss Grayling thought the team deserved a special tea.'

'Not just the team,' Pamela explained. '*All* of us. This isn't St Hilda's.'

'No, thank goodness.' A grin spread across Darrell's face. 'This is Malory Towers!'

CHAPTER TWENTY-FIVE

IT WAS early morning, and Darrell sat on her bed cross-legged, books open around her. Everyone else was asleep, but she was studying for the first-form exam. Darrell was determined to do well. It was hard to concentrate, though, with Matron snoring loudly in her camp bed. Darrell flinched at a particularly loud snort, but kept her eyes fixed on her book.

'Arrgh!' Alicia groaned, opening her eyes. 'Irene had better hurry up and stop sleepwalking. I can't take this much longer!' She sat up, grabbed her pillow and aimed it in Matron's direction.

'Don't!' Darrell chuckled. 'You'll get an order mark.'

Alicia pulled a face. She tossed the pillow down, and a few tiny white feathers floated out. 'I don't want to listen to this racket on my birthday!' she grumbled.

'It's your *birthday*?' Darrell was surprised. Alicia hadn't mentioned it until now.

'Look!' Alicia said, amused, pointing at Matron. One of the feathers had landed on her nose, and it was moving up and down a little as she snored.

Then Matron snorted loudly and sniffed the feather

right up her nose. Darrell and Alicia giggled. Immediately Matron let out a giant sneeze that woke her up. '*Atishoo!*' she spluttered, coming bolt upright. She rubbed her nose. 'What was *that*?'

Alicia blinked and yawned as if she'd just woken up herself. 'Matron! Did you smell the ghost?' she asked, pretending to be very afraid. 'Lady Jane IS HERE!'

'There's no such thing as ghosts, you silly girl.' Matron climbed out of bed, looking worried and trying to stare at her nose. It sent her cross-eyed. Alicia laughed, then groaned as Darrell picked up her book again. 'Stop revising, will you?' she scolded. 'The exam isn't for *ages*.'

'It's *tomorrow*!' Darrell said.

'Like I said. Ages!' Alicia shrugged. 'Hurry up, there's a surprise at breakfast.'

'Sorry, Alicia, I really need to stay here and revise,' Darrell insisted.

The breakfast tables were set, but the North Tower girls weren't interested in eating. Apart from Darrell, who was still in the dorm, they were all clustered around Alicia, gazing eagerly at the large hamper in front of them. It had arrived from Alicia's family in Canada.

'What's in it?' Gwendoline asked, unable to wait any longer. She tried to sneak a peek, but Alicia batted her hand away.

'I'll do it,' Alicia said. Almost reverently she lifted

the lid off the hamper, and everyone gasped in awe. It was packed to the brim with delicious tuck. The girls crowded round, and a wide-eyed Mary-Lou pulled out a large bar of milk chocolate.

'This must be two weeks' ration coupons at least!' she gasped.

Irene pounced on a packet of biscuits. 'Can't believe Darrell stayed in the dorm revising.' She sniffed the packet of biscuits longingly. 'Imagine revising when you could be sniffing custard creams!'

'Sherbet!' Gwendoline said greedily. 'Tinned pears!'

'Oh!' Mary-Lou sighed dreamily. 'Fruit cake!'

'Listen,' Alicia whispered. 'Midnight feast. Tonight!'

There was a murmur of excitement.

'I'm going to go and tell Darrell,' Alicia said. 'She'll be thrilled!' And she scooted off to the dorm.

Darrell had finished revising and was already on her way down to breakfast when she met Alicia on the stairs, staggering under the weight of the hamper. She was as excited to see the treats as the others, but when Alicia mentioned the midnight feast Darrell shook her head.

'I can't come,' she told Alicia quietly as they carried the hamper to the dorm.

Alicia's mouth dropped open. 'What do you mean, you can't come?'

'I have to do well in the exam tomorrow,' Darrell explained. 'I need my sleep.'

'But you've been working really hard!' Alicia protested.

'I can't.' Darrell bit her lip. She hated missing all the fun, but she'd promised Miss Potts she'd do her absolute best. 'Sorry.'

Jean and Gwendoline, who were behind them, heard this.

No one had begged *her* to go the midnight feast, Gwendoline thought sourly.

'Oh, let Darrell be boring if she wants, Alicia!' Gwendoline sneered.

'Darrell probably wants to do well because our parents are given our exam marks at the Open Day next week,' Jean said coolly. 'So if you've been telling them you're top of the class, and you aren't, they'll find out.'

'What!' Gwendoline exclaimed. Her face was a picture of utter horror. Saying nothing more, she darted away. Jean grinned.

Gwendoline was now on a mission to find Miss Potts, and she managed to corner the teacher in the corridor just before the first lesson.

'Miss Potts?' Gwendoline said earnestly. 'Can I have a quick word? It's just that – well, do you agree that I'm not doing as well in class as I should be?'

'I do,' Miss Potts said, slightly suspicious.

'And that's my old governess's fault,' Gwendoline said quickly. 'Not *yours*.'

She put a reassuring hand on Miss Potts's arm, and the teacher raised her eyebrows. 'What's all this about, Gwen?'

'It's been very hard for me being so far behind.' Gwendoline forced tears to her eyes. 'I think I need more time to do a formal exam. Especially if the results are made public.'

Miss Potts looked thoughtful. 'I see.'

'I'm thinking of *you*, Miss Potts.' Gwendoline played her last card. 'A terrible mark would reflect badly on my teachers.'

Miss Potts smiled breezily. 'I'll cope. You're going to take this exam, Gwen. It'll do you good.'

'So you really won't come to the midnight feast?' Alicia asked as she and Darrell lugged the heavy hamper towards the dorm.

'No.' Darrell felt terrible but stuck to her guns. 'I'm sorry.'

'Girls!' Matron strode up behind them, and Darrell and Alicia stared at each other in alarm. 'What's in that box?' She lifted the lid and gazed at the luscious contents in amazement. 'I see. *I'll* take this.'

'No!' Alicia protested.

'Yes, indeed.' Matron commandeered the hamper. 'You girls will stuff yourselves silly and get sick. I shall dole it out sensibly little by little.'

'But it's Alicia's birthday present!' Darrell said, stunned.

Matron put the hamper on a nearby chair and opened a tin of biscuits. She took out a small, plain one and handed it to Alicia. 'Happy birthday,' Matron said grimly. Then she walked off down the corridor with the hamper.

Darrell and Alicia were fuming when they rushed into the dorm. They found Irene and Jean there and told them what had happened.

Alicia sighed, dejected. 'That's the end of my birthday fun.'

'It's so unfair!' Darrell was outraged on her friend's behalf. 'We should just go and get it back!'

Alicia jumped up, eyes gleaming with mischief. 'That would be AMAZING! How?'

Darrell was a little shocked. She'd meant it as a joke. 'I don't know . . .'

But almost instantly an idea popped into her head.

'Better be quick or Matron will have scoffed the lot!' Jean advised.

'I *might* have an idea,' Darrell confessed. 'But we'll need a diversion.'

'Leave that to me,' Jean said confidently.

'Ooh, can I help?' Irene bounced on her bed. 'No one ever asks me to do this kind of stuff!'

Alicia glanced eagerly at Darrell who nodded.

'Let's do it!' said Darrell with a grin.

CHAPTER TWENTY-SIX

ALICIA STOOD outside the san, banging frantically on the door. After a moment Matron opened it, looking highly irritated at being disturbed.

'It's Jean, Matron!' Alicia gasped. 'She's got her finger stuck in a bedspring!'

'*What?*' Matron's irritation increased. 'All right, wait there.' She disappeared inside the san, emerging a few moments later with a first-aid kit and a bunch of keys.

'Oh, please hurry!' Alicia begged as Matron closed the door behind her. 'Jean's finger's gone all white – what if it falls off? Come on, *please*!' And she hustled Matron off down the corridor before she had a chance to lock up.

Jean was sitting on her bed, groaning loudly, her little finger jammed in one of the small wire coils that connected the bedsprings to the frame. Matron stared at her, stunned. 'How have you managed to do *that*?' she snapped.

Jean shrugged helplessly. 'Ow!' she moaned theatrically. 'It's stuck, Matron!'

Behind Matron's back, Alicia gave Jean a thumbs up

and tiptoed away to the door. Meanwhile, Matron took a tube of cream from her bag and began briskly greasing Jean's finger. Then she pulled it hard.

'OW!' Jean yelled out in genuine pain, freezing Alicia in her tracks. 'It's actually REALLY stuck!'

'Yes, you said!' Matron growled. 'Now hold on!' She took a firmer hold of Jean's finger and prepared to pull again. Jean's panic-stricken eyes met Alicia's.

'Go!' Jean mouthed at her. 'I'll be fine!'

Alicia shot off at once. They didn't have much time! She raced out of the dorm and hurtled round the corner towards the san. Irene was already on guard in the corridor outside.

'Remember, if you see Matron . . .' Alicia panted as she flew past Irene.

'Yes, yes, I'll shout like anything!' Irene assured her.

Darrell was already inside the san, searching one of the two large cupboards beside Matron's desk when Alicia charged in.

'Found the tuck?' asked Alicia hopefully.

'Not yet,' Darrell replied.

Alicia flung open the other cupboard and burrowed inside. 'Thanks for this. I know you wanted to study. You're a brick, Darrell Rivers.'

Darrell smiled. 'Alicia, how come your parents sent all that food?' she asked a little awkwardly. 'I mean . . . just food? No books or games or clothes?'

Alicia pulled a pile of towels out of the cupboard, followed by a glass jar containing a set of false teeth. She grimaced. 'No real presents you mean, Darrell?'

'Well . . . yes.'

Alicia shrugged. 'I'm full board here. I only see my parents maybe once a year.' She gave a yell. 'Irene?'

'ALL CLEAR!' Irene shouted back.

'They used to send stuff,' Alicia went on. 'Dolls. Pink frilly dresses. All my favourite things.' Her voice was muffled because she was rummaging at the back of the cupboard, but Darrell could hear the sarcasm. 'In the end I told them to just send food. Because everybody eats, right?'

For the first time ever Darrell felt sorry for Alicia. She whisked a pile of newspapers off the top shelf of the cupboard and grinned. 'Talking of food, here's yours!'

Alicia applauded, and between the two of them they tugged the hamper off the shelf.

'Irene?' Darrell called.

'ALL CLEAR!' Irene yelled back, annoyed. 'I'd say if it wasn't! It's all clear. All clear. All cleeeear . . .' Quietly Irene repeated the words over and over, fitting them to a simple tune. 'All, clear, all clear,' Irene sang, testing out her tune. 'Hmm, needs woodwind.' She hummed away. 'All cleeear . . .'

Irene was so lost in music, she didn't notice a grim-looking Matron marching down the corridor towards her, Jean trailing along behind. Jean was glumly holding her hand in the air, a coil of wire, detached from the bed, still curled round her finger.

Inside the san, Darrell and Alicia were emptying the hamper.

'Looks like Matron hasn't touched it,' Alicia observed with relief. 'No, wait – the cake's not here.'

'It's there.' Darrell pointed at Matron's desk. Half hidden behind piles of paperwork was Alicia's fruit cake. It had a huge slice missing.

'That beast!' Alicia groaned. 'She's had nearly half. Well, she's not having any more!' She moved to grab the cake, but Darrell held her back.

'She'll notice,' Darrell pointed out. 'We can replace the hamper, and Matron won't know we've been in here. But if the cake goes missing just after you've knocked at the door?'

'You're right.' Alicia cast a sad look at the cake and reluctantly left it where it was. 'Ooh, that woman!'

Darrell hefted the hamper back on to the top shelf. 'Let's go' she muttered.

The two girls tiptoed over to the door, and Alicia opened it just a crack. They could hear Irene singing to herself outside.

'Irene Edwards!' Matron roared as she spotted Irene loitering dreamily in the corridor ahead of her.

Alicia and Darrell exchanged panic-stricken glances. 'This is *why* we don't involve Irene in this sort of stuff!' Alicia whispered.

Matron was now hustling both Irene and Jean towards the san. 'Malory Towers girls do not *loiter*, Irene,' she said reprovingly, pausing outside the san door.

At that moment Alicia peeped outside and realised how close Matron was. She glared at Irene.

'Sorry!' Irene spluttered to Alicia. 'I mean, sorry, Matron.'

'Well, as you're here, you can help me with Jean,' Matron replied frostily. 'I need someone to hold a pair of pliers.'

Jean gulped.

'NO!' Irene gasped desperately as Matron turned to push the door open. Inside the san Darrell and Alicia could hardly breathe. How could they escape? 'I mean, I wonder if Jean should just keep that on her finger till it falls off?' Irene continued.

Matron spun round to stare at Irene in disbelief. She now had her back to the door, and Irene flapped her hands frantically at Alicia. Carrying armfuls of tuck, Darrell and Alicia sneaked out of the san while Matron's back was turned and hurried soundlessly down the corridor.

'Or we could wait until Jean's finger falls off, whichever happens first,' Irene added, embroidering her suggestion to give Darrell and Alicia time to escape. They did. The two of them rushed round the corner and collapsed into giggles once they were safely out of Matron's sight.

Later that afternoon, everyone met up in the dorm to view the tuck laid out on Alicia's bed. There was a chorus of cheers, but Gwendoline was the only one who didn't join in. She was sitting on her bed, trying to read two books at once.

'Good show!' Jean slapped Alicia on the back. Her injured finger was tied up in a large white bandage.

'You're so brave!' Mary-Lou said to Darrell admiringly.

'Shhh!' Gwendoline snapped. 'Some of us are trying to study, you know.'

Alicia grinned wickedly at her. 'I thought you didn't care about "the stupid exam"?'

Gwendoline scowled back.

'Are you all right, Jean?' Darrell asked.

'Looks worse than it is.' Jean held up her bandaged finger. 'I didn't think it would *really* get stuck! It must have swollen up while I waited for Matron.'

'Matron!' Katherine exclaimed, pointing at the camp bed in the corner. 'She's sleeping in here. How are we going to get out for the midnight feast?'

'Sorted.' Alicia winked. 'Betty's just come down with

a *terrible* sore throat.'

'Oh, poor her,' Irene said sympathetically.

'Irene!' Jean groaned.

'Oh, I get it – she's faking it so we can have our feast!' Irene finally realised.

'Yes, Matron will be busy in the san all night,' Alicia said gleefully. 'Here's the plan. Darrell and I will stay up and wake everyone—'

'Alicia, I'm still not coming,' Darrell interrupted quietly. 'I need to be fresh for the exam tomorrow.'

'The feast's not happening without you,' Alicia said immediately.

'We went to all that effort for nothing?' Irene exclaimed.

'Darrell, please come,' begged Sally.

'Or we'll *all* miss out,' Emily added.

Darrell wavered. How could she let everyone else down? 'All right,' she agreed at last. 'I'll come.'

'We'll be back by one,' Alicia said, smiling. 'Promise.'

CHAPTER TWENTY-SEVEN

WHILE THE rest of Malory Towers slept the North Tower first-form girls were enjoying a magnificent midnight feast in the common room by candlelight. Darrell was glad she'd agreed to come along, even though the thought of the exam tomorrow was still worrying her.

'Here, try these.' Alicia held out a huge box of chocolate biscuits. Darrell hesitated, unable to make up her mind, so she chose two. Alicia grinned as Darrell took a bite from each alternately.

'I can't believe Emily persuaded me to come, and now she's staying in bed because she's too tired!' Darrell grumbled, allowing the delicious milky chocolate to melt on her tongue.

'Oh, pipe down and have another crunchy caramel!' said Alicia. She flicked a sweet at her. Darrell had her hands full of biscuits, so she caught it neatly in her mouth. Alicia applauded.

Mary-Lou, Irene and Jean were sitting in a circle, each of them holding a shelled prawn.

'Alicia told me this is frightfully delicious,' Irene

informed the other two, opening a packet of sherbet. 'You dip the prawn in the sherbet, then bite.'

'You sure about this?' Jean asked doubtfully.

'After three then,' said Mary-Lou. 'One, two, three.'

The three of them dipped their prawns in the sherbet and bit into them.

'Oh!' Irene gasped blissfully. 'That's just –' she spat the prawn out – 'utterly DISGUSTING!'

Jean and Mary-Lou grabbed cans of ginger beer and glugged them down, trying to wash the taste away.

'You didn't *believe* me, did you, Irene?' Alicia said, amused.

Jean and Mary-Lou groaned and began pelting Irene with sweets.

'Ssh!' Katherine warned them as the noise rapidly got out of hand.

'Sorry!' Irene threw out her arms and bowled over the nearby umbrella stand. It clattered heavily to the floor. The girls glanced at each other, horrified.

'Do you think Matron heard?' Mary-Lou whispered. At that moment the light clicked on in the corridor outside.

'Quick!' Darrell said urgently, 'Clear everything up and let's get out of here!'

The girls began scooping the leftover food into their dressing-gown pockets, Gwendoline taking care to grab handfuls of her favourite pink wafers. Then they rushed for the door.

Candle in hand, Matron stepped out of the san. 'Who's there?' she called suspiciously.

The girls scurried down the darkened corridor, Alicia leading the way. Then, to their dismay, a light flicked on at the other end of the corridor.

'Oh, cripes,' Jean breathed.

There was the sound of footsteps, and suddenly a huge shadow loomed on the wall ahead of them. Matron was about to round the corner and catch them red-handed.

'Back the other way, quick!' Alicia ordered.

'We won't make it to the end of the corridor,' Sally gasped.

'Any girl found out of bed will be scrubbing bedpans till the cows come home!' Matron threatened as she strode in their direction.

Darrell, at the back of the group, grasped the nearest door handle and turned it. The door wasn't locked. 'In here!' she whispered.

'We can't!' Katherine was scandalised. 'It's Miss Grayling's study!'

'It's this or be caught,' Darrell replied. 'Come on!'

The girls hurtled inside, and Darrell closed the door. Mary-Lou was white with fear. 'We shouldn't be in here,' she squeaked. 'It's totally forbidden.'

Alicia was already boldly prowling around. 'Miss

Grayling lives like a king!' she whispered. 'Look – toasting-fork, tea and she's even got *bananas*!'

'I haven't seen one of those since I was tiny,' Jean said longingly.

Katherine had her eye to the keyhole. 'Matron's coming!' she gasped.

The petrified girls rushed to hide – Darrell, Mary-Lou and Alicia behind the curtains, Jean and Sally under Miss Grayling's desk and the others behind the cupboards. The door creaked open, and everyone held their breath.

Matron switched the light on. She stood in the doorway, looking around and listening. Darrell thought they were sure to be discovered. But eventually Matron turned out the light and left. The girls breathed a sigh of relief – until they heard the sound of a key turning in the lock.

'She's locked us in!' Katherine groaned.

The girls were panic-stricken. What *now*?

'This was a fantastic idea!' Gwendoline said sarcastically.

'There must be another key in here somewhere,' Sally guessed. 'Everyone look.'

The girls spread out around the study, searching for a spare key. Darrell started with Miss Grayling's neat and tidy desk. In the first drawer she opened she noticed a booklet pushed to the back. On the front was written *First Form General Exam.*

Darrell blinked. Was she dreaming? The answers to the exam questions were right here in her hands! The exam she was so determined to do well in . . . She lifted a corner of the booklet, unaware that Gwendoline was watching her. What was Darrell up to? Gwendoline wondered, nibbling on a pink wafer.

Pulling herself together, Darrell closed the booklet and left it where she'd found it. She wasn't a cheat.

'Found it!' Alicia held up the spare key. 'It was hidden inside the Chinese vase.'

'What's that booklet?' Gwendoline asked nosily, catching a glimpse of it as Darrell closed the drawer.

'The answers for tomorrow's exam,' Darrell replied uncomfortably.

Gwendoline couldn't believe her ears. 'Ooh, let's have a look!'

'No, we can't,' Darrell said firmly.

'Cheating is VILE,' Alicia added, eyeing Gwendoline with dislike.

Gwendoline opened her mouth to argue, but suddenly a loud cry echoed along the corridor outside.

'What was that?' Darrell asked as the girls clutched at each other in terror. The scream was followed by low moans and whimpers of pain.

'Someone's hurt!' Alicia guessed. 'You lot take the food back to the dorm –' she stuffed her tuck into

Katherine's arms – 'and I'll go and see what's happened.'

'I'll come with you.' Darrell handed her food to Sally. Alicia unlocked the door, and then she and Darrell ran down the corridor. Sally, Katherine and the others hurried off the other way, leaving Gwendoline lagging behind . . .

Darrell and Alicia followed the direction of the noise. They were shocked to find Emily lying in the corridor underneath the portrait of Lady Jane Malory. She was moaning and clutching her ankle, face screwed up in agony.

'Are you all right?' Darrell asked anxiously. She and Alicia attempted to help Emily up, but she collapsed to the floor again, squealing with pain. 'Ow! My ankle!'

'What happened?' said Alicia.

'I was coming to find you, and I fell,' Emily explained shakily.

Darrell was puzzled. 'But this isn't the way to the common room.'

'No.' Emily stared at her in a panic. 'But I saw something. A hooded figure. I was so scared, I ran off, and then I tripped . . .' She winced as she moved her foot. '*Ow!*'

'I can hear you!' Matron's voice suddenly echoed down the corridor. 'Stay right there!'

Darrell glanced at Alicia, then at Emily. They couldn't run off and leave her. Matron had finally caught them!

Matron charged round the corner, red-faced and fuming.

'Matron, thank goodness you're here!' quick-thinking Alicia said brightly.

Matron frowned, wrong-footed. She'd been about to bawl the girls out for being up after lights out.

'Emily's hurt herself,' Alicia explained.

'Why on earth are you all out of bed?' Matron demanded.

'Emily heard a noise and went to investigate,' Alicia said. 'She saw a hooded figure – the ghost!'

'So she ran.' Darrell backed Alicia up.

'And I fell,' Emily added.

'We heard her cry out, so we got up and came to find her.' The expression on Alicia's face was one of pure innocence.

Matron's eyes narrowed. 'I see. This is exactly why you're meant to stay in your dorm after lights out. Back to bed immediately.'

Darrell sighed silently with relief. They'd got away with it! Between them, she and Alicia helped Emily hobble back to the dorm where Matron bandaged up her ankle.

'Come to the san in the morning,' Matron instructed. She stared suspiciously around the dorm. All the other girls *seemed* to be asleep. She left, closing the door behind her.

A moment later the dorm erupted. Everyone leapt out of bed and crowded around Darrell and Alicia.

'What happened?' asked Jean.

'Did you get into *trouble?*' Mary-Lou gasped.

'Alicia talked us out of it,' said Darrell with an admiring glance at her friend.

'Emily saw a hooded figure,' Alicia said gleefully. 'Lady Jane's ghost rides again!'

The sound of footsteps outside sent them all scurrying back to their beds. But it was only Gwendoline. 'You ran off and left me, you horrid things!' she complained, closing the dorm door behind her.

'You're too unfit to keep up, you mean!' Alicia scoffed. 'Right – bed, everyone. It's half past three.'

'What?' Darrell stared at her, aghast. 'Oh, no! My brain's going to be scrambled for the exam tomorrow!'

Gwendoline slipped into bed. Under cover of the darkness, she secretly pulled out a piece of blue paper that had been stuffed into her sleeve. She unfolded it, and the pale moonlight lit up the list of answers she'd copied down from the booklet in Miss Grayling's desk.

Gwendoline closed her eyes and fell asleep smiling.

CHAPTER TWENTY-EIGHT

EARLY THE following morning Miss Potts and Mam'zelle Rougier entered Miss Grayling's study to collect the exam papers.

'The papers for the second and first forms are in Miss Grayling's desk,' Miss Potts was saying, when she suddenly came to such a dead halt that Mam'zelle Rougier almost cannoned into the back of her.

A half-eaten pink wafer biscuit lay on Miss Grayling's desk. Frowning, Miss Potts pointed it out to Mam'zelle Rougier. 'Miss Grayling hates biscuits,' Miss Potts said.

'She has impeccable taste,' Mam'zelle Rougier agreed. 'She would not eat these lurid pink wafers!'

Miss Potts hurried round to the other side of the desk, where her suspicions only increased. Two drawers were half open. One held a stack of blue paper, the other the first-form exam booklet.

'And Miss Grayling never leaves her desk drawers open.' Miss Potts looked very shaken. 'Mam'zelle Rougier, please tell the first form that their exam will be delayed.'

A couple of hours later the first-form girls sat in rows in the dining hall, waiting for the exam to start. Darrell yawned as two of the older prefects walked between the rows, placing an exam paper face down on each desk. There was a low hum of chat, mostly speculation about why the exam had been mysteriously delayed.

'Why *are* they so late starting?' Darrell sighed, rubbing her eyes. She was worried and wanted to get it over with.

'Relax,' Alicia told her. 'You could do this exam in your sleep. Which is lucky!'

Darrell didn't even smile. She looked so tired and stressed Alicia felt a bit guilty. She glared at Gwendoline who was smiling confidently. 'Why are *you* looking so smug?' Alicia demanded.

Gwendoline felt the comforting rustle of the sheet of blue paper tucked inside her sleeve. 'Pretty sure I'm going to ace this,' she replied airily.

Grim-faced, Miss Potts strode to the front of the room. 'Girls, I am *shocked*,' she said quietly. 'Last night someone entered Miss Grayling's study.' The North Tower girls shot alarmed glances at each other. 'Furthermore, we believe that they looked at today's exam paper.'

Darrell almost fell off her chair while the rest of the hall gasped.

'I was very sure no Malory Towers girl would ever cheat,' Miss Potts continued. 'But then again, I was very sure none of you would ever invade the privacy of the headmistress's room.' Darrell felt hot and cold all over with shame and embarrassment. 'So you can see that we had no choice but to change the exam paper,' Miss Potts concluded.

Gwendoline sat bolt upright, the smile wiped right off her face.

'And if no one owns up to this after the exam, then I'm afraid the parents' Open Day will be cancelled. Cheating will NOT be tolerated at Malory Towers.' Miss Potts gave them all a hard stare. 'You may begin.'

The girls turned over their papers. Darrell didn't look at the other girls as she turned her paper over. She breathed in deeply and then exhaled. She knew what she had to do. Darrell took up her pen and began to write . . .

The exam had finished, and the girls streamed out into the corridor, glad to be free. Gwendoline, however, was in floods of tears.

'Jeepers, Gwen, if that's how you ace a test, I'd hate to see you flunk one!' Alicia joked.

'We didn't cheat!' Jean complained. 'Potty can't stop us seeing our parents.'

'This is so unfair,' Mary-Lou agreed.

'It's all Darrell's fault,' Gwendoline sobbed accusingly. '*She's* the one who took us in there.'

Alicia glanced over her shoulder. 'Where *is* Darrell?' she asked.

Darrell had gone straight to Miss Potts after the exam finished. Her heart was pounding, but her gaze was steady as she faced her form mistress.

'*You* were the girl in Miss Grayling's study?' Miss Potts repeated, eyebrow raised. Matron, who was also present, shook her head in disgust.

'Yes, Miss Potts. I'm very sorry.' It was only fair that she took the blame, Darrell had decided. It had been *her* idea to hide in the study.

Miss Potts eyed her sternly. 'I am VERY disappointed in you, Darrell. Cheating? I would not have expected—'

'I didn't cheat!' Darrell broke in defensively. 'I did see the paper. I touched it. But I promise I didn't look.'

Miss Potts stared appraisingly at Darrell who returned her gaze with an open, honest expression.

'Who was with you?' Matron snapped disapprovingly. 'Alicia? Emily?'

Outside the classroom, Alicia, Sally, Mary-Lou, Emily, Katherine, Jean and Irene were squashed against the door, listening.

'Well?' Matron said grimly.

Darrell took a breath. This time she'd have to lie. 'It was just me. No one else.'

Suddenly the door burst open, and Alicia flew in. The other girls tumbled in behind her, landing on the floor in an untidy heap.

'I was there!' Alicia panted. 'And Darrell *didn't* cheat. I promise!'

Sally struggled to her feet. 'Miss Potts, I want to own up too.'

'So do we!' Mary-Lou and Katherine chorused.

Irene and Jean couldn't untangle themselves from each other, but they were determined to have their say.

'We had a midnight feast—' Jean said.

'Prawns and sherbet!' Irene interrupted. 'And we hid, but no one cheated!'

Katherine, Mary-Lou and Emily helped each other up as Gwendoline sidled in. 'Miss Potts,' Katherine began.

Miss Potts held up a hand. 'Let me guess. You were all there, and no one cheated?'

Gwendoline fiddled with her sleeve, pushing the blue paper out of sight, and nodded eagerly.

'You didn't need to do this,' Darrell whispered to Alicia.

'We're your friends, dummy!' Alicia whispered back. ''Course we did.'

Miss Potts regarded the girls closely for a moment. 'Very well,' she said, 'I believe you. You made a grave error of judgement, but I no longer think any of you –'

her gaze lingered on Gwendoline for a moment – 'are cheats. You can still see your parents on Open Day.'

Matron frowned as Alicia grinned cheekily at her.

'But you're restricted to grounds until I say otherwise,' Miss Potts said. 'Now! Out!'

Gratefully the girls rushed out, relieved to have got off relatively lightly.

'Now we've just got one problem left,' Alicia announced. Everyone was puzzled, except Gwendoline who looked fearful. 'What are we going to do with all those leftovers?' Alicia said with a laugh, and Gwendoline muffled a sigh of relief. 'What about a *midday* feast?' There were cheers as the girls hurried eagerly back to the dorm to polish off the remaining tuck.

'The way you all ran in!' Darrell said with a sigh, handing round a box of chocolate biscuits. 'Thank you *so* much.'

'That's all right,' Gwendoline said sweetly.

'Says the last through the door!' Alicia pointed out.

Gwendoline scowled.

Mary-Lou dabbed a liquorice stick into a container of sherbet. 'A midday feast is a lot less scary than a midnight feast,' she said thoughtfully.

The girls giggled, and Alicia held up a tin of condensed milk in a toast. 'To Darrell!' she cried.

Everyone applauded, except Gwendoline who rolled her eyes.

Darrell held her chocolate biscuit aloft. 'To us all!' she declared.

CHAPTER TWENTY-NINE

'Malory Towers, Malory Towers,
Your cliff-top days and golden hours . . .'

The sound of sweet, harmonising voices, accompanied by a piano, drifted around the school corridors. Everyone was preparing for Open Day tomorrow. There were girls standing on stepladders pinning artwork to the walls while others rushed past carrying armfuls of flowers. Miss Potts and Mam'zelle Rougier were teetering on chairs, trying to hang a huge banner that read *Open Day! Welcome, Parents!*

'It's too high on your side,' Miss Potts complained.

'It's too low on *your* side,' retorted Mam'zelle Rougier.

'Will guide us through our adult years,
Hand in hand with the friends we made as girls . . .'

Darrell and Alicia were hurrying down the corridor carrying equipment for the athletics events – race numbers, batons for the relay and a coil of finishing-line rope.

'The hundred-yard dash always draws the biggest crowd,' Alicia was saying.

'Hope I can beat my time!' Darrell replied eagerly.

Alicia grinned. 'I hope I win and beat *you*!'

> *'Four tall towers,*
> *The train blasts steam*
> *Oh, that cliff corner view*
> *Of the school of our dreams!'*

Carrying a tray of crockery for the Open Day refreshments, Mary-Lou paused in the common room doorway. Irene was at the piano, and Katherine and Jean were singing along. Sighing with pleasure, Mary-Lou closed her eyes and lost herself in the music.

> *'Four tall towers*
> *That teach us how to strive,*
> *To be women the world can lean on,*
> *Women who will thrive . . .'*

The music stopped. Mary-Lou opened her eyes and gave a little squeal of embarrassment when she saw the other girls staring at her in amusement. Blushing, Mary-Lou scuttled away.

By the following morning, after a good deal of hard

work, the school was ready for Open Day. Even the dorms had been spruced up. The beds were neatly made, and there were vases of flowers on each bedside table. The girls stood to attention when Matron marched in to carry out her inspection. She had dolled herself up for the occasion and had even curled her hair.

'Well, this dorm is *spotless*.' Matron sounded slightly disappointed. 'Shame you didn't keep it this tidy when I was sleeping in here. Now, step forward if your parents are attending the Open Day.'

Some of the girls, including Darrell, stepped forward, and Matron took a stack of envelopes from her pocket. 'These are your half-term results. The rest will go out in the post.'

Darrell eyed the envelopes nervously as Matron handed them out. 'I have to give my results to my parents *today*?' she whispered. 'What if I haven't done well?'

'Then you'll have a jolly awful picnic!' Alicia chuckled. She sobered up though when she noticed Darrell's expression. 'Oh, don't worry! You've worked harder than any of us.'

Darrell cheered up a little. 'I can't wait for you to meet my parents. Mother's bringing cold chicken and pickles for our lunch – two weeks' rations!'

'Oh, didn't I tell you?' Alicia shrugged. 'Sorry, Betty's parents decided to come after all, so I'm spending the day with them instead.'

Darrell's face fell. She'd asked Alicia *weeks* ago. Now she was being dropped in favour of Betty.

'She is my best friend after all,' Alicia said breezily as Matron slapped an envelope into Darrell's hand.

When Matron had left, the girls with envelopes raced into the bathroom, led by Alicia. Darrell followed dispiritedly.

'What if you joined my family for the picnic, then Betty's for the concert?' she asked.

Alicia was busy filling a sink with hot water. 'I promised her the whole day. Why don't you just ask someone else?' She took Jean's envelope, and they all watched as she held it over the steam rising from the sink. Alicia slid her finger underneath the flap, and it opened neatly without tearing.

Jean drew out her results card. 'Not bad!' she said, skimming through it. 'At least I won't end up in dreaded remedial.'

'What's *dreaded remedial*?' asked Darrell.

'It's for girls who aren't up to snuff,' Alicia replied, taking Gwendoline's envelope.

'They give you piles of extra work,' Jean said. 'By the way, Darrell, you *could* ask Mary-Lou to lunch. Her grandmother's ill and can't come.'

'She'd faint with joy if you did,' Gwendoline snorted mockingly.

Darrell smiled. 'Yes, I think I will.'

Alicia held out the open envelope to Gwendoline who took it and peeked inside at her results. Her expression unreadable, she walked off. Then Alicia turned to Darrell, but she shook her head and shoved the envelope into her pocket. 'No, I don't want to go behind my parents' back,' Darrell said. 'I did my best. I just hope my results are good.'

Darrell followed Gwendoline out. Further along the corridor, she was surprised to see Gwendoline tearing up pieces of paper and throwing them into the grate where a fire burned. Darrell was shocked. 'Are those your results?' she asked.

'Of course not!' Gwendoline snapped.

'Look, Gwen, I know what it feels like,' Darrell said sympathetically. 'But your parents will find out eventually . . .'

'Shut up and leave me alone!' Gwendoline tossed away the last scrap of paper and marched off.

Darrell went looking for Mary-Lou. As she rounded a corner she bumped heavily into Jean, who was carrying a pile of sheet music. The sheets flew up into the air and scattered.

'Oh, no!' Jean groaned.

'Sorry!' Darrell got down on her hands and knees to help retrieve them.

Inside the nearby classroom the two girls could hear Miss Potts and Mam'zelle Rougier talking. They were laying out the girls' work for parents to view.

'I meant to ask, how did the new girls do in their French exam?' Miss Potts enquired.

'There were some surprising results,' Mam'zelle Rougier replied. 'Darrell Rivers, *par exemple* . . .'

Darrell's ears pricked up.

'Her exam was *très décevant*,' Mam'zelle Rougier went on.

'As was her English exam,' Miss Potts agreed. 'Now, what about Sally Hope?'

'What's *décevant*?' Darrell whispered as she and Jean scooped up the last few sheets.

Jean shrugged. 'Don't know. But I'm sure it's jolly good!'

In the common room Irene was at the piano practising the song 'Four Tall Towers' for the concert, while Mary-Lou arranged flowers on the mantelpiece.

'We're one girl short,' Irene said between chords. 'Helen caught whooping cough, and now she sounds like Humphrey Bogart. Would you sing with us, Mary-Lou?'

'Me?' Mary-Lou gasped, eyes shining.

'Oh, Mary-Lou, there you are,' Gwendoline said, marching purposefully into the common room. She glowered as Irene began to play a mournful, tragic little tune to mark her arrival. 'Your granny isn't coming,

Mary-Lou?' Gwendoline cooed sympathetically. 'Poor thing. You mustn't be alone today – you can come with me and Mother!'

Mary-Lou tried to hide her horror as Irene flung her a sympathetic glance. 'H-how kind,' Mary-Lou stammered. 'But I won't be alone. I'm singing in the concert.'

Irene beamed at her, but Gwendoline roared with laughter. 'A little mouse like you?' she scoffed. 'Don't be silly!' She eyed Mary-Lou's neat pigtails. 'You'd better go and do your hair or Mother will notice. Go and brush it out. Here!' She handed Mary-Lou a flowery Alice band. 'Go on.'

Mary-Lou hesitated. Then dutifully she took the Alice band and went out, leaving Gwendoline smiling complacently.

Darrell was still searching for Mary-Lou. Unable to find her downstairs, she went to check the dorm. Mary-Lou was standing in front of the mirror, her hair loose. She had the fussily decorated Alice band perched on her head. 'I look like a French poodle,' Mary-Lou was saying mournfully to Sally, who was sitting on her bed.

'Mary-Lou!' Darrell exclaimed. 'I've been searching everywhere for you.' Mary-Lou looked pleased. 'Sorry to hear about your granny. Would you like to join me for a family picnic instead?'

'Oh, yes!' Mary-Lou gasped. 'But . . . Gwendoline just asked me to go with *her*.'

'What!' Darrell was annoyed. 'She knew I was inviting you!'

'I'd much rather go with you,' Mary-Lou admitted.

'Wizard! Then go and tell Gwen.'

'But I can't . . .' Mary-Lou stared at Darrell in distress. 'She'd be so angry.'

Darrell's temper flared. 'For goodness' sake, Mary-Lou!' she snapped. 'What happened to trying to be a LITTLE bit braver?'

Tears sprang to Mary-Lou's eyes. She turned and fled from the dorm.

CHAPTER THIRTY

'YOU WERE quite hard on her,' Sally observed.

'I know.' Darrell sighed. 'It's just that my family will think I'm awfully lonely if I don't bring a friend. And Mother will worry . . .'

'At least your family are coming,' Sally said quietly.

'Yours aren't any more?' Darrell asked. Sally just shrugged. 'Sorry. Would *you* like to join my family for lunch?'

'How sweet,' Sally said drily. 'Was I your first choice?'

A car horn blared outside.

'The parents are starting to arrive!' Darrell bit her lip. 'Please come, Sally?'

'I can't.' Sally swung her legs off the bed. 'I'm going for a walk. *Alone.*'

Rebuffed, Darrell watched her run out of the dorm. She *had* to find someone to invite to the picnic, Darrell thought distractedly, otherwise her mother would be upset . . .

Out in the corridor, Gwendoline was fussing with Mary-Lou's hair. Emily was sitting on the floor, back to the wall, working on a piece of intricate needlepoint.

'Keep still!' Gwendoline snapped, adjusting the Alice band.

'Ow!' Mary-Lou protested. 'Um . . .' She gathered her courage. 'Gwen, Darrell's also invited me to lunch, and—'

'Awful girl!' Gwendoline interrupted. 'She *knew* I was going to ask you. You wouldn't want to go off with a girl who thinks you're so feeble, would you?'

Mary-Lou's face fell as Gwendoline marched her away. Darrell passed them at the corner, and Mary-Lou kept her head down guiltily, but Darrell ignored her. She rushed on, almost tripping over Emily's feet, and her results envelope fell out of her pocket.

Darrell bent to pick it up. 'Sorry, Emily.'

'My fault.' Emily grinned. 'Foolish place to sit.'

'Shouldn't you be outside with the others?' asked Darrell. 'The parents are here.'

'My mother's not coming.' Emily folded her needlework. 'She works such long hours.'

'She works?' Darrell was impressed. 'I say, would you like to join me and my family?'

Emily smiled joyfully. 'I'd be delighted!'

Darrell was utterly relieved. Then the envelope in her hand jogged her memory. 'Emily, are you any good at French? Do you know what *décevant* means?'

'Oh, I do,' Emily chuckled, 'but not because I'm *good* at French! Mam'zelle Rougier writes that on my prep all the time – it means "disappointing".'

Darrell was dumbstruck. *Disappointing!* After all the work she'd done!

'Are you all right, Darrell?' asked Emily.

'Fine,' Darrell muttered. 'Come on.'

Outside the front of the school cars were sweeping up the drive in a long procession, honking their horns. Excited groups of girls stood around waving as their parents arrived. Darrell spotted Alicia and Betty with Betty's parents and stared longingly at them, unaware that Mary-Lou was watching Darrell and Emily with exactly the same expression.

'Mother, you simply must meet Mary-Lou!' Gwendoline pulled her over to Mrs Lacey. She spoke loudly, hoping Darrell would hear. 'It's so lovely to have a best friend.'

Darrell *did* hear but was soon distracted as a familiar black car purred up the drive, and she almost burst with joy.

'Mother! Daddy!' Darrell ran to the car as Mr Rivers helped Mrs Rivers out and handed her a walking-stick. Emily trailed after her.

'There you are, darling,' Mr Rivers said as Darrell flung herself into his arms.

'You don't normally use a stick,' Darrell said anxiously when she hugged her mother in turn.

'Don't worry.' Mrs Rivers patted Darrell's cheek.

'We've got a lot of ground to cover today!'

'We have a surprise for you.' Mr Rivers opened the back door of the car. Felicity leapt out and into Darrell's arms.

'Felicity!' Darrell gasped. 'What are you doing here?'

'Daddy has a medical conference at the Truro Grand Hotel, so we're here for the weekend!' Felicity explained with shining eyes. She stared at Emily. 'Hallo, are you Darrell's best friend?'

'I don't think—' Emily began.

'Oh, we're all good friends here,' Darrell broke in quickly.

'Is that Sally Hope, over by the steps?' Mrs Rivers asked. Darrell glanced over and saw that it was indeed Sally, talking to Jean's parents. 'I had tea with her mother and baby Daphne last week.'

'How strange.' Darrell looked bemused. 'Sally *insists* she hasn't got a sister.'

'Oh, darling, you must have misunderstood.' Mrs Rivers waved. 'Sally! Sally Hope!' But Sally didn't even look as she hurried away in the opposite direction.

'Come on.' Darrell linked arms with Felicity. 'I'll tell you all the secrets of Malory Towers . . .'

After showing them round the school, Darrell took her family to the lacrosse pitch where a running track had been marked out, ready for the athletics later. 'This is where we beat St Hilda's,' she explained.

'St Hilda's?' Her mother looked concerned.

'Don't worry, Mother, we thrashed them!' Darrell eyed her sister mischievously. 'Hey, Felicity, you'd better watch out, you know!'

'That's where Lady Jane's ghost likes to stand!' Emily added, joining in the teasing. Felicity shrieked and jumped off the spot.

'You absolute beast, Darrell! And you too, Emily!' Felicity chased after the two laughing girls.

On the other side of the lacrosse pitch Mary-Lou watched miserably as Darrell and Emily enjoyed themselves. Gwendoline was waving a lacrosse stick around to impress her mother, but she had no idea how to hold it properly.

'Everyone agrees I'm a natural, but I'm not even on the team!' Gwendoline complained.

'Well, I shall speak to that Potts woman immediately,' Mrs Lacey said indignantly.

'No, Mother, it was my decision,' Gwendoline explained in a saintly manner. 'I'll join next year when the others have reached my level.'

Mary-Lou blinked. This wasn't the first lie Gwendoline had told her mother today by any means. How Mary-Lou wished she'd had the courage to stand up to Gwendoline and refuse her invitation . . .

Mrs Lacey spotted Darrell running across the pitch. 'Now there's a nice athletic girl,' she said approvingly.

'Let's say hello to her.'

'No, Mother!' Gwendoline was alarmed, but Mary-Lou took charge. 'Darrell!' she called. 'Mrs Lacey wants to meet you.'

Darrell immediately ran over, despite Gwendoline's sour face.

'I'm Sylvia Louise Mary Lacey.' Mrs Lacey extended her hand graciously. Darrell blinked, somewhat taken aback. 'Are you taking part in the athletics, Darrell?'

'Yes, the hundred-yard dash,' Darrell replied. 'I'm hoping for second or third.'

Mrs Lacey smiled. 'Lucky for you that Gwendoline focused on swimming this term, or you'd have had a real race on your hands!'

Darrell threw back her head and laughed. 'Focused on swimming?' she chuckled. 'It takes Gwendoline two hours to get one toe wet!'

'I beg your pardon?' Mrs Lacey was puzzled. Darrell glanced at Gwendoline whose face was bright red with fury. Oops! Darrell realised she'd well and truly put her foot in it!

'Um – but she's *very* good at other things,' Darrell babbled brightly, moving hastily away. 'Lovely to meet you!'

Thankfully Darrell shot off back to her family, leaving Gwendoline glaring after her.

CHAPTER THIRTY-ONE

'NOW, SHALL we head to the beach for our picnic?' Mr Rivers suggested as Darrell rejoined them.

As they set off towards the car an envelope fell from Darrell's blazer pocket. Felicity swooped on it. 'Darrell! Are these your—'

'Shhh!' Panicked, Darrell dropped back, worried her parents might hear. But they were ahead, chatting to Emily. 'Give it to me.' And she grabbed the envelope.

'I'm top of my class in French and second in maths,' Felicity chattered brightly. 'Soon I'll be a Malory Towers girl too, and—'

'Malory Towers girls don't boast,' Darrell snapped, but then immediately felt contrite when Felicity blushed. 'Sorry, Fee.' She gave her sister a squeeze. 'Come on.'

Quickly Darrell slid the envelope back into her pocket. She couldn't bear to spoil the day by giving it to her parents. Not yet ...

It was a perfect sunny afternoon. The sky was cloudless and the brightest cornflower blue, the sea a deep, clear green. As the foamy little waves washed up on to the sand Mr Rivers spread out a blanket to sit on, and they all tucked into the picnic. It was a feast – cold chicken, pickles, butter and freshly baked bread. Darrell was a little quiet and subdued, however, because all she could think of was the envelope in her blazer pocket.

'What do your parents do, Emily?' asked Mrs Rivers, handing her a plate of chicken.

'Oh, my mother's a nurse,' Emily said hesitantly.

'Which hospital?' Mr Rivers unscrewed a jar of pickles. 'I might know her.'

'She's at the . . .' Emily gasped with embarrassment, clapping a hand over her mouth. 'Oh, how silly of me – I've gone blank!'

'Are you all right, Darrell?' Mrs Rivers eyed her closely.

'Of course!' Darrell made a huge effort to pull herself together. 'I'm just – nervous. About the race.'

'But you're the best runner in the form!' Emily said supportively. 'She's marvellous at lacrosse too,' she told Mr and Mrs Rivers.

'Darrell's fire serves her well on the games field,' Mr Rivers remarked, smiling at his daughter.

'And in the pool, right, Darrell?' Emily nudged her. 'She gave a most *exasperating* girl exactly what she deserved!'

'You didn't lose your temper, did you, Darrell?' her father asked.

'Only once! Or maybe twice.' Darrell felt highly uncomfortable and was desperate to change the subject. 'Did you know Emily saw a ghost?'

'A *real* one?' Felicity's eyes were out on stalks.

'I think so,' Emily replied solemnly.

'Lady Jane herself!' Darrell grabbed Felicity and tickled her. 'She visits our dorm at night . . .'

At the same time a very different kind of picnic was taking place in the Malory Towers gardens. A table had been set up and laid with a white cloth, along with crockery, glasses and cutlery and a variety of odd-looking dishes.

Mrs Lacey and Gwendoline were delicately eating a pink mousse. Mary-Lou valiantly took a mouthful from her own bowl but was unprepared for the strong fishy taste.

'Mam'zelle is very pleased with me, of course,' Gwendoline told her mother.

More lies! Mary-Lou stared incredulously at Gwendoline who noticed and gave her a kick under the table.

Mary-Lou squealed with pain. 'Sorry,' she apologised to Mrs Lacey. 'I think I accidentally bit my tongue when I ate some of this – this . . .'

'Pickled crab in aspic, dear,' said Mrs Lacey.

Appalled, Mary-Lou grabbed a glass of water and

took a swig, trying to get rid of the fishy taste.

'So wonderful about your French!' Mrs Lacey beamed at Gwendoline. 'And top of the class in English too.'

Mary-Lou burst out laughing, spraying water everywhere. There was a horrible silence for a few moments . . .

'So you're not taking part in *anything*, Gwendoline?' Mrs Lacey handed Mary-Lou her dessert.

Mary-Lou gulped. It was a large portion of prune flan.

'No, Mother, I told you,' Gwendoline said virtuously. 'I have to give the others a chance.'

Mrs Lacey clasped her hands. 'My sweet, unselfish Gwendoline! But how *rude* of that girl to make fun of your swimming.'

'Nobody likes Darrell,' Gwendoline said spitefully. 'She thinks far too highly of herself. Isn't that right, Mary-Lou?'

Deliberately Mary-Lou took a huge bite of the disgusting prune flan, so she wasn't forced to agree. She pointed at her full mouth apologetically.

'We'll wait,' Gwendoline said coldly.

Bravely Mary-Lou swallowed the flan and stood up. 'I have to go,' she said, her knees knocking together with fear. 'I can't *bear* to—'

'Yes?' Gwendoline said sweetly.

'I can't bear to – to have my hair in such a mess,'

Mary-Lou blurted out. 'I must go and redo it.' And she walked away, furious with herself for not having the courage to stand up for Darrell . . .

The Rivers family and Emily were also enjoying their dessert – scones with clotted cream, jam and juicy strawberries. Felicity was fascinated by the story of Lady Jane Malory and couldn't stop questioning Darrell and Emily about the ghost.

'The window in the dorm opened by *itself*?' Felicity asked, breathless with excitement.

'But I set a ghost trap after that, and it's never been sprung,' Darrell replied. 'Don't worry, Fee. Ghosts aren't real. But it's a bit of a mystery.'

'There will, of course, be a practical explanation.' Mr Rivers took a bite of scone.

'Perhaps I should do a bit of detective work,' Darrell said, only half joking.

'Or *perhaps* Lady Jane would prefer to rest in peace,' suggested Emily.

'If anyone can solve a mystery, it's Darrell,' Mr Rivers stated confidently. 'She's like a dog with a bone, that one! So determined.'

'She is,' Emily agreed. 'She works so hard at her prep. I'm sure she'll get good exam results.'

Horrified, Darrell rushed to change the subject yet again. 'Fee, shall we skim some stones?'

Felicity nodded eagerly and jumped to her feet.

'So do the exam marks arrive in the post?' Mrs Rivers asked.

'No, Mother,' said Felicity, 'Darrell's got them in—'

'The dorm,' Darrell broke in desperately. 'I left them there for safekeeping.'

Felicity got the message and said no more, but Darrell was racked with guilt. Her parents had been so marvellous to her after everything that had happened at St Hilda's, and now she'd let them down *again* . . .

'Hey, buck up!' Alicia said sharply when she and Darrell met a few hours later for the start of the races. The girls were lined up in their heats and doing a few stretches, but Darrell was feeling sick and rubbing her stomach. 'Don't do a Sally on me. I want to beat you fair and square.'

Darrell's parents and Felicity approached them.

'Is it your turn coming up, darling?' Mrs Rivers asked.

'I think we'll just have time to watch before our meeting with Miss Grayling,' said Mr Rivers.

Darrell's heart jumped into her throat. 'You're meeting *Miss Grayling*?'

'First form, one hundred yards,' Miss Potts's voice rang out. 'Rivers, Johns, Winlow, Cunningham, Bradley.'

The Rivers family went to take their seats while

Darrell stumbled to the start line, reeling from what she'd just heard. She had no chance of keeping her disappointing exam results quiet *now* . . .

'On your marks, get set . . .' Miss Potts called.

Eagerly Darrell lunged forward.

'False start, Darrell!' Miss Potts reprimanded her. 'Do that again, and you're disqualified.'

Darrell was almost in tears as she took her place again. Why couldn't *something* go right for her?

As the girls lined up again Pamela approached Darrell after noticing the anguished expression on her face. 'You can do it, Darrell,' Pamela said, placing her hands supportively on Darrell's shoulders. 'You can do anything you set your mind to.'

Gratefully Darrell nodded. Back in position, she waited for Miss Potts's whistle, determined not to make the same mistake again. When the whistle shrilled out Darrell, afraid of being disqualified, got off to a slow start. But she put on a spurt and, arms pumping, caught up with Alicia who'd gone off like a rocket.

The crowd were on their feet cheering the two girls who were neck and neck. Even Mrs Lacey joined in, much to Gwendoline's disgust. As they raced towards the finishing line Darrell pulled ahead and hit the tape first. She'd won!

CHAPTER THIRTY-TWO

'FIRST PRIZE in the hundred-yard dash goes to Darrell Rivers!' Miss Potts announced.

Everyone was in the marquee, enjoying bowls of strawberries and cream as the prizes were handed out. Bursting with pride, Darrell threaded her way through the applauding crowd towards the podium where Miss Potts waited with her prize winners' ribbon.

'Good for you!' Miss Potts said warmly, pinning the ribbon on Darrell's shirt. She glanced at Mr and Mrs Rivers beaming in the front row. 'And aren't your parents sensible? They know exam results aren't everything.'

Darrell was flooded with guilt. She stepped off the podium and ran straight to her parents. 'I'm sorry!' she said.

'What do you mean?' Mrs Rivers looked perplexed.

'I lied about not having my results!' Darrell blurted out. 'Because they're *awful*!' She pulled the envelope out of her pocket and handed it to her surprised mother.

'I'm sure they're not,' Mrs Rivers said, opening it up. But she frowned when she glanced at the report card inside.

'And Emily's lovely, but she's *not* my best friend.' Darrell burst into tears. 'B-because I haven't got one. I wanted today to be perfect for you, and it's all gone wrong!'

'Perfect for us?' It was her father's turn to look puzzled. 'Today is about *you*.'

Mrs Rivers glanced at her husband. 'Darling, will you go and see Miss Grayling?' she asked. 'I'll join you later. I want to talk to Darrell.'

Wiping her tears, Darrell sat down by her mother and Felicity. 'I'm sorry,' she said shakily. 'I promised not to let you down.'

'You *haven't*.' Mrs Rivers put her hand over Darrell's.

'I lied to you!' Darrell groaned.

'And then you told the truth. You mustn't be so hard on yourself. As for a best friend . . .' Mrs Rivers smiled, slipping her arms round her daughters. 'I didn't find a best friend until I was eighteen! You know, it can take a long time to find someone who truly knows you and accepts you for who you are.'

Reassured, Darrell hugged her mother close.

All too soon the Open Day was coming to an end. Darrell and Felicity sat on the main entrance steps waiting for their parents. Around them girls were saying their goodbyes to their families, and although there were a few tears, there was also a good deal of chat and laughter.

Not for Gwendoline, however. Scarlet-faced, she was enduring a stern scolding from her mother.

'I didn't know you had a meeting with Miss Grayling!' Gwendoline muttered sullenly. 'You always said exam results didn't matter so long as I'm ladylike and pretty.'

'They matter to your father!' Mrs Lacey declared grimly.

Darrell was watching for her parents to appear. When they did her stomach lurched sickeningly.

'What did Miss Grayling say?' Darrell asked, apprehensive.

Her father smiled. 'That you're talented, spirited and clever.'

Instantly Darrell's face lit up. 'She DID?'

'Your results were lower than expected, however,' Mrs Rivers added gently. 'So there'll have to be some changes . . .'

'You'll be sitting in the front row,' Mr Rivers said. 'Away from a distracting young lady called – Alicia, is it?'

Darrell nodded unhappily. 'All right.'

'And since you need more time to study, we've agreed you'll give up lacrosse,' said Mrs Rivers.

'*No!*' Darrell gasped, horrified.

'You have to strike a balance, darling.' Mrs Rivers gave Darrell a loving hug and then settled herself inside the car. 'Never forget we are *so* proud of you.'

Felicity hugged Darrell and then hopped in herself, but Mr Rivers hung back. 'Life will always put up obstacles,' he said. 'You have to find your *own* way through, my dear.' And he winked at her before climbing into the driver's seat.

Darrell's head was in a spin as the car drove off. No lacrosse! How could she bear it? And yet it was almost as if her father was trying to tell her something . . .

'What a day!' Alicia dashed over and slapped Darrell on the back. 'Did you hear Gwen's dear mama? Great win, by the way!'

Darrell nodded weakly.

'What?' Alicia asked. Darrell showed her the report card, and Alicia's eyebrows flew up. 'Oh, no!' she groaned. 'Did Miss Grayling put you in dreaded remedial?'

'No,' Darrell replied.

'That's something. Imagine all that extra work!' Alicia shuddered in mock horror. 'I can't think of anything worse.'

Frowning, Darrell watched Alicia rush over to Betty. *Extra work?*

Ten minutes later Darrell was standing in front of Miss Grayling's desk. 'I've been waking up two hours early every day to do my prep,' she explained earnestly to the headmistress. 'But it still isn't enough. Giving up lacrosse isn't the answer, though. Sport helps me work through my temper.'

'That's very observant of you.' Miss Grayling nodded approvingly. 'What do you propose then?'

Darrell took a breath. 'I'd like to be put in dreaded remedial.'

'Just "remedial" will do,' said Miss Grayling, hiding a smile.

'I can improve, I know I can,' Darrell said confidently. 'I just need a little help.'

'Very well,' Miss Grayling replied. 'I agree to your proposal. You may continue with lacrosse.'

'I won't let you down,' Darrell assured her.

'Coming to me took a lot of courage, Darrell,' Miss Grayling said. 'Well done.'

'Thank you, Miss Grayling, but I'm just finding my own way though the obstacles,' Darrell replied, remembering her father's words.

Out in the corridor some of the girls were taking down the banners and artwork and clearing up the refreshments. Darrell was glad to see things were getting back to normal. She wasn't looking forward to the extra work, but it'd be worth it if she could improve her results *and* continue playing lacrosse.

Later that afternoon, when Darrell was up in the dorm with the others, Pamela popped her head round the door.

'Darrell? Super race today!'

Darrell blushed. 'Thanks.'

'Miss Grayling's asked me to be your student teacher this term,' Pamela continued. 'Does that suit you?'

Darrell was thrilled. 'Oh, yes!'

'I was in the remedial programme myself,' Pamela told her. 'Now I run it.'

Darrell could scarcely believe her ears. '*You* were in remedial?'

Pamela nodded. 'And I hope I can help you as much as it helped me.'

Aglow with happiness, Darrell watched the head girl leave. There was a good deal of hard work ahead of her, but with Pamela to help her she didn't mind half as much . . .

CHAPTER THIRTY-THREE

THE FIRST-FORM ballroom dancing class was not going well. Mam'zelle Rougier groaned as Gwendoline and Irene, who were dancing together, both stepped forward at the same time and banged heads.

'Listen to the *music*!' she yelled. 'Oh, these English girls – impossible!'

'I can see stars!' Gwendoline complained. 'I should probably go and lie down, Mam'zelle?'

'*Non!*' Mam'zelle replied sharply. 'Once more, please.'

Darrell and Alicia grinned as they twirled past.

'How can Irene be so wizard at music but make such a meal of a waltz?' asked Darrell.

'How can Gwen make such a meal of EVERYTHING?' Alicia shot back, and Darrell chuckled.

As the two of them danced alongside Sally and Jean, Darrell noticed an envelope fall from Sally's pocket. It landed at Darrell's feet, and, when she retrieved it, she could see a baby photo through the torn flap.

'Aw, is that your baby sister?' Darrell exclaimed. 'She's a darling, Sally –'

'Give that here.' Her face grim and unsmiling, Sally

grabbed the envelope and hurried to the door. Darrell made to follow, but Alicia prevented her.

'No point. She's been in an absolute grump since yesterday.'

'Probably upset because her parents couldn't come,' Darrell suggested.

Irene and Gwendoline were still stumbling around the room together, and suddenly there was a scream of pain from Mam'zelle Rougier. Irene had trodden heavily on her toes. The class ended in chaos as Mam'zelle limped furiously out of the room.

Darrell slipped quickly away to collect her books for her first remedial session with Pamela, but the other girls left in a more leisurely fashion, giggling about Irene's clumsiness.

'You got Mam'zelle right on the big toe, Irene!' Alicia chuckled as they strolled along the corridor.

Suddenly there was a huge crash directly behind them. Gwendoline shrieked with fear, and Mary-Lou clutched at Jean in a panic.

Hearts racing, they all turned as one, dreading what they would see. The portrait of Lady Jane Malory had fallen off the wall and was lying face down on the floor of the corridor.

There was a shocked silence.

'Don't you ever get *tired* of trying to terrify us, Alicia?' Gwendoline made a brave attempt to sound normal, but her voice was shaking.

'It wasn't me.' Alicia shrugged. 'Lady Jane's getting more active because Miss Grayling's away today. Remember Emily actually *saw* her hooded figure walking the corridors!'

Emily was inspecting the back of the portrait. 'The cord's broken. I'll tell the caretaker.'

'When you saw Lady Jane did she have her hood up or down?' Alicia enquired.

'I don't want to talk about it,' Emily said shortly, and Mary-Lou looked relieved.

'You lot are no fun!' Alicia complained. 'Where's Darrell when you need her?'

Darrell was up in the dorm, collecting her books together. She spotted some scrunched-up paper on the floor and, thinking she'd dropped it herself, picked it up. But it was the photo of Sally's little sister. Darrell smoothed the photo out and turned it over. Written on the back was *Daphne, 1946. Your little sister is getting bigger!*

Perplexed, Darrell turned to Alicia who'd just darted in. 'Sally *can't* have meant to throw this away—' Darrell began.

'Oh, never mind mopey old Sally Hope!' Alicia interrupted impatiently. She took some scissors and a sheet of black card from her bedside locker. 'I've had the *best* idea! We can do it together in prep.'

'I can't.' Darrell was embarrassed, but firm. 'I've joined remedial.'

'You've *joined*?' Alicia repeated, eyes widening. 'Deliberately? After I warned you about it? Why didn't you tell me?'

'It only happened yesterday,' Darrell replied.

'They say it's deadly dull. And utterly boring—'

'Gosh,' Darrell broke in sarcastically, 'I wonder *why* I didn't tell you!' She swept her books up into her arms, put the baby photo on top and left.

There was a notice on the common room door that read *Quiet, please – remedial class in progress*. Darrell hesitated outside, hoping she was doing the right thing. Then Irene arrived, also clutching a pile of books. 'Darrell!' she gasped. 'Are you the girl starting today? We'll have such fun!'

Darrell was stunned. 'But you *can't* be in remedial, Irene. You're a genius!'

'Maybe at music and maths, but I'm really slow at everything else,' Irene confessed shyly. 'Pamela's the only thing keeping me from being bottom of the form.'

Irene opened the door, and the two girls went in. There was a record playing on the gramophone, and Pamela was pouring hot cocoa into mugs. She smiled at them. 'Darrell! Good to see you.'

'I've brought an essay I need to redo for tomorrow, and I have a whole lot of tricky spellings,' Darrell said anxiously. '*Schism. Emblem. Rhythm—*'

'First things first.' Pamela handed the surprised Darrell a mug. 'Sit down and drink your cocoa. Miss Potts has given us the rest of the week to work on your essay. And don't worry about the spellings.' Pamela picked up a piece of chalk. 'Rhythm Helps Your Two Hips Move.' She wrote the initials of the words on the blackboard as she spoke.

'I've never spelt *rhythm* wrong once since Pamela showed me that,' Irene said proudly.

Darrell relaxed in her chair and took a sip of cocoa. This was much better than she was expecting! But then a discordant, crashing noise unexpectedly disturbed the peaceful atmosphere. Someone was bashing tunelessly away at a piano elsewhere in the school.

Darrell pulled a face. 'Who's making that racket?'

'Sally's in a mood again.' Irene shrugged. 'Wonder what's set her off this time?'

Darrell glanced down at the baby photo on top of her books. She could guess . . .

'Sally?'

Darrell paused in the doorway of the room. Sally was still banging away on the piano an hour later and didn't hear Darrell call her name. Darrell could see her wincing every so often as if she was in pain.

Her ears ringing, Darrell went in and put a hand on

195

Sally's shoulder. Sally jumped up, surprised. Then she saw the baby photo in Darrell's hand, and her eyes narrowed. 'What are you doing with *that*?' she snarled.

Darrell was taken aback. 'I found it. You can't have meant to throw it away. It's your *sister.*'

Sally gasped and clutched her stomach. 'I told you, I don't have a baby sister!' she panted.

'But you *do*!' Darrell was perplexed beyond belief. 'My mother's *met* her.'

'Your mother's a liar!' Sally snapped, her face chalk-white.

'My mother wouldn't lie!' Darrell cried furiously.

Sally ignored her, sat down at the piano and began playing at full volume again.

'Why are you so rude?' Darrell yelled. 'What's the matter with you?'

Sally jumped up, bursting with anger. '*You're* the matter with me!' she shouted. 'You and your stupid mother!'

'My mother's *not* stupid!' Darrell blazed back.

'She's an interfering busybody!' Sally retorted. 'And so are you! Get out of my way, Darrell Rivers!'

Sally tried to shove Darrell out of her way and, incandescent with rage, Darrell pushed her back, but a little too roughly. Sally went sprawling, knocking over a pile of sheet music, and her stomach crashed very hard into the piano stool. She moaned in agony.

'Sally, are you all right?' Darrell asked anxiously. 'Did I hurt you?'

Sally scrambled to her feet. 'Just leave me alone!' she muttered, and stumbled from the room.

CHAPTER THIRTY-FOUR

FULL OF remorse, her anger gone, Darrell picked up all the sheet music from the floor, then hurried after Sally. There was no sign of her in the corridor, however. The supper bell rang, but food was the last thing on Darrell's mind. She went to the dorm, but it was empty. Everyone else had gone down to eat.

Darrell stuck her head into the bathroom and called, 'Sally?' There was no answer. She was about to leave when she heard a small, soft groan. Dashing back into the bathroom, Darrell found Sally crouched on the floor behind the showers, doubled up with pain.

'I'm so sorry I pushed you,' Darrell said tearfully. 'I didn't mean to hurt you.'

'You – didn't,' Sally gasped with difficulty. 'It's my tummy. It makes me a terrible grump.' She took a breath and winced. 'I shouldn't have said that about your mother. I'm sorry.'

Darrell was extremely worried. 'Please let me take you to the san, Sally,' she pleaded. 'If it's nothing, you can tick me off later. But what if it's serious?'

Exhausted, Sally nodded. Darrell helped her up,

noting anxiously how Sally trembled with pain at every movement.

It seemed to take ages to get to the san. Even leaning on Darrell, Sally couldn't walk very fast, and Darrell was acutely aware that every step was agony for her. Her anxiety increased. When they finally reached the san, Darrell banged on the door and yelled 'Matron!' several times.

'Darrell Rivers, stop that racket at once!' Matron flung open the door in a temper. She was wearing a smart coat and had her handbag, ready to go out for the evening.

'Sorry, Matron, but Sally's really poorly,' Darrell gasped.

Sally moaned and doubled up again as an intense wave of pain washed over her. Matron frowned. 'Margaret!' she yelled. 'Get this child inside!'

Margaret came running and helped Sally into the san.

'I think I know what caused it, Matron,' Darrell said miserably. 'It's my fault. I pushed—'

'Thank you for your opinion, Doctor Rivers!' Matron snapped. 'Dorm! Now!' And she slammed the door shut in Darrell's face.

Inside the san, Sally was sitting on a bed, whimpering.

'Should I call the doctor?' Margaret asked, concerned.

Matron shook her head. 'This always happens after Open Day,' she said briskly. 'Too much strawberries and cream! Just keep an eye on her.'

'Of course, Matron.'

'Now I'll be late for the pictures,' Matron muttered grumpily, checking her watch. 'And no calling the doctor while I'm out, Margaret. You're a soft touch, and these girls know it!'

'Yes, Matron,' Margaret replied obediently, but there was a worried expression on her face.

Back at the dorm, Darrell was supposed to be getting ready for bed. Instead, still in her uniform, she was sitting on the bathroom floor writing a letter.

'Look lively!' Alicia, in her pyjamas, stuck her head round the door. 'I'm about to start.'

'I'm busy,' Darrell said distractedly.

'Doing what?'

'Writing to Sally's mother to explain.' Darrell looked downcast. 'You see, we had a fight—'

'A *fight*?' Alicia whipped the letter from her hands and screwed it up, much to Darrell's dismay. 'That's for your own good *and* Sally's,' Alicia continued. 'You'll both be in trouble if you send that letter. Aren't your parents staying just down the road at the Grand? Potty could have them back here in five minutes!'

'But I'm worried about Sally,' Darrell said, sighing.

Alicia ignored her and skipped away, taking the letter with her. Frustrated, Darrell began to brush her teeth.

The dorm was now in uproar. Alicia was standing on her bed, a blanket wrapped round her, while Irene beat out a sound like horses' hooves on the furniture. Everyone was gripped by the scene, except Gwendoline, who was brushing her hair.

'A dark, hooded figure gallops across the cliff with her love.' Alicia struck a dramatic pose. 'Her cloak billows behind her as they career through the fog . . .'

Shivering, Mary-Lou pulled the bedcovers right up to her chin.

'Alicia!' Katherine said sharply. 'Lights out.'

'Darrell's still in the bathroom,' Alicia replied. 'Anyway, Matron or Margaret will come and do it.'

'One hundred!' Gwendoline said triumphantly, laying her brush down. 'First time all term! And Katherine's right, Alicia – we need our beauty sleep. I'll turn the lights out *myself*.' She headed self-righteously towards the switch.

'Don't be such a goody-goody!' Alicia said and fired her pillow across the dorm. As Gwendoline turned to switch off the lights, the pillow hit her squarely in the back and burst open, showering both her and the dorm in white feathers.

Gwendoline gave an outraged shriek. 'How dare you!' She grabbed the nearest pillow and threw it back at Alicia. Within seconds the whole dorm was screaming with laughter and chucking pillows at each other.

Katherine watched helplessly for a moment. Then she slipped out and hurried to the san.

Margaret was holding a cold cloth to Sally's forehead with one hand and had the telephone receiver in the other when Katherine walked in. She was shocked to see how pale and ill Sally looked.

'We thought it was too many strawberries at first,' Margaret was saying. 'And you can't come any earlier? All right, thank you, Doctor. We'll see you in the morning.'

'Margaret, we need someone for lights out,' Katherine said as Margaret hung up. But then Sally coughed and was sick all over the floor.

'Sorry, Katherine, could you do lights out yourself tonight?' Flustered, Margaret ran for a mop and bucket.

The pillow fight in the dorm was still in full swing when Katherine returned. 'I've been told to do lights out,' Katherine said firmly, as Darrell came out of the bathroom in her pyjamas, and she flipped the switch, leaving the dorm in darkness.

'Isn't Margaret coming?' Darrell asked Katherine.

'She's too busy with Sally,' Katherine replied.

Miserably Darrell climbed into bed. Sally was desperately ill, and it was all *her* fault. As Darrell lay there worrying Alicia suddenly shot upright.

'Emily, you said Lady Jane was wearing a hooded cloak when you saw her, didn't you?' Alicia enquired.

'Don't remember,' Emily said sleepily.

'You DID!' Alicia launched into full dramatic mode. 'I think SHE'S HERE!'

Mary-Lou peeped out from under her covers. She stiffened with terror as she saw an elongated silhouette of a girl in a hooded cloak on the wall. The shadow of the girl was moving straight towards her bed! Mary-Lou let loose a terrified scream.

Katherine leapt out of bed and switched on the lights to reveal Alicia holding a torch and a shadow puppet of a figure in a hooded cloak, cut from black card. She was in fits of helpless laughter.

'That's enough, Alicia Johns!' Katherine said sternly. 'Pity *you* didn't eat too many strawberries yesterday and end up in the san like poor Sally!'

Suddenly alert, Darrell sat up. 'Is that what the doctor said?'

'The doctor's not there,' Katherine replied. 'It's just Margaret.'

Darrell felt cold all over. 'Katherine, I need to go down to the san right away.' She swung her legs out of bed. 'Sally hasn't told them what really happened.'

'NO!' Katherine said firmly. 'Leave it to the grown-ups, Darrell. Now, everyone, lie down and go to sleep.'

Darrell lay down, but there was no way she was going to sleep. Impatiently she waited until the dorm was quiet, and there was no more movement. Then she slid out of bed, pushed her covers into a heap and crept out.

CHAPTER THIRTY-FIVE

HUMMING 'GREENSLEEVES' to herself, Matron stood in the san, taking off her gloves. Her mind was on the film she'd just seen, but then a cry of pain caught her attention. Matron swung round. She took one look at Sally's grey, drawn face and panicked. 'Margaret!' she roared. 'How long has she been like this?'

Margaret hurried out of Matron's room, carrying a clean bowl. 'An hour, maybe a little more,' she confessed.

Matron's alarm intensified. 'Call the doctor, you fool!'

'I did!' Margaret replied defensively. Neither she nor Matron noticed Darrell appear at the open door. 'He's busy. The hospital too. No one can come till morning.'

'Matron . . .' Darrell said anxiously.

Matron whirled round. 'What are *you* doing out of bed?' she shouted. 'Back to the dorm immediately!'

'No!' Darrell said desperately. She wouldn't be silenced – this was too important. 'The reason Sally's sick – it can't be because of the food at Open Day. She didn't eat anything! It's because, well, she fell on to her tummy just before I brought her here.'

'She had a fall?' Matron said through gritted teeth. 'Why didn't you say so?'

'I tried,' Darrell replied dismally.

Matron turned to Margaret. 'Wake Miss Potts and tell her we need a doctor NOW!'

'She's already ringing round.' Margaret placed the bowl on Sally's bed. 'But no luck yet.'

'I know who to call!' Darrell's face lit up with relief. 'The Truro Grand—'

Furiously Matron rounded on her. 'Are you still here?' she thundered. 'Go to bed – you've done enough damage as it is!' She thrust Darrell outside and slammed the door.

Darrell stood outside the closed door, fists clenched in frustration. Then, making a sudden decision, she hurried back to the dorm. No one stirred as Darrell collected her purse and left.

A few moments later Darrell was downstairs at the payphone. She dropped her money into the slot and asked the operator to put her through to the Grand Hotel in Truro.

'Hello?' Darrell said eagerly when the receptionist answered, 'I need to speak to Mr Rivers, please. He's one of the speakers at the medical conference.'

'I'm afraid Mr Rivers and the other speakers have gone out for the evening,' the receptionist replied. Darrell's shoulders drooped. 'They should be back very soon. May I take a message?'

'Yes, please,' Darrell said shakily. 'Ask him to call his daughter at Malory Towers as soon as he can. *Please.*'

Darrell hung up. What if the receptionist forgot to give her father the message, she thought, chewing at her lip. Sally might get even worse . . .

Suddenly Darrell's gaze focused on the notice-board in front of her. Pinned to it was a map of the area, and the Truro Grand Hotel was marked on it. Without hesitation Darrell unpinned the map. Then, fastening her dressing gown, she rushed out of school and down the driveway into the dark shadows of the night . . .

Back in the dorm, Mary-Lou was in the throes of a very frightening nightmare. She was thrashing around in bed, yelling, '*No! No! Help me!*'

The noise woke the others up, and an annoyed Alicia reached over and shook her. 'Pipe down, Mary-Lou!' she ordered.

Mary-Lou woke up, wild-eyed and breathing hard. 'It was Lady Jane! I saw her!'

Katherine glared at Alicia. 'I TOLD you to stop that nonsense!'

'Look, Sally's still not back.' Irene pointed at the empty bed. 'She must be really ill.'

Alicia frowned, remembering her conversation with Darrell in the bathroom. 'Darrell?' She leant over and poked the heap of blankets in the bed. To Alicia's shock they collapsed. There was no one there.

'Katherine, Darrell's gone!' Alicia cried.

'We can't do this, Katherine,' Alicia said, as she, Katherine, Gwendoline, Irene and Jean approached Miss Grayling's study. 'It's sneaking!'

'It's *not*,' Jean argued. 'Darrell could be in real danger.'

'This isn't like when she went to the village looking for Gwen,' Katherine hissed, raising her hand to knock on the door. 'We don't have a clue where she is.'

Alicia caught Katherine's hand before she could knock. 'I won't let you drop her in it!' Alicia said through her teeth. Then an expression of utter fury crossed her face as Gwendoline stepped forward and rapped smartly at the door.

After a moment's delay, Miss Potts opened it. She had the phone in her other hand. 'I'm sorry, can you hold?' she said into the receiver. Then: 'Girls, what in heavens' name?'

'It's Darrell, Miss Potts,' Katherine blurted out. 'She's disappeared!'

Darrell was running along a narrow, dark country lane. She'd just passed a signpost reading *Truro 10 miles*, but even that hadn't deterred her. A car raced past her, just a little too close, horn blaring. Darrell cowered back on to the verge and hurried on. Then, when a second car approached, she stepped off the road into the shadows to make sure she didn't get knocked over.

The car passed Darrell, but then there was a squeal of brakes. The car reversed back towards her, and the driver's window was wound down.

'Darrell?' said a familiar voice.

Darrell's heart lifted. 'Daddy! Oh, Daddy!' she exclaimed, overjoyed beyond belief.

Mr Rivers leapt out of the car and swept her into his arms. 'What are you doing out here?'

'Coming to fetch you!' Darrell said, breathless with happiness.

'By yourself? In the dark?' Mr Rivers frowned. 'Who gave you permission?'

'No one,' Darrell said in a small voice.

'Darrell, you simply *cannot* walk off school grounds like this,' Mr Rivers said sternly. 'Not in the day, and absolutely not at night!'

'Sorry.' Darrell was close to tears, her teeth chattering.

'You're freezing!' Mr Rivers wrapped her in his coat and opened the car door for her. 'I'm sorry I missed your call. I rang back, and your form mistress answered. Apparently there's a very sick girl in the san who's had a fall.'

'It's Sally,' Darrell told him. 'You have to help her, Daddy!'

'Of course I will,' Mr Rivers assured her.

Even though Darrell thought she'd walked miles, the drive back to Malory Towers only took ten minutes. As Mr Rivers picked up his medical bag Darrell caught his arm.

'Daddy, I must tell you something,' she said quietly. 'About Sally. It wasn't just an ordinary fall. She fell *really* hard on her tummy. Because I pushed her . . .'

CHAPTER THIRTY-SIX

MR RIVERS looked very concerned, and Darrell hung her head, feeling thoroughly ashamed of herself. 'When was this?' he asked.

'This afternoon,' Darrell whispered. 'You see, it's all my fault.'

'Oh, Darrell.' Her father shook his head. 'Why didn't you tell someone?'

'I tried!' Darrell said miserably. 'Do you think you'll be able to make her better?'

'I'll do my very best,' her father replied.

At that moment Miss Potts hurried out to meet them. 'Darrell!' she exclaimed, relieved. 'We've been out of our minds! Thank heavens you found her.'

'Lucky I did,' Mr Rivers said coolly.

'I am SO sorry, Mr Rivers,' said Miss Potts contritely.

'I should think so. But we have more urgent things to focus on tonight.' Darrell's father lifted an enquiring eyebrow. 'Which way to the san?'

'Straight down the corridor, third door on the left,' Miss Potts replied.

As Mr Rivers strode away Darrell stared pleadingly

at Miss Potts. 'Can I wait up—' she began, before being overtaken by the most enormous yawn.

'Come on.' Miss Potts put her arm round Darrell and guided her upstairs. 'Back to bed.'

But Darrell knew she wouldn't sleep. Not until she discovered whether Sally was going to be all right or not . . .

In the san Mr Rivers was already examining Sally.

'Does this hurt?' he asked, pressing down on her abdomen.

Sally groaned.

'And this?'

Sally yelped with pain and doubled over.

'I need to operate,' Mr Rivers said immediately. 'Right away.'

Matron looked panic-stricken. 'Margaret, bring hot water and clean towels,' she yelled.

Quickly Margaret prepared a bowl of steaming water and soap. While Mr Rivers scrubbed his hands, she unfolded a green cloth and began laying out his surgical equipment, including a sharp scalpel and a steel kidney dish. Matron eyed these with alarm and began backing away. 'Well, I'll leave you to it, Doctor,' she muttered.

Mr Rivers stared at her in surprise. 'I thought you'd be assisting, Matron? Unless you don't feel able . . .'

Matron looked affronted. 'I'll have you know I've assisted at *countless* operations, Doctor.'

In the dorm Darrell was tossing and turning, unable to sleep. She lay on her back, staring up at the ceiling, her cheeks wet with tears. What was happening in the san? She longed to know. Her father was a brilliant doctor, but Sally had been so very poorly ... Would she recover?

The operation was now underway. Matron was busying herself laying out the rest of the surgical equipment, while Mr Rivers bent over Sally, scalpel in hand.

'Matron,' he called, 'the kidney dish, please.'

Matron steeled herself. 'One second, Doctor,' she said in a quavering voice. 'I'm not feeling too good myself ...'

Matron took a deep breath and turned. Her eyes almost popped out at the sight of Sally on the operating table. Gasping, she slid to the floor in a dead faint, pulling the green cloth and the surgical instruments with her.

'Oh, good heavens!' Mr Rivers exclaimed, exasperated.

Darrell woke with a start. She'd eventually fallen asleep, but she'd only dozed lightly. It was very early, and no one else in the dorm was up yet. Darrell jumped out of bed, flung on her dressing gown and rushed to the san.

She crept through the open door. There was Sally in bed, white and motionless. Fear and guilt clutched at Darrell's insides. Was Sally better – or worse?

Mr Rivers was leaning over Sally, checking her pulse. He went to pick up his surgical bag and saw Darrell frozen with anxiety in the doorway. 'Daddy, how is she?' Darrell whispered, dreading what the answer might be. 'Were you able to help her?'

Her father put his arms round her. 'Sally is going to be just fine.'

Darrell burst into tears of relief.

'And it wasn't your fault at all,' Mr Rivers went on. 'Sally had appendicitis. It was nothing to do with her fall.'

Darrell raised her head to look at him. 'Are you *sure*?'

Her father laughed. 'Quite sure. Her appendix was infected. Very inflamed. She was lucky it didn't burst. That would have been even more serious.'

'She's had tummy-aches all term,' Darrell said. 'Can I see her? Please?'

'Two minutes only,' Mr Rivers said firmly. 'She needs quiet, calm and rest.'

He went out to put his bag in the car, and, smiling, Darrell tiptoed over to Sally's bed.

Sally's eyes opened, and she smiled weakly at Darrell.

'How are you?' Darrell asked sympathetically. 'Was

it awful? Does it hurt?'

Sally nodded. 'But nothing like yesterday,' she whispered.

'Did you get to keep the appendix?' Darrell teased.

'No!' Sally giggled, then winced. '*Ow!* Don't make me laugh!'

'I'm so glad you're all right.' Darrell stuck her hand in her pocket of her dressing gown. 'And since you're feeling better, might you want this?' She pulled out the photo of Sally's baby sister.

Sally's smile vanished. She reached out and snatched the photo from Darrell. 'Why do you have to bring this up again?' Sally moaned, tears springing to her eyes. She clutched her stomach. 'Mr Rivers! Mr Rivers!'

Darrell's father hurried back into the san. 'Darrell!' He was annoyed. 'I said CALM and QUIET!'

'I don't feel well,' Sally whispered. 'Can you please ask Darrell to leave?'

Darrell backed away, very puzzled indeed. Why was Sally behaving so strangely?

'Darrell, we need to talk about *thinking* before you *act*,' Miss Potts said sternly. She was sitting in Miss Grayling's chair, alongside Mr Rivers and Matron.

'I know I shouldn't have pushed Sally,' Darrell admitted.

'It's not just that,' Mr Rivers said. 'You left school in

the middle of the night – without telling anyone!'

'But I had to do something,' Darrell defended herself. 'No one would listen!'

'*I* would have listened,' Matron said piously.

Darrell stared at her, appalled by her lies.

'Darrell, adults are here to *help* you,' Miss Potts said, 'so talk to us. You must *never* go off on your own. Now . . .' She sounded kinder. 'Say your goodbyes to your father.'

Darrell flung herself into Mr Rivers' arms. 'Goodbye, Daddy,' she said. 'Thank you! And give my love to Mummy.'

'Do you think she took any of that to heart?' Miss Potts asked Mr Rivers when Darrell had gone.

Mr Rivers sighed. 'The trouble is, she's right. If she hadn't listened to her gut instinct, Sally could have been very seriously ill indeed.'

Matron pursed her lips disapprovingly. 'Darrell won't *always* be right, though, will she?'

Later that day, Darrell and Irene were in their remedial class with Pamela. Darrell was scribbling in her rough book, and Irene took a peek at her work. 'Crikey!' she groaned. 'if that's our French translation, I'm in trouble!'

'Shhh, it's not French,' Darrell whispered. 'It's about Sally. There's something wrong.'

'Yes, appendicitis.' Irene looked puzzled. 'I thought your dad fixed it?

'It's something else,' Darrell said. 'Walk to the Post Office with me later?'

Intrigued, Irene nodded, and Darrell continued scribbling away. At the top of the page she'd written *Dear Mrs Hope* . . .

CHAPTER THIRTY-SEVEN

SALLY WAS sleeping peacefully in the san. Although she was still recovering from the operation four days earlier, she already looked better, and there was more colour in her pale cheeks. She breathed deeply and evenly.

CREEEEEAK!

Sally's eyes opened. A noise had awakened her. What was it?

CREEEEEAK!

There it was again. Gingerly Sally pulled herself upright, grimacing a little, and peered through the darkness. There was a night light on her bedside table, but it was very dim.

'Who's there?' Sally called. She squinted into the shadows – and saw a dark figure in a hooded cloak disappear inside the tall cupboard.

'Margaret!' Sally yelled at the top of her voice. 'MARGARET!'

The door of the first-form dorm was flung open, and Miss Potts bustled in. 'Wakey, wakey, rise and shine!' She strode over to the window and yanked the curtains back, allowing the morning sunlight to pour in. Alicia groaned loudly. 'The early bird catches the worm!' Miss Potts added briskly.

'But the early worm gets eaten!' Alicia grumbled, eyes still closed. 'Can't I stay in bed?'

'Interesting that you see yourself as the worm in this scenario, Alicia.' Miss Potts smiled coolly. 'Now, I need you all to help pack up Sally's trunk.'

'Is she going into hospital?' Alicia asked.

Mary-Lou looked anxious. 'Has she taken a turn for the worse?'

'No, she's on the mend.' Miss Potts opened Sally's bedside locker. 'But her parents have decided she will be leaving the school.'

The girls gasped in surprise, and Darrell almost fell out of bed she was so shocked. Sally – leaving Malory Towers? Guilt swamped her. 'You mean, for good, Miss Potts?' Darrell whispered.

'I'm afraid so.'

'Why?' asked Emily.

'That's between Sally and her parents,' Miss Potts replied, going over to the door. 'We'll need to organise a little send-off for her.'

As soon as the teacher had left the girls burst out into chatter and speculation.

'Maybe her father's gone BANKRUPT!' Alicia said dramatically.

'Maybe they just miss her,' was Jean's suggestion.

'Or maybe Sally *wants* to go.' Katherine looked sober. 'She's never seemed very happy here.'

Feeling guiltier than ever, Darrell turned to Irene. 'It can't be because of that letter I sent,' she murmured. 'Can it?'

Irene shrugged nervously and pulled a face.

'Oh, no!' Darrell groaned. 'What if this *is* all my fault?'

In the san Sally had had a restless night after spotting the shadowy figure in the hooded cloak. Margaret had gone to the kitchens to collect Sally's breakfast, and she was on her way back to the san when Matron marched along the corridor towards her. 'Chop chop!' Matron said snappily. 'I need Sally fed, watered, up and dressed.'

Margaret was puzzled. 'Isn't she supposed to be on bed rest?'

'The powers that be have other plans,' Matron replied, heading into the san where Sally was sitting up in bed waiting for her.

'Matron!' she said eagerly. 'Has Margaret told you? I saw someone in the san last night.'

'What?' Matron swung round to look at Margaret.

'Whoever it was went in there!' Sally pointed at the tall cupboard. 'I heard the door creak open.'

'She must have been dreaming,' Margaret murmured to Matron.

'I wasn't!' Sally insisted. 'She was *real!* A girl in a black hooded cloak, like the portrait of Lady Jane!'

Matron looked alarmed.

'Maybe her fever's back?' Margaret suggested. Immediately Matron fetched a thermometer and put it into Sally's mouth.

'Open the cupboard!' Sally mumbled through a mouthful of thermometer. 'Please! You have to believe me!'

Margaret did as Sally asked and opened the creaky cupboard door. Both Sally and Matron braced themselves. However, the cupboard was empty.

'It *can't* be!' Sally gasped as Matron whipped the thermometer out. 'I've been watching the door ever since.'

Matron was checking the thermometer. 'Normal.' She eyed Sally grimly. 'My suspicion, Miss Sally Hope, is that you're getting bored and making things up to amuse yourself! You're *quite* ready to get out of bed, which is just as well as your mother is on her way.'

A fleeting mix of emotions swept across Sally's face – disbelief, confusion, hope. 'Mother's coming to visit me?'

'Not to visit.' Matron began washing her hands at the sink. 'To take you away.'

Sally's face drained instantly of colour. She stared at Matron in shock.

Darrell and Irene were attending a remedial class with Pamela. They had their books open, but both of them had other things on their minds.

'*Bricks . . . tricks . . .*' Irene said under her breath. 'What else rhymes with *appendix*, Darrell?'

'I need to get to the san,' Darrell muttered.

'That doesn't rhyme AT ALL!' Irene said, annoyed. 'Concentrate, Darrell – this is for Sally's goodbye song.'

Pamela looked up from her book. 'Shhh, you two!' she said. 'What's wrong with you today? Darrell, stand up and read aloud. Maybe that will help calm you down.'

Darrell stared at the poem she was studying. As usual she had trouble focusing on the page, and she had to keep blinking to try to clear her vision.

'"The Charge of the Light Brigade" by Tennyson.' Darrell cleared her throat. '*Half a league, half a league, half a league, half a league, half a league, half a league . . .*' Her voice faltered.

'So many leagues?' Irene asked, open-mouthed.

'*How* many leagues, Darrell?' Pamela probed. 'It's only three, I think.'

Darrell held the book closer, squinting at the page. 'Sorry, the words are jumping about again.'

'That's the worst excuse I ever heard!' Irene teased her.

Darrell rubbed her eyes, wishing she could explain a little better why she found reading and writing so hard.

'Are you all right, Darrell?' asked Pamela.

'No, not really.' An idea had just surfaced in Darrell's head. 'My eyes are very sore. I think I ought to see Matron.'

'Very well,' Pamela agreed. 'But hurry back.'

Darrell nodded, left the common room and shot off down the corridor at speed. She hurried to the san, past the classroom where Alicia and the others were just finishing an English class with Miss Potts.

'Now, girls,' Miss Potts was saying as she collected their books, 'as Sally is leaving, Pamela will require a replacement monitor.'

'I know Darrell would love to—' Mary-Lou began, but Gwendoline's hand had shot up, and she was waving eagerly at Miss Potts. 'Me, please! I'll do it!'

Miss Potts raised her eyebrows. 'Goodness, Gwendoline, I've never seen you so enthusiastic! Well, since you're so keen . . .'

Gwendoline beamed happily.

In the san Matron was giving Darrell an eye test while Sally watched listlessly from her bed. 'Read this,' Matron said, tapping the smallest row of letters on the chart.

'A, C, E, O, B, N,' Darrell read with ease.

Matron bent over and peered intently at her eyes. 'Nothing wrong at all,' she said with a sniff.

'I can see the letters, Matron,' Darrell explained. 'But sometimes they jump around.'

Matron stood up. 'I suggest you stop fooling about and wasting everyone's time,' she said coldly. 'Miss Potts will hear of this!'

As soon as Matron left the san, Darrell hurried over to Sally. She looked pale, exhausted and miserable.

'Have you heard what's happening?' Sally asked shakily.

'Potty told us,' Darrell replied. 'You didn't *ask* to leave, did you?'

'No, why would I?' Sally said. 'I *love* it here.'

'Maybe your mother's worried about you?' Darrell suggested awkwardly. 'What if – someone wrote to her? Not about your appendicitis, but about other things . . .'

Sally stared at her. 'Did *you* write to my mother, Darrell?'

Darrell looked hugely guilty.

'What did you say?' Sally demanded.

'Just that you kept denying you had a little sister,' Darrell confessed. 'And that you always seemed unhappy.'

'Only when you keep talking about her!' Sally shot back.

'So you DO have a sister?'

'Why do *you* care?' Sally cried.

Darrell shrugged, frustrated. 'I just don't understand why you keep denying it, that's all.'

Sally hid her face in her hands. 'Because everything changed when she was born,' she said in a muffled voice.

'Things always change when a new baby comes,' Darrell said, remembering when Felicity arrived.

Sally looked up, and Darrell saw tears in her eyes. 'I was sent away to Malory Towers the day Mother and the baby arrived home from hospital. They don't want me any more!'

'But – that's terrible!' Darrell said, appalled.

Matron appeared. 'Still here?' She directed a very sour look at Darrell. 'Off with you!'

Upset, Darrell stumbled out. Poor Sally!

'Matron, may I speak to Miss Grayling?' Sally pleaded.

'She's still away.' Matron went over to her desk and picked up some paperwork. 'And Miss Potts isn't to be bothered unless absolutely necessary.'

'I don't want to go home,' Sally said, frustrated. 'I don't want to leave Malory Towers.'

Matron burst out laughing. 'You don't get a say! When will you girls learn that your elders and betters know what's best for you?' Clutching the papers, she went out.

Sally lay for a moment, thinking. Then, pushing back the covers, she reached for the crutch at the side of her bed and hauled herself to her feet.

CHAPTER THIRTY-EIGHT

PAMELA WAS in the common room, marking the remedial class's work, when Gwendoline knocked at the door. 'Hello, Pamela,' she said brightly. 'Gwendoline Mary Lacey, your new monitor! Shall I tidy your things?'

'Maybe later,' Pamela replied with a smile. 'Actually, a cup of cocoa would be lovely.'

'Of course,' Gwendoline said obligingly, although she'd never made cocoa in her life. She picked up the pot of cocoa and attempted to undo the lid.

Pamela was flicking through Darrell's rough book. *There's something strange going on here*, she thought.

'Gwen, does Miss Potts ask you to write your homework out in rough first, then copy it up neatly later?' she asked.

'Of course not,' Gwendoline replied, still struggling with the cocoa pot lid. 'That would take twice as long.'

Pamela turned back to Darrell's rough book. The pages were messy with lots of crossings-out. Some words were written several times so Darrell could test the spelling, and some of the letters were back to front.

Gwendoline was still trying to open the cocoa pot.

Suddenly the lid popped off, and a huge cloud of cocoa powder puffed out.

'Gwendoline!' Pamela exclaimed.

'I'm so sorry!' Gwendoline gasped, wiping her eyes. 'I've never made cocoa before.'

'You'd better clean yourself up,' Pamela said. 'You look like a panda!'

Gwendoline caught a glimpse of herself in the mirror and let out a horrified squeal.

Cup of tea in hand, Matron strolled into the san, humming 'Greensleeves'. She was brought up short by the sight of Sally's empty bed. Her pyjamas lay on the covers, and her school uniform was gone.

'Sally!' Matron called in a panic. There was no reply. Flustered, Matron dashed out of the san and made for the first-form dorm.

The girls were in the dorm packing Sally's trunk. Darrell was folding her lacrosse kit neatly while Irene put the finishing touches to Sally's leaving song. The only one who wasn't helping was Gwendoline. She was lying on her bed, complaining loudly.

'I'm exhausted,' Gwendoline groaned. 'I've been working like a carthorse! I'm supposed to be Pamela's assistant, not a maid.'

'Poor old Gwen-derella!' Jean said, and the others chuckled.

Matron charged in. 'Girls! Has anyone seen Sally Hope? She's vanished from the san!'

Everyone shook their heads, surprised.

Darrell felt guilty all over again, wishing she'd never sent the letter to Mrs Hope.

'Jean, Darrell, Irene, Mary-Lou, go and look for her,' Matron ordered distractedly. 'You others, set up tea for Mrs Hope in the common room. She'll be here any minute!'

The girls scattered. What Matron didn't know, however, was that Mrs Hope had arrived already and was being greeted by Miss Potts.

'I'm afraid Miss Grayling's away at the moment,' Miss Potts said as she led Sally's mother along the corridor. 'Family reasons.'

'Oh dear.' Mrs Hope sighed. She was an attractive woman with a warm smile, but she seemed very tired and stressed. 'I'd hoped to speak to her—' She stopped dead, hand to her forehead, swaying a little.

Miss Potts caught hold of her elbow. 'Are you all right?'

'Just a little dizzy,' Mrs Hope murmured, closing her eyes. 'It was a long day of travelling, and I've been very ill since having baby Daphne. This is the first time I've left her.'

'It must be difficult,' Miss Potts said sympathetically.

'And now this trouble with Sally ...' Mrs Hope

looked upset. 'My daughter is in your care, Miss Potts. I should be informed immediately if something is wrong!'

'We telephoned the moment she was ill—' Miss Potts began.

'Not the appendicitis,' Mrs Hope broke in. 'The unhappiness!'

Miss Potts was bemused. 'But Sally is thriving here.'

'That's not what *this* says!' Mrs Hope thrust a piece of paper into Miss Potts's hand. The teacher stared down at the letter in confusion.

'Sally! Sally! Sal, Sal, Sally!' Irene skipped past, singing tunefully. Both Miss Potts and Mrs Hope turned to look at her. 'Oh, hello, Miss Potts,' Irene went on brightly. 'And hello . . . ?'

'This is Sally's mother,' said Miss Potts.

'Why were you calling Sally?' Mrs Hope asked Irene.

'Because I'm looking for her,' Irene replied.

'She's in the san,' Miss Potts chimed in.

'Oh, she's back?' Irene looked pleased. 'Good show! Who found her?'

'What are you talking about?' Miss Potts asked, suspicion growing.

Realising her mistake, Irene began to back away. 'Oh, nothing . . . I'd best be off anyway . . .'

'Irene!' Miss Potts said sternly.

'Sorry,' Irene mumbled, 'but Matron didn't want to worry you.'

Mrs Hope looked very frightened. 'What's happened?' she cried.

Outside, Darrell, Jean and Mary-Lou were searching the school grounds for Sally.

'She won't be able to walk far,' Mary-Lou pointed out. 'She'll still be weak from the operation.'

'She must be here *somewhere*.' Frustrated, Darrell glanced up at the dorm – and unexpectedly saw a very familiar figure at the window. 'Hang on!'

Sally's eyes met Darrell's. She shook her head frantically, then ducked down out of sight.

'What?' Mary-Lou asked.

'Um – I just thought – wouldn't it make more sense to split up?' Darrell suggested, thinking fast. 'I'll circle the building; Jean, you take the lacrosse pitch; and, Mary-Lou, you go down to the pool.'

'Yes, we can cover more ground that way,' Mary-Lou agreed.

Darrell waited until Jean and Mary-Lou had run off, then she dashed back into school.

CHAPTER THIRTY-NINE

AS MISS Potts and Mrs Hope hurried to the san Miss Potts was reading Darrell's letter:

> ...so you see, Sally is sad, even thouwgh her appendix is better – and she still seys she dosent have a litel sister. I wundered if seeing you mite make it better ...

Miss Potts was so intent on the letter she didn't notice Pamela running downstairs with an armful of papers. The two of them collided heavily. Miss Potts dropped Darrell's letter, and Pamela's papers flew everywhere.

'Look where you're going, Pamela!' Miss Potts groaned.

'Sorry!' Pamela said quickly, gathering her papers up, 'It was actually *you* I was coming to see. I think I know why Darrell's timed work looks so different from her prep.'

Pamela held out Darrell's rough book. It was open at the page where Darrell had practised writing to Mrs Hope.

'Thank you,' Miss Potts said, scooping Darrell's letter off the floor of the corridor. 'But I'm afraid it'll have to wait.' She glanced very briefly at the rough book, but her attention was caught when she realised it was the first version of the letter to Mrs Hope. 'It's the same!' Miss Potts said, surprised. 'In a way . . .'

Miss Potts held the neatly written letter against the rough copy in Darrell's book and compared the two. The difference in the handwriting and general presentation was striking. The first version was a lot messier. And even though there were spelling mistakes in the letter sent to Mrs Hope, there were twice as many in the first draft.

'Oh my goodness!' Miss Potts exclaimed, staring at the rough version. 'Look at the date. 1647 instead of 1947!'

'Darrell does everything in rough first,' Pamela said. 'The first time round so much is back to front. That's why everything takes her so long.'

Miss Potts gave Pamela an approving look. 'Pamela, you really are an excellent remedial tutor.'

Pamela beamed at her.

Having shaken off Jean and Mary-Lou, Darrell made her way to the dorm. At first glance it appeared to be empty. But then Darrell saw a crutch sticking out slightly from behind Sally's bed.

'Thanks for not giving me away,' Sally murmured when Darrell approached her hiding place.

'Everyone's looking for you,' said Darrell.

Sally's bottom lip trembled. 'I don't want to leave Malory Towers.'

'But what can you do?' Darrell asked sympathetically.

'I can hide until Mother goes.'

'She won't leave without you!'

'Oh, yes, she will,' Sally said bitterly. 'She'll need to get back to BABY. You go back to the others and pretend you haven't found me.'

'I can't.' Darrell shook her head. 'That's a downright lie.'

'You owe me, Darrell Rivers,' Sally said angrily. 'Your letter started all this.'

Darrell stared at her guiltily. But before either of them could speak, they heard Matron's voice outside and footsteps approaching the dorm. 'The girls have packed all her things away for you,' Matron was saying.

Grimacing with pain, Sally crawled underneath the bed, dragging the crutch with her. After a moment of hesitation Darrell did the same. 'I won't have to lie if they can't find me either!' she whispered.

Sally managed a tiny smile and put her finger to her lips as Mrs Hope entered the dorm, accompanied by Irene and Matron.

'You're not to worry, Mrs Hope,' Matron said

robustly. 'Sally is a sensible girl.'

'But I *am* worried,' Mrs Hope insisted. 'This is so out of character.'

Sally's face had brightened when she heard her mother's voice. For a moment Darrell thought she might scramble out from under the bed to greet her, but she didn't.

'She really DID come without Baby!' Sally whispered, eyes shining.

Exhausted, Mrs Hope sat down on Sally's bed. The mattress sagged, and Darrell and Sally exchanged alarmed looks.

'Ah, here are Sally's friends,' Matron said as Alicia, Mary-Lou, Gwendoline and Katherine arrived. 'Any sign of Sally, girls?'

The girls shook their heads.

'Are any of you Darrell Rivers?' Mrs Hope asked.

'Certainly not!' Gwendoline replied with a sniff.

'She wrote me a letter saying Sally was unhappy here,' Mrs Hope continued. 'Is that true?'

None of the girls really knew how to respond.

'Sally's a brilliant lacrosse player,' Alicia said.

'She's one of the cleverest in the class,' Mary-Lou offered.

Under the bed Sally couldn't help smiling.

'She's a great swimmer.' That was Irene.

'She was the head girl's monitor,' Gwendoline said

eagerly, 'and I'm *sure* she could step *right* back into that role, if you let her stay.'

'Be quiet, Gwendoline,' Matron snapped.

'But is she happy?' asked Mrs Hope.

Everyone hesitated, unsure how to answer. They were saved from replying by Miss Potts entering the dorm. 'Thank you, girls,' she said. 'If I could have a moment alone with Mrs Hope, please . . .'

Mrs Hope waited till everyone had left, then she turned to Miss Potts. 'I think I've let Sally down terribly,' she confessed, her voice breaking with emotion. Sally bit her lip, hearing her mother's distress.

'You can't blame yourself,' Miss Potts said.

'I do, though.' Mrs Hope sighed, tears welling in her eyes. 'We should have come to Open Day. The letter said Sally was upset we didn't. But we *wanted* to come. It was Sally who insisted otherwise!'

Under the bed Darrell glanced at Sally in surprise.

'We thought she was being thoughtful, giving me more time with baby Daphne.' Mrs Hope took a tissue from her handbag and dabbed her eyes.

'Yes, especially as you've been ill,' Miss Potts pointed out.

Mrs Hope suddenly looked rather uncomfortable. 'But we didn't *tell* Sally I'd been ill . . .'

Darrell glanced at Sally who looked completely shocked.

'Why not?' asked Miss Potts.

'We didn't want to worry her while she was away at school,' Mrs Hope explained. 'I was so weak . . . I could barely look after myself, never mind Daphne . . .'

'Poor Mother,' Sally murmured, gripping Darrell's hand. 'I never knew!'

'You know, we can only make sense of the world through the information we're given,' Miss Potts said diplomatically. 'I think Sally may have created a story to fit the only facts she had.'

'What do you mean?'

'Well,' Miss Potts said gently, 'when you and the baby returned from hospital Sally was sent away . . .'

Mrs Hope looked perplexed. 'But she knows we love her!'

A little cry of joy escaped from Sally at her mother's words. Holding her side, she pulled herself painfully out from under the bed. 'Mother!'

Mrs Hope gasped with surprise and then clasped her daughter thankfully in her arms.

'I feel so silly, Mother,' Sally said. 'I thought you didn't care about me any more now you have Daphne, but you've been ill!'

'We should have told you,' Mrs Hope said, holding on to her daughter tightly. 'All we wanted was the best for you. Of course you're welcome back home if you want to come.'

236

As they embraced Darrell crawled out from underneath the bed too.

Miss Potts looked alarmed. 'Any more of you under there?' she enquired.

Sally giggled, then groaned, holding her side. 'Mother, this is my friend Darrell who wrote you the letter.'

'I'm sorry if I caused any trouble,' Darrell said earnestly. 'I was only trying to help.'

'You have,' Mrs Hope assured her. 'Thank you.'

'Darrell, a word!' Miss Potts said, indicating the door.

Darrell sighed and followed her form mistress out.

CHAPTER FORTY

'DARRELL, REMIND me what we said about thinking before you act.' Miss Potts's voice was gently sarcastic. She was sitting at Miss Grayling's desk, Pamela at her side. 'About not interfering and trusting adults to help you?'

'I'm trying, Miss Potts,' Darrell replied earnestly. 'But sometimes helping and interfering can seem quite similar!'

Miss Potts hid a smile. 'Well, it *was* a good impulse of yours to alert Sally's mother to her distress. Keeping her problems and worries to herself wasn't doing Sally any good.'

'I'm glad they got a chance to talk,' Darrell said, relieved.

'Yes.' Miss Potts looked thoughtful. 'Pamela and I were wondering if you might have any problems or worries of your own to share with us, Darrell?'

Surprised, Darrell shook her head.

'Are you sure?' Miss Potts placed Darrell's rough book on the desk.

'Jumping letters?' Pamela prompted. 'Dancing words?'

Darrell shrugged. It had been happening all her life, and Matron had said her eyes were fine. There was nothing to be done about it.

'Writing things out over and over again must take a lot of extra time,' Miss Potts observed.

'I get up early,' Darrell replied, 'or I work in break.'

'You've been covering up how hard you have to work,' Pamela pointed out. 'It can't be easy.'

'I'm just slow,' Darrell said. 'I'm sorry.'

'There's nothing to be sorry for, Darrell,' Miss Potts replied. 'We believe you have a condition called "word-blindness". You'll need a proper diagnosis, of course, but—'

'"*Word-blindness*"?' Darrell repeated, stunned. 'It sounds *dreadful*.'

'Not at all.' Miss Potts spoke firmly. 'It's just something that needs the right kind of attention.'

'It means there's a reason for your problem,' Pamela said comfortingly.

'But I don't *want* to have problems,' Darrell muttered, still trying to process what Miss Potts had said. 'I want to be normal . . .'

'Having problems *is* normal,' Miss Potts reminded her kindly. 'No one gets through life without them. 'You. Sally. All of us. Overcoming problems helps to make us stronger. And we can help you . . .'

* * *

Sally lay on her bed in the dorm, crutch propped up on her bedside locker. She was exhausted, but happy.

She slipped her hand into her pocket and pulled out the photo of baby Daphne that Darrell had returned to her. A loving smile curved her lips.

She raised her head curiously, hearing the scuffling of feet outside in the corridor. She could also hear muffled giggles, whispering and lots of shushing going on. Then there was a burst of song.

> *'Sally, Sally, what a to-do,*
> *Sing this song and you won't feel so blue!'*

Sally recognised the voices and smiled. Next moment Irene flung open the door, and Sally's classmates rushed in, led by Darrell and Alicia.

> *'You had pain all term in your tummy,*
> *It wasn't very funny,*
> *But Darrell's dad fixed*
> *Your poor appendix*
> *And now you're good as new!'*

Matron was strolling along the corridor to the san when she heard the girls' singing. She scowled. 'What in the Devil's name . . . ?'

> *'Sally, Sally, things have been quite tough,*
> *You braved it out until it got really rough,*
> *Matron thought it was ice cream and berries*
> *That gave you a pain in your belly!'*

At the sound of her name Matron gave a shout of rage. She ran helter-skelter down the corridor and barged her way into the dorm where the girls, conducted by Irene, were just finishing their song.

> *'But Darrell's dad fixed*
> *Your poor appendix*
> *And now you're back with us!'*

'Get away with you all!' Matron hollered furiously. 'What *is* this caterwauling?' She grabbed a mop from a nearby bucket and, shaking it threateningly, charged towards the girls. Sally giggled, cradling her stomach as Matron shooed the others out of the dorm.

'Out of here!' Matron roared. 'And, Sally, back to the sanatorium! Now!'

Back in bed in the san, a contented Sally lay humming Irene's goodbye song. When Darrell popped her head warily round the door Sally beckoned her in. Matron had gone to speak to Miss Potts.

Darrell scurried inside, followed by Alicia and Mary-

Lou, and the three of them gathered round Sally's bed.

'Listen here, Sally!' Alicia said firmly. 'You just can't leave. The lacrosse team won't survive!'

'Nor will Pamela,' Mary-Lou chimed in. 'Gwen's a dreadful monitor!'

Sally smiled, but Darrell noticed she was shivering slightly. 'You're cold,' Darrell said, 'I'll get a blanket.' She went over to the tall cupboard. The door creaked when Darrell opened it, and then, as she rummaged for a blanket, she let out a shocked gasp. 'Oh, my word!'

Hanging inside the cupboard was a long hooded cloak made of black velvet. The four girls stared at it, dumbfounded.

'I knew it!' Sally murmured.

'Oh, my five wits!' Mary-Lou whispered, petrified. 'So there really *is* a ghost!'

'No,' Darrell said decisively. 'A ghost doesn't wear real clothes. Someone's wandering the school at night dressed in this cloak.'

Mary-Lou didn't look very convinced.

'See? We *need* you, Sally!' Alicia said urgently. 'We need your detecting skills here in the san.'

At that moment Matron returned and looked extremely annoyed to see them. 'Girls, I'm at the end of my tether!' she announced melodramatically. 'The san is *not* a playground.'

'We've just come to say goodnight to Sally, Matron,'

Darrell hastened to explain.

'Really?' Matron said with heavy sarcasm. 'And here was me thinking you'd all come for a good dose of cod-liver oil. Line up!'

'It's quite all right, thank you, Matron,' Alicia said, bolting for the door, Mary-Lou at her heels. Matron followed them, still issuing threats, and for a few moments Darrell was left alone with Sally.

'What are you going to do?' Darrell asked.

'Well, Mother said she'd love to have me back home,' Sally replied cheerfully.

'I'm happy for you.' Darrell looked downcast. 'But I'll miss you.'

Sally shook her head. 'No, you won't. You *really* won't. Mother knows what's best for me . . .' Her face split into a huge grin. 'And that's Malory Towers. I'm staying!'

Darrell felt enormously relieved.

'I have to stay because they tell me the lacrosse team can't manage without me,' Sally joked. 'And anyway, Darrell Rivers, you and I have got some serious ghost-detecting to do!'

CHAPTER FORTY-ONE

A few days later Darrell and Alicia walked down the front steps of the school, deep in a discussion about the 'ghost'. A delivery van, back doors open, was parked at the bottom of the steps, but neither girl took much notice of it.

Gwendoline and Mary-Lou were approaching the steps from the other direction.

'O.B.L.I.Q.U.E, oblique,' Gwendoline was saying.

'Spot on!' Mary-Lou nodded approvingly, then consulted her list. 'Obstinate.'

'O.B.S.T.I.N.A.T.E,' Gwendoline spelt out. 'Obstinate.'

'Correct!'

'What are you two up to?' asked Alicia.

'Practising spellings,' Gwendoline replied. 'I heard Potty likes to surprise everyone with a spelling test towards the end of term.'

Darrell was dismayed. 'Aren't surprises supposed to be *good* things?' she groaned.

The delivery man passed by them and went up the steps. He was carrying a large white box tied with a stylish crimson and gold ribbon.

'Now that's a good surprise if ever I saw one!' Gwendoline remarked, staring at the box with envious eyes.

'It's a *box*,' Alicia murmured.

'Not just *any* box,' Gwendoline said longingly. 'See the ribbon? That's a couture dress or I'm a Dutchman!'

The girls glanced at each other uncertainly.

'A *designer* dress.' Gwendoline rolled her eyes. 'It's the season.' More blank looks. 'Malory Towers must have a *debutante*!'

Alicia shrugged. 'What's a "debutante"?'

'A girl who's taking her first steps into society,' Gwendoline explained in a superior manner. 'Coming of age – meeting the king!'

'King George?' Alicia's eyes widened. 'The *actual* king?'

'At Buckingham *Palace*?' Mary-Lou asked, impressed and scared at the same time.

'What are we waiting for?' Alicia said. 'Let's go and see who it's for!'

Gwendoline and Alicia raced up the steps into school. Mary-Lou hung back, noticing Darrell still looked worried. 'I could help *you* practise your spellings too, if you want,' she offered shyly.

Darrell sighed. 'Thanks, Mary-Lou but there's no point. My spelling is appalling. A.P.A.L—'

'Actually, it's double P,' Mary-Lou interrupted awkwardly.

'You're not helping, Mary-Lou.' Darrell forced a smile, but now she really was worried.

The box had been delivered to the art classroom where Margaret was carefully unpacking it from its tissue-paper layers. Humming 'Greensleeves' to herself, she arranged the snow-white satin gown on a tailor's mannequin, spreading out the full skirt and attaching the belt with its intricate pattern of seed-pearls.

Outside in the corridor Alicia and Gwendoline were arguing.

'He went the other way!' said Gwendoline.

'No, this way!' Alicia insisted. She burst into the art room, Gwendoline behind her.

'That's ridiculous!' Gwendoline cried. 'The art room's the last place—' She came to a dead halt, mouth falling open in delight. 'Oh, it's a *ball gown*! It's *stunning*! Is it Dior?'

'No, but it is couture,' Margaret replied, packing the tissue paper back into the box. 'Beautiful, isn't it?'

'Can I...?' Reverently Gwendoline stretched her hand out towards the spotless satin, but Margaret immediately stepped between her and the dress. 'No one goes near it till the final fitting,' she warned.

'Look at the belt,' Gwendoline gasped, eyes aglow.

'All those different-sized pearls! Who's the debutante, Margaret?'

'The Honourable Camilla in West Tower?' Alicia suggested.

'Lady Sarah in the upper sixth?' said Gwendoline.

'Not my place to tell,' Margaret said firmly. 'Now, scoot!'

Outside, Darrell and Mary-Lou were lying on the grass, practising spellings, when an excited Gwendoline and Alicia rejoined them.

'*Medicine*.' Darrell tried to sound the word out as she wrote down various spellings. 'MedEH – medI – medUH—'

'We could stake out the art room,' Alicia was suggesting. 'See who goes in to try on the dress?'

Gwendoline looked glum. 'That could take DAYS!'

'Maybe whoever it is doesn't *want* to be found,' Darrell said, throwing her book down.

'Any girl would be proud to be a deb,' Gwendoline replied sternly. 'She'll have been preparing for this her whole life!'

Darrell shrugged. 'What's so great about frilly dresses and dances and curtsying?'

Alicia plonked herself down next to Mary-Lou. 'You know, Mam'zelle told me Lady Jane Malory was a debutante,' she said wickedly. Mary-Lou shivered.

'That's probably why she ran away!' Darrell said, only half joking.

Gwendoline tutted loudly. 'A coming-out ball is the start of your adult life,' she lectured. 'It's a chance to marry well.'

'I'm not sure I want to get married straight out of school,' Darrell said thoughtfully.

'Oh, I remember. You want to be a *doctor*.' Gwendoline glanced down at Darrell's book and smirked. 'You'd better learn how to spell "medicine" first!'

Mortified, Darrell gathered her books together and left for her first remedial lesson of the day with Pamela. But Gwen's malicious words haunted her. Staring at the work she was doing for Pamela, with its ink blots and multiple crossings-out, Darrell threw down her pen in defeat.

'I'm never going to be able to do it,' she said miserably to Pamela. 'Now we know I have word-blindness, what's the point?'

'We can start to remedy it,' Pamela pointed out gently. 'That's why it's called "remedial"!'

'I used to think I wanted to be a doctor.' Darrell stared despairingly at her messy work. 'I'm awful at exams, though. And will I even get to university?'

'Darrell, the important thing is not to give up,' Pamela said firmly. 'You *have* to follow your dream.'

Darrell smiled at her. 'I suppose if *you* got through

remedial and got a place at college, then I can too . . .'

Pamela looked a little awkward, but they were interrupted by Gwendoline rushing in, carrying a plate of burnt toast.

'Breakfast as ordered!' Gwendoline announced grumpily, thrusting the plate at Pamela and turning to leave.

'Gwen, wait!' Pamela said. 'Forgive me, but I don't think your heart's in this any more?'

Gwendoline squirmed a little but looked relieved. 'I was actually hoping to have a word with you about that. There's a debutante in the upper sixth, and I think my skills would be more useful to *her*.'

Pamela glanced at the burnt toast, and Darrell smothered a smile.

'You're such a sport, Pamela,' Gwendoline continued, edging away. 'It's been an honour, but I'm ready to move on!' And she hurried out.

'Shall I make more toast?' asked Darrell.

Pamela nodded. 'It looks like I have a vacancy for a monitor,' she said with a smile. 'Interested?'

Darrell beamed. 'Yes, please!'

After the remedial class was over Darrell joined the other girls in the art room. The satin dress had been covered with a protective sheet and placed out of danger behind a screen. However, all the girls were enthusiastically sketching their dream ball gowns, apart from Darrell. Her drawing was of a female doctor at a patient's bedside. Miss Potts surveyed it, nodding approvingly.

'Were *you* a debutante, Miss Potts?' asked Mary-Lou.

'Goodness, no!' Miss Potts replied, amused. 'I went to teacher training college. Now, please fold your easels and tidy up. We have the lower sixth in here next.'

The girls did as they were told. Meanwhile, Miss Potts took a stack of leaflets and began laying them out on the tables. Darrell noticed a name handwritten in the top corner of one of the leaflets – *Pamela Worthington*.

'Why is Pamela's name on this one, Miss Potts?' Darrell asked curiously.

'She lent it to me,' Miss Potts replied. 'We're discussing career options for the lower sixth. This one –' Miss Potts tapped the leaflet – 'is for *my* old college, Gosworth.'

'Pamela would be a brilliant teacher,' Darrell said eagerly.

'I agree, Darrell, but Pamela's plans have changed.' Miss Potts sighed. 'She isn't staying for the upper sixth. Now, hurry up, girls . . .' She continued laying out the leaflets, leaving Darrell in shock.

'I don't understand!' Darrell said to Mary-Lou. 'Pamela's so clever. Why *wouldn't* she go to college?'

'Maybe she can't afford to stay another year,' Mary-

Lou suggested. 'Lots of families are having money problems after the war.'

'It's so *unfair*!' Darrell complained, immensely frustrated. 'When some people have hundreds of pounds to spend on white-satin dresses and going to balls . . . Poor Pamela!'

CHAPTER FORTY-TWO

IT WAS the middle of the night, and Mary-Lou awoke with a start to hear footsteps running lightly down the corridor. Petrified, she stared round nervously, then almost leapt out of her skin as Irene appeared at her bedside.

'Are you sleepwalking?' Mary-Lou whispered.

'No,' Irene replied. 'Someone just ran out of the dorm. Come on, let's follow them.'

Mary-Lou shuddered. 'I'm not going anywhere!'

'Fine.' Irene scurried over to the door and along the corridor, listening for the footsteps. She paused at the corner. There were the footsteps again. And this time they were coming from *behind* her!

Irene shrieked, spun round, and then sagged with relief as Emily appeared. 'What are *you* doing here?'

'Following you!' Emily replied. 'I thought there must be a midnight feast no one had told me about.'

'I heard footsteps.' Irene glanced around anxiously. 'I think it's the ghost!'

Emily sighed. 'Don't say you still believe in that nonsense?' She hurried off towards the dorm. An owl hooted loudly, and Irene, unnerved by the spooky sound, fled after her.

'Miss Potts?' The following morning, Darrell stood hesitantly in the doorway of the classroom where Miss Potts was at her desk, preparing for first lesson. 'May I speak to you about something . . . delicate?'

Miss Potts was intrigued. 'Of course. Sit down.'

Darrell did so, wondering nervously how to begin. 'If I had a friend,' she began, choosing her words carefully, 'a friend who'd been in remedial, but was now doing really well . . . might there be a chance of a scholarship? If this girl was truly exceptional?'

'I understand.' Miss Potts nodded. 'If your parents are having financial problems, Darrell, they should talk to Miss Grayling.'

'No!' Darrell exclaimed, more uncomfortable than ever. 'It's not *me*.'

'Then who?'

'Pamela,' Darrell blurted out. 'I think her family must be having money troubles, and that's why she isn't going to college.'

Miss Potts stood up. 'Come with me, Darrell,' she said kindly.

In the art room one of the older girls was wearing the white ball gown so that Margaret could adjust the fit. A small crowd of excited first-formers, including

Gwendoline and Alicia, were clustered around, trying to get a glimpse of the mysterious debutante, who had her back to them and was shielded from their view by Margaret.

When Miss Potts led Darrell into the room all a confused Darrell could see was a white flowing skirt and glossy hair, neatly pinned up and held in place by a shimmering tiara.

'Girls!' Miss Potts clapped her hand. 'Please leave.'

'How come *Darrell* gets to stay?' Gwendoline asked, disgruntled.

'Because helping with a dress fitting is part of a monitor's job,' Miss Potts replied coolly.

'That's why I'm here!' Gwendoline bounced up and down with eagerness. 'I want to be the debutante's monitor.'

Miss Potts smiled. 'Until yesterday you were . . .'

Gwendoline's face was a picture of puzzlement. Then Margaret stepped aside, and the debutante turned to face them all. It was Pamela.

Gwendoline could not believe her eyes as the girls stared at Pamela in awe and wonder. She looked breathtaking, the full-skirted gown sweeping to the floor, tiara sparkling, the seed-pearl belt glistening at her waist. Devastated, Gwendoline groaned softly. She'd lost her chance!

But Gwendoline wasn't the only girl in the art room

who was upset. Darrell's world had also turned upside down, and her face was white and drawn as she gazed at Pamela in utter dismay . . .

As the girls crowded round Pamela, bursting with admiration and buzzing with questions, Darrell left quietly and ran to the san. There she poured her heart out to Sally.

'So Pamela can't be poor if she's a debutante,' Sally said thoughtfully. 'She's just *choosing* not to go to college.'

'Maybe her family are making her do it,' Darrell suggested. 'I'm sure it's not what she wants.'

'You mean it's not what YOU want,' Sally said.

Darrell was taken aback. 'What do you mean?'

'She's been good to you, so you want her to stay another year—'

'It's not about me!' Darrell broke in, affronted. 'We know she's a marvellous teacher, and now she's going to be stuck in a frilly frock, practising curtsies!'

'She might be perfectly happy about it,' Sally suggested. 'Have you thought about that?'

Darrell wasn't convinced. She was determined to speak to Pamela, and she got her chance a little later that day. Margaret was pinning up the hem of the dress while Darrell sat on the floor, holding the box of pins. Pamela was adjusting her tiara, which had slipped sideways, in the mirror.

'I need a hairpin.' Pamela frowned at her reflection. 'Darrell, could you—'

'I'll go!' said an eager voice from the doorway. Gwendoline had been hovering there for the last fifteen minutes. 'I've got an antique hairpin with a pearl. It'd match *perfectly*.'

'Thanks, Gwen, but it's my monitor's job to help me,' Pamela said, holding the tiara in place. 'A plain hairpin will be fine.'

Darrell found a hairpin in Margaret's sewing-box, while a deflated Gwendoline disappeared.

'You never said you were leaving this term,' Darrell said, handing Pamela the hairpin.

'Well, I only found out recently myself,' Pamela murmured. 'What do you think of my dress, Darrell?' She smiled. 'To die for, isn't it?'

'What about Gosworth College?' Darrell persisted.

Pamela's smile faded. 'What about it? College isn't for me now.'

'But why not?' Darrell cried. 'You told *me* to follow my dream!'

'Maybe –' Pamela's voice wavered a little – 'maybe it *isn't* my dream.'

'I don't believe you!' Darrell said, distraught.

'I have responsibilities, Darrell. To my family.' And Pamela turned away, shutting down the conversation.

Darrell said no more. An idea was forming inside

her head, but was it helping or was it interfering? Darrell wasn't sure and didn't care. She ran downstairs to the payphone.

'Hello, Operator?' she said breathlessly. 'Could you put me through to Gosworth College, please?'

'DO YOU really believe it was the ghost we heard last night?' Mary-Lou said miserably. She was playing cards with Alicia and Irene in the common room, but her mind wasn't on the game.

'It makes sense,' Alicia replied, slapping down her king of clubs. 'Debutante season is a *very* traumatic time for Lady Jane.'

'Why?' Mary-Lou asked anxiously.

'She was madly in love,' Alicia said with a melodramatic sigh. 'She didn't want to marry anyone else . . .'

Mary-Lou and Irene listened avidly.

'So, on the night of her first ball, her highwayman crept in and tied a love-knot to her door,' Alicia continued, 'to show her his heart was hers, no matter what.'

'Oh, that's actually quite a sweet story.' Mary-Lou brightened. 'I was expecting something creepy.'

'Now her ghost, in its debutante dress, returns every year.' Alicia's voice was doom-laden. 'To look in vain for the love-knot at her door.'

Mary-Lou's face fell. 'Yes, THAT'S the sort of thing I was expecting.'

'Wait!' Alicia exclaimed. 'What if there's a way to put the ghost of Lady Jane Malory to rest for ever?'

'How?' Irene asked.

'What if, this year, the love-knot was there?'

'You mean, we tie it on the door ourselves?' Irene was breathless with excitement.

'Exactly.' Alicia nodded. 'It might be all Lady Jane needs to find peace and stop haunting Malory Towers.'

Irene glanced at Mary-Lou. 'Let's do it tonight!'

'I have some ribbons in my locker!' Mary-Lou told her. The two of them threw down their cards and skittered out of the room, chattering animatedly.

Left alone, Alicia smiled to herself. Honestly, those two would believe anything!

The art room was empty. Pamela's dress hung on the tailor's mannequin, the heavy white folds spread out around it.

The door creaked open a little way, and Gwendoline peeped in, checking the coast was clear. She slipped into the room, closing the door, heart beating fast. Then she tiptoed over to stand in front of the ball gown.

Gwendoline stroked the white satin gently, enjoying its cool smoothness under her fingers. She put a fold of the fabric gently against her cheek. Then, gathering her courage, she undid the zip.

The door opened. Scarlet with embarrassment at

being caught, Gwendoline whirled guiltily round. 'What are *you* doing here?' she snapped defensively.

'Pamela asked me to fetch her shoes.' Darrell stared at Gwendoline suspiciously. 'What are *you* doing?'

Gwendoline blushed an even more fiery red. 'I just wanted to *feel* it.' She stretched out her hand to the dazzling white fabric once more.

'Careful!' Darrell warned.

'Satin is so flattering to the skin,' Gwendoline said dreamily. 'It makes you GLOW!'

Darrell shrugged. 'It's just a *dress*.'

'It's the most beautiful thing I've ever seen!' Gwendoline gushed. 'I can't believe you don't want to try it on – I do!'

'I *don't*!' Darrell said firmly.

'You saw what it did to Pamela.' Gwendoline sighed longingly. 'One minute she was just a schoolgirl. The next, she was a princess!'

'She's still the same old Pamela,' Darrell pointed out.

'Don't you want to know how that feels?' Gwendoline persisted. 'To be grown-up?'

Darrell fell silent. She couldn't deny that secretly she was a *tiny* bit tempted to find out . . .

Downstairs, Miss Potts was marking essays at her desk when Pamela arrived and knocked at the open door.

'You wanted to see me, Miss Potts?'

'Ah, yes, Pamela.' Miss Potts laid her pen down. 'I thought we'd agreed you wouldn't be trying for Gosworth College any longer?'

Pamela was puzzled. 'We did. And I'm not.'

'Then why did the college call me about your Open Day place?' Miss Potts asked, exasperated.

'My what?'

'If you go, another girl may lose her chance,' Miss Potts pointed out. 'I spoke to the head, and she said you called this morning.'

'But I didn't!' Pamela insisted.

'Then who did?' Miss Potts asked crisply.

In the art room Darrell stood in front of the mirror, eyes tightly closed.

'Well?' Gwendoline said eagerly.

Darrell took a long breath, opened her eyes and gazed at herself in the mirror. Pamela's dress was too long and a little big for her, but the feel of the heavy folds of satin swishing round her legs was quite delightful, Darrell had to admit.

'I suppose it's pretty,' she said grudgingly.

Gwendoline sniffed. 'Rainbows are pretty. This dress is *breathtaking*.'

Darrell peered at her reflection. 'It's just not ME, though.'

'That's the point!' Gwendoline said, rolling her eyes.

'I shouldn't have put it on. Please help me out of it before someone sees!'

Gwendoline moved to unzip the dress, but before she could the door opened. Darrell and Gwendoline were rooted to the spot, like rabbits caught in headlights.

'Darrell!' Pamela was so shocked she could hardly get the words out. 'What on earth?'

'I'm sorry!' Darrell gasped, mortified.

'Take it off!' Pamela ordered. 'Right now! I trusted you, Darrell. I'm deeply disappointed in both of you.'

Quickly Gwendoline fumbled for the zip with trembling hands as Pamela turned to leave. Darrell waited impatiently, so embarrassed she couldn't *wait* to take it off.

Pamela turned back as if a thought had just struck her. 'It was you, wasn't it, Darrell?' Her tone was accusing. '*You* phoned the college and booked me a place on the Open Day.'

Darrell flushed as Gwendoline wrestled with the zip. 'I'm *so* sorry, Pamela. I was just trying to help—'

'How dare you!' Pamela interrupted furiously. 'Do you really think you know better than I do what I want from my life?' She stormed out, slamming the door behind her.

'What is she talking about?' Gwendoline asked, pulling the zip downwards.

'Just help me out of this,' Darrell replied, tugging distractedly at the straps of the dress. 'I have to go and apologise – OH!'

The threads on the seed-pearl belt had snapped. Darrell and Gwendoline watched in utter horror as all the pearls cascaded to the floor with a clatter and rolled away in different directions.

'Now look what you've done!' Gwendoline wailed.

'It was *both* of us!' Darrell retorted, wishing desperately that she'd resisted the temptation to try on the dress. 'And now we have to fix it *together* – before Pamela finds out!'

CHAPTER FORTY-FOUR

THE OTHER girls were in the dorm preparing for lights out. Emily was embroidering a handkerchief, sewing-box open on her knees, when Darrell and Gwendoline flew in. 'Emily!' Darrell gasped. 'We need you!'

Startled, Emily moved her sewing-box and threw back the bedcovers.

'No, bring that with you,' Gwendoline ordered, indicating the sewing-box. 'And be quick!'

'But – why?' Emily began, puzzled. However, she barely had time to grab her slippers and dressing gown before she was hustled out of the dorm by Darrell and Gwendoline and down to the art room.

'Oh!' Emily murmured when she saw the satin ball gown lying on one of the tables. Her seamstress's eye quickly noted the broken threads at the belt. 'Where are the pearls?'

'Gwendoline and I collected them off the floor.' Darrell handed Emily a small box with the pearls inside. 'We *think* we found them all. Can you fix it, Emily?'

Silently Emily inspected the damage as Darrell and

Gwendoline stood side by side in a state of high anxiety. Neither girl knew who reached for whose hand first, but they both found comfort in the other's touch.

'I'll try.' Emily opened her sewing-box. 'Look, the dress is getting crumpled. Let's get it on the mannequin.'

'I'll put it on,' Gwendoline offered eagerly. This was her chance! 'It'll be easier that way . . .'

The three girls weren't the only ones who'd sneaked out of the dorm. Alicia, Irene and Mary-Lou were outside in the corridor where Alicia was fashioning a love-knot from two ribbons, one red, one pink.

'Right!' Alicia pulled a torch and a sheet of paper from her dressing-gown pocket. 'Read this. It's a message to the ghost.'

'This had better not be one of your pranks, Alicia,' Irene muttered suspiciously.

Alicia looked wounded. 'How could you think that? I'm trying to help you! Quick, before Matron comes for lights out – read it!'

'*Lady Jane Malory, hear us, we implore,*' Irene and Mary-Lou read together. '*Find peace in the other world with your love for ever more!*'

'Again, like you mean it!' Alicia said impatiently. 'Maybe you should sing it?'

'We're *not* singing it!' Irene and Mary-Lou chorused.

* * *

In the art room a starry-eyed Gwendoline stood admiring herself in the mirror, arranging the satiny folds of the dress around her, while Emily stared critically at the seed-pearl belt. She'd finished attaching all the pearls, and the dress looked almost perfect. But there was one large pearl missing.

Darrell was crawling around on all fours, searching underneath the furniture and getting hot, dusty and flustered in the process.

'It must be there *somewhere*!' Gwendoline said.

'If it is, I can't see it.' Frustrated, Darrell sat back on her heels. 'Emily, isn't there anything you can do?'

'Not without the last pearl,' Emily replied.

'Wait!' Darrell said suddenly. 'Gwen, didn't you say you have a hairpin with a pearl on it?'

'Yes . . .' Gwendoline sounded wary. 'So what?'

Out in the dark corridor Alicia had tied the love-knot to a door while Irene and Mary-Lou sang the message to Lady Jane by torchlight.

> *'Lady Jane Malory, hear us, we implore.*
> *Find peace in the other world with your love for*
> *ever more!'*

They all waited, Alicia struggling to conceal her laughter.

'It's not working,' Irene said, disappointed.

'Maybe we got the wrong door,' Mary-Lou fretted. 'Or maybe we need more love-knots.'

'Or maybe I just made the whole thing up?' Alicia suggested, unable to control herself any longer. She burst into giggles as Irene and Mary-Lou stared at her in disgust.

'Not funny, Alicia,' Irene snapped, snatching the sheet of paper from Mary-Lou and crushing it.

'Why would you do that?' asked Mary-Lou in distress.

'To teach you a lesson,' Alicia replied, still laughing. 'Don't believe everything you're told!'

But Mary-Lou was now staring wide-eyed over Alicia's shoulder and into the distance. 'What's *that*?' she whispered, the colour washing from her face.

Irene and Alicia turned to look.

In the flickering torchlight a ghostly figure in a long white dress was gliding swiftly along the corridor. The sight was terrifying. Irene was as pale as Mary-Lou as they clutched frantically at each other, fixed to the spot with fear. Meanwhile, Alicia, her face as white as the ghost's dress, whirled round with a terrified shriek and ran for her life back to the dorm.

'Hold on,' Irene muttered, squinting down the corridor. 'Is that *Gwen*?'

Gwendoline hurried back into the art room and

reluctantly held out her antique pearl-topped hairpin to Emily. She compared it with the pearls on the belt.

'It matches!' Emily said with satisfaction. 'It's *perfect*.'

'Can we use it, Gwen?' Darrell asked eagerly. 'To save the day for Pamela?'

Gwendoline pouted. 'It's very special to me. And I'd never get it back . . .' She thought for a moment. 'All right.' She rolled her eyes, her tone martyrish. 'I'll make the sacrifice.'

Darrell was thrilled and relieved. 'Oh, Gwen, I could hug you!'

'I'd rather you didn't,' Gwendoline said tartly.

'I need to go and find Pamela,' Darrell said as Emily threaded her needle. 'Cover for me with Matron, will you?' And she dashed out.

It took Darrell a while to find Pamela. She was in the common room, checking Darrell's and Irene's work. 'I've been looking for you everywhere, Pamela,' Darrell said awkwardly.

'Hello, Darrell.' Then there was an uncomfortable silence for a few moments.

'I just had to tell you how sorry I am!' Darrell burst out remorsefully. 'I shouldn't have interfered.'

'I'm sorry too.' Pamela sounded sincere. 'I shouldn't have snapped.'

'I know I shouldn't have called the college,' Darrell said, 'but I thought you were being forced to give up your dream . . .'

'Dreams can change.' Pamela smiled at her. 'I did think, once, that I'd like to teach. But my mother was a deb. That's how she met my father—'

'You don't have to do it just because your mother did!' Darrell broke in.

'It's not just about being a deb,' Pamela said gravely. 'It's a whole tradition. I have no brothers, so the family estate will pass to me. And I'll need to run it with a husband at my side. It's my family's way of life. And one that's dying . . .'

Darrell looked confused. 'But do you *want* to do it?'

'I love that there are girls out there who are breaking old traditions and choosing other paths,' Pamela replied, 'but, yes, Darrell. This is what I want, for my family and for myself.'

Darrell sighed despondently. 'I don't know what I'll do without you next year.'

'Miss Potts and Miss Grayling will see you through,' Pamela assured her. 'They know much more about "word-blindness" than I do.'

Tears welled in Darrell's eyes. 'I didn't mean schoolwork . . .'

'Write to me after I've left.' Pamela squeezed her shoulder warmly. 'We can stay friends.'

'I'd love that.' Darrell swiped a hand across her wet face.

'So, I've heard rumours about a spelling test.' Pamela changed the subject. 'Is it bothering you?'

Darrell nodded.

'Come on then.' Pamela beckoned to Darrell to sit down beside her. 'It's late, but we might just manage to squeeze in a lesson . . .'

The girls were gathered at the bottom of the staircase with Miss Potts. It was the day of the ball, and they were intending to give Pamela a good send-off.

'I can't believe you thought Gwen was a ghost!' Irene teased Alicia.

'Alicia thought Gwen was a *ghost*?' Darrell said, surprised.

'We'll tell you about it later,' Mary-Lou said with a grin.

'No, you won't,' Alicia snapped, stony-faced.

'Here she comes!' Gwendoline cried.

A smiling Pamela appeared at the top of the stairs. She was a vision of the perfect princess in her sweeping white ball gown and glittering tiara, and there were gasps of admiration as she walked elegantly down the staircase, holding up her skirts.

'Have a wonderful ball!' Darrell cried.

'I want to hear all about it tomorrow,' Gwendoline gushed.

'And good luck with your curtsy,' Mary-Lou added.

'Hurry, Pamela, your car's waiting,' Miss Potts said. 'And, the rest of you – time for class.'

'She's wearing my pearl, you know!' Gwendoline said proudly as, waving, Pamela headed out to the car.

Everyone was already seated in the classroom when Miss Potts came in. 'Tell me, girls,' she said briskly. 'Do you like surprises?'

Darrell glanced at Mary-Lou.

'I was thinking,' Miss Potts went on, 'it's such a lovely day – we should have a spelling test.'

Everyone groaned except Darrell and Mary-Lou.

'You can do this,' Mary-Lou whispered to her.

'I know,' Darrell said confidently, picking up her pen.

'Number one,' said Miss Potts. 'APPALLING.'

The two girls grinned at each other, and Darrell began to write. A.P.P—

CHAPTER FORTY-FIVE

GWENDOLINE POPPED her head round the dorm door. Darrell and Alicia were playing cards, and Mary-Lou was tidying a pile of stockings on Darrell's bed.

'Oh, there you are, Mary-Lou,' Gwendoline said. 'I need a friend to help me with French prep.'

'Actually, I'm quite busy reorganising Darrell's stockings,' Mary-Lou said hesitantly.

Gwendoline scowled.

'But the stockings are all the same colour,' Darrell said, confused.

'I'm pairing them by thickness,' Mary-Lou replied.

'True friendship!' Alicia said mockingly.

'Hero-worship, you mean!' muttered Gwendoline.

'Jealous?' Alicia teased.

'She follows Darrell everywhere,' Gwendoline complained. 'She's her shadow.'

'Leave her alone,' Darrell said, turning her top card over. 'She means well.'

There was suddenly a loud shriek from Mary-Lou, swiftly followed by the crash of breaking glass. Immediately Darrell leapt up from Alicia's bed and rushed over to her.

'Spider!' Mary-Lou screamed, pointing at the floor.

Darrell glanced down, but the first thing she noticed wasn't a spider. The sound of breaking glass had been her precious family photo tumbling off her bedside locker. Now it lay in broken pieces on the floor.

Upset, Darrell tried to fish the photo out from behind the smashed glass, but it tore right across her mother's face.

Mary-Lou looked on, aghast. 'Sorry!' she murmured tearfully.

Alicia strolled over and spotted a tiny money spider clinging to one of the bedposts. 'For goodness' sake, Mary-Lou!' she exclaimed, scooping up the spider and releasing it out of the window. 'It's *tiny*.'

'Just leave my things alone!' Darrell said hotly.

'Sorry,' Mary-Lou said again. 'I'm just terrified of spiders.'

'Well, if it keeps you out of my hair, maybe I should send more spiders your way!' Darrell snapped, unaware that Gwendoline was listening closely.

'I'll buy you a new frame,' Mary-Lou said shakily. 'I'll save up all term.'

But Darrell, still picking up the pieces, gestured to her to back off. 'Forget it. Just keep away from my things.'

Mary-Lou's face crumpled and she hurried from the dorm.

'Mary-Lou, wait!' Darrell called, suddenly feeling bad. But Mary-Lou had fled to the common room. There she curled up in an armchair by the window and sobbed.

'Here you are.' Gwendoline came in and sat down beside her. Mary-Lou turned away, but Gwendoline ignored the hint. 'It's not *your* fault you're afraid of spiders. Darrell had no excuse to be so horrid.'

'It's not Darrell,' Mary-Lou said miserably. 'I always mess things up.'

'Here.' Gwendoline offered Mary-Lou a delicate lace handkerchief. Mary-Lou wiped her face and blew her nose loudly into the handkerchief. Gwendoline looked rather disgusted, shaking her head when Mary-Lou offered it back. 'You keep it,' Gwendoline went on. 'Then, anytime you're upset, you'll remember you have a friend.'

Mary-Lou sniffed. 'Why are you being so nice to me?'

'Because you need a *real* friend,' Gwendoline replied. 'Not one who seems nice but says mean things behind your back.'

'Who says mean things behind my back?' asked Mary-Lou.

'Don't worry,' Gwendoline assured her, 'they're the same about me. That's why we need to stick together.'

Mary-Lou smiled weakly at her, and Gwendoline smiled back . . .

A science lesson was about to begin. Miss Potts, wearing goggles and gloves, was at the front of the classroom pouring liquid into a small bowl. Darrell hurried in last and went to her desk, passing Mary-Lou on the way.

'Darrell, I really am so sorry,' Mary-Lou said quietly.

'No, *I'm* sorry.' Darrell smiled at her. 'I shouldn't have snapped.'

'Indeed you shouldn't,' Gwendoline hissed from the seat beside Mary-Lou.

Miss Potts clapped her hands for silence, and Darrell hurried to take her place by Alicia.

'Now, last lesson we were discussing physical and chemical changes—' Miss Potts began.

'What on *earth* is that smell?' Jean interrupted, wrinkling her nose.

'That odour, Jean, is the result of adding acetic acid to iron filings,' the teacher explained. 'Thus creating a . . .?' She looked around for someone to answer.

'Stink?' Alicia suggested, grinning. The girls giggled.

'The answer I was looking for was "chemical change",' Miss Potts answered drily. 'But, yes, it is quite pungent. Now, girls, groups of three, please!'

'Mary-Lou,' Darrell called, 'come and join us.'

Gwendoline bristled. 'Why on earth would Mary-Lou want to join *you*?' But a beaming Mary-Lou was already gathering up her books and pens.

Gwendoline glared at her. 'Mary-Lou,' she said

275

cuttingly, 'what will it take to show you Darrell Rivers is *not* your friend?' Mary-Lou didn't reply because she was already heading towards Darrell and Alicia. Bitterly Gwendoline watched the three girls chatting happily together. Something would have to be done about this . . .

Gwendoline didn't concentrate on the science lesson at all because she was making secret plans.

That evening she sneaked out of school and into the gardener's shed in the grounds. The shed was rickety, dark and swathed in cobwebs. As she pushed the creaking door open Gwendoline gulped nervously. It was all rather spooky. But it was an essential part of her plan . . .

Taking an empty matchbox out of her pocket, she began searching the shelves gingerly. She peered behind boxes and garden tools, looking for something. But when Gwendoline cautiously lifted a plant pot to check underneath, soil poured out of the hole in the bottom, staining her uniform. She groaned, turned and walked face-first into an enormous cobweb. Gwendoline shrieked loudly.

'Everything all right?' Ron had walked in. 'What are you up to?'

Gwendoline thought quickly. 'I'm doing a project on spiders. I need some to study.'

'There's a big one right behind you,' Ron pointed out. Gwendoline let out a terrified yelp, and Ron looked amused. 'Why study spiders if you're scared of them?'

'Perhaps you could help instead of laughing at me?' Gwendoline said tearfully.

Ron looked embarrassed. 'Sorry. I can catch the spider for you if you like?'

Gwendoline handed him the matchbox, and Ron shooed the spider safely inside.

'Thank you,' Gwendoline said with dignity. 'I won't keep you from your work.' She pointed at the spilt soil. 'You can clean that up for a start!' And she marched off, holding the matchbox out in front of her.

CHAPTER FORTY-SIX

THE NEXT morning, Gwendoline stole into the classroom, matchbox in hand. She made her way straight towards Mary-Lou's desk and lifted the lid. But before she had a chance to release the spider Gwendoline heard familiar voices outside. Darrell and Alicia! They mustn't find her here . . .

Swiftly Gwendoline ducked down behind the teacher's desk as they entered. They were carrying watering cans as they were on plant duty that week.

'I don't understand why Gwen's suddenly chumming up to Mary-Lou,' Darrell remarked as she and Alicia watered the plants on the windowsill. Gwendoline's ears pricked up at the sound of her name.

'No one else would have her?' Alicia suggested airily.

Behind the desk, Gwendoline scowled.

'It can't be easy trying to make friends if you've been taught by a governess all your life,' Darrell pointed out. Gwendoline was rather surprised and pleased to hear Darrell sticking up for her.

'I don't know.' Alicia shrugged. 'I mean, she shouldn't find it hard to make friends. She's pretty, blonde, angelic-looking . . .' Gwendoline beamed. 'Hard to believe she's so horrid underneath it all,' she added. Gwendoline hastily stifled a gasp of rage and seethed quietly.

Then Darrell approached to water the plant on the teacher's desk. Gwendoline shrank back into her hiding place, grimacing as a few drops of water landed on her. She stayed put until Darrell and Alicia had left, then she hurried over to Mary-Lou's desk, lifted the lid and gingerly opened the matchbox . . .

Up in the san Sally was feeling much better. Matron had taken her temperature and was studying the thermometer carefully. 'Very good,' she pronounced.

Sally beamed. 'I feel so much better. I'm ready to go back to the dorm.'

'*I'll* decide when you're ready,' Matron said sternly as Darrell and Alicia entered with their watering cans. 'And what do *you* two want?'

'We're on plant duty this week,' Darrell replied.

Matron rolled her eyes in irritation and marched out.

'Oh, I'm NEVER going to get out of here!' Sally groaned. 'I'm so *bored*!'

'Better the san than the subjunctive with Mam'zelle Rougier,' Alicia joked, watering the plants on Matron's desk.

'I'd swap Matron for TEN Mam'zelle Rougiers any day!' Sally said fervently.

The lesson bell echoed along the corridor.

'Listen up,' Alicia said, eyes dancing, 'I've got a plan . . .'

Unfortunately Matron returned at that moment and Alicia could say no more. 'Leave it with me,' she whispered, grinning mischievously.

The girls' French lesson with Mam'zelle Rougier had just begun, and Gwendoline could barely contain her excitement. She couldn't take her eyes off Mary-Lou, anticipating the moment when she opened her desk lid.

Mary-Lou noticed Gwendoline staring and smiled uncertainly at her before opening her desk. Gwendoline tensed, watching avidly. Mary-Lou took out her book and closed her desk again. Gwendoline was so frustrated she could have screamed.

'Take this down, *s'il vous plaît*,' said Mam'zelle Rougier, writing on the board.

Everyone started writing except Mary-Lou. Her pen wasn't working. She shook it a few times, then gave up and opened her desk to find another. Gwendoline watched breathlessly.

Mary-Lou was scrabbling through her belongings, searching for a pen. All of a sudden she let go of the desk lid and screamed at the top of her lungs. The lid banged shut. The girls stopped writing and turned to stare.

'*Tiens!*' Mam'zelle Rougier exclaimed sternly.

'Mary-Lou! Have you gone mad?'

Gwendoline smirked.

'Oh, Mam'zelle!' Terrified, Mary-Lou jumped to her feet and backed away across the classroom. 'There's a simply gigantic spider in my desk!'

'*Une petite araignée?*' Mam'zelle Rougier raised her eyebrows. 'And you scream like this? Sit down!'

'Oh, but I daren't!' Mary-Lou wailed. 'It might come out. Mam'zelle, it's enormous!'

Gwendoline tried not to giggle. Her plan was working beautifully.

'I remember first-form tricks,' Mam'zelle Rougier said with deep suspicion. 'We shall see if this spider exists.' She threw the desk lid open dramatically while Mary-Lou retreated further off.

The girls stared, enjoying the drama as Mam'zelle Rougier searched inside the desk thoroughly. She found nothing. Scowling furiously Mam'zelle turned on Mary-Lou. 'You bad girl!' she snapped. 'So quiet, so good. Yet you too try to deceive me!'

'I promise there *was* a spider...' Mary-Lou began weakly.

'Go straight to Miss Potts!' Mam'zelle Rougier thundered. 'You can tell *her* all about this invisible –' Mam'zelle noticed something moving on her arm and glanced down – 'SPIDER!' she roared in an absolute panic.

The class collapsed into hysterical laughter. Mam'zelle Rougier was jumping around, flailing her arms and legs in an effort to shake the spider off. 'Girls, where is the monster?' she shrieked. 'Get it off me!'

The door opened, and Miss Potts came in. 'Mam'zelle, *what* is all this commotion?' she asked.

'*Une araignée très, TRÈS grande!*' Mam'zelle gasped, trying to compose herself. 'Running along my arm!'

Gwendoline was enjoying herself enormously. This had gone even better than she'd expected! However, she received a huge shock when she bent to scratch her leg. There was the spider, crawling up her sock.

Gwendoline let out a scream loud enough to shatter glass. She leapt to her feet in a panic and began dancing up and down, trying to shake the spider off too. The watching girls roared with laughter, holding their aching sides.

'It's on my leg!' Gwendoline squealed. 'Help me!'

'Gwen!' Miss Potts said sternly as the spider fell to the floor and scuttled away. 'Outside – now!'

Humiliated, Gwendoline slunk out of the classroom. This *hadn't* been part of her plan at all . . .

The girls were in the changing room, preparing for games. Gwendoline had bagged the seat next to Mary-Lou, and they were sympathising with each other about the enormous spider.

'Where's my kit?' Mary-Lou asked suddenly.

'Is this it?' Irene picked up a sodden shirt and games skirt from a puddle in the corner.

Mary-Lou was perplexed. 'But I left my kit on my peg!'

'I bet it was Alicia and Darrell,' Gwendoline said loudly. 'We all know they love a prank.'

'That's not a prank,' Alicia said. 'That's just horrid.'

'But your pranks *are* horrid,' Gwendoline insisted. 'I wouldn't be surprised if you hid that spider in the classroom too.' She did a fake double-take as if she'd just realised something. 'You and Darrell were in the classroom right before it appeared!'

Alicia shrugged. 'Just watering the plants.'

Gwendoline played her ace. 'Darrell said she'd like to send more spiders Mary-Lou's way. Didn't she, Mary-Lou?'

Mary-Lou nodded reluctantly.

'It wasn't us.' Alicia had changed now, and she made her way to the door. 'Not our style. Cross my heart, Mary-Lou. We did NOT put that spider in your desk.

She walked out, and Gwendoline turned to Mary-Lou. 'I don't know about you, Mary-Lou,' she said, 'but I don't trust those two one inch.'

Mary-Lou didn't reply, but she looked worried.

CHAPTER FORTY-SEVEN

'I wish I'd seen Mam'zelle's face!' Sally chuckled.

'It was something like this.' Darrell imitated an exaggerated terrified expression, and both girls giggled.

'I do hate missing all the fun.' Sally sighed as Matron came into the san. She didn't look at all pleased to see Darrell there.

'On your way, Miss Rivers,' Matron ordered.

Darrell squeezed Sally's hand and left, passing Gwendoline and Mary-Lou in the doorway. Matron flung her hands in the air. 'More visitors!' she remarked grimly. 'It never ends.'

'Someone put Mary-Lou's kit in a puddle,' Gwendoline explained.

Mary-Lou sneezed loudly.

'And you wore it?' Matron shook her head disapprovingly. 'No wonder you caught a chill. Wait here.' She went over to the medicine cabinet.

'How do you know it was put there?' Mary-Lou asked Gwendoline.

'Someone's got it in for you,' Gwendoline said firmly. 'It's obvious after the spider affair.'

Sally wondered what was going on. It was worrying that someone could be so spiteful, and poor Mary-Lou looked very unnerved.

Matron returned with a spoonful of tonic. 'Open wide!'

Mary-Lou paled, but heroically she swallowed down the foul-tasting medicine.

'Here's a note to excuse you from games for the rest of the week.' Matron handed a paper to Mary-Lou. 'Now go and get some rest. Silly girl.'

Later that evening Darrell and Alicia sneaked into the san while Matron was having her dinner downstairs. Alicia wanted to scope out the lie of the land for her secret plan to get Sally back to the dorm. But when Sally told Darrell what Gwendoline had been saying to Mary-Lou Darrell became extremely upset.

'Mary-Lou needs saving from that beastly Gwendoline,' Darrell said, frowning.

'The only person who can save her is Mary-Lou herself,' Sally said wisely. 'She has to find the strength to tell Gwendoline to leave her alone.'

Alicia was peering underneath all the beds, but now she straightened up and shook her head. 'Some chance!'

Darrell sighed. 'I wish there was some way we could help Mary-Lou find her confidence.'

'And get out from under Gwen's control . . .' Sally's

eyes gleamed suddenly. 'Hang on!'

'What?' Darrell asked eagerly.

'Mary-Lou's off games, right?' said Sally. 'So she'll be by the side of the pool when everyone else is swimming.' She gazed at Darrell. 'What if you pretend to have a cramp in the water and call her for help—'

'And she'll throw the lifebelt in and save me!' Darrell finished with a huge grin. 'That's—'

'A terrible plan!' Alicia broke in quickly. 'What about the lifeguard? She'll save you before Mary-Lou does.'

'Not if someone distracts the lifeguard,' Sally suggested. 'What about a race at the other end of the pool?'

'Maybe.' Alicia still didn't look convinced. 'But you know how hopeless Mary-Lou is. If she freezes and does nothing, you won't give her confidence. You'll destroy it.' She turned to Sally. 'Being in the san is addling your brain,' Alicia said. 'We really HAVE to get you back to the dorm!' And she marched out.

Darrell and Sally glanced at each other, deflated.

'Alicia's awfully smart,' Darrell said slowly.

'She is,' Sally agreed. 'But she's forgotten something very important.'

'What?'

'That it's YOU Mary-Lou would be saving,' Sally said. 'Alicia thinks Mary-Lou is weak. But she could be much more than that – for the sake of someone she

286

really cared about.'

Darrell wasn't sure if Sally was right, but she decided it was worth a try. So the following day, when the first-formers went down to the pool, Darrell hung back to speak to Alicia. Everyone was in swimwear and robes, except for Mary-Lou.

'Really?' Alicia said sceptically. 'You're doing this?'

'I'm going to try,' Darrell said with determination. 'Will you help me or not?'

'It's going to backfire,' Alicia said confidently. 'But sure, I'll help.'

Darrell smiled her thanks and then fell into step with Mary-Lou who was walking with Gwendoline. 'Mary-Lou, will you throw pennies in the deep end, so I can dive for them?' asked Darrell.

'She's not your servant!' Gwendoline snapped at exactly the same time as Mary-Lou said, 'I'd love to.'

Darrell handed Mary-Lou a couple of pennies and exchanged glances with Alicia. The first part of the plan was complete!

Alicia turned to the others. 'Who's up for a swimming race? Come on. You too, Gwen!' Gwendoline threw her a resentful look, but reluctantly followed the other girls to the shallower end of the pool.

Meanwhile, Darrell threw off her robe, then dived into the deep water to retrieve the penny Mary-Lou had tossed in. She surfaced, holding the coin triumphantly and placed it on the side. 'Again!' she called.

Smiling, Mary-Lou threw in another penny as Alicia marshalled the other girls for their race. The sixth-former who was the lifeguard was watching them.

'Barbara?' Alicia waved at the lifeguard. 'We're racing – will you be our judge?'

Barbara nodded and moved up the pool to watch the race. The girls were splashing around noisily in the shallow end, getting into position, as Mary-Lou tossed a coin in. Darrell dived down to find it while Alicia made a huge, distracting fuss about the race.

'No, Jean, not there! Gwendoline goes at the end – we have to give her a head start. Now wait for me to count. One, two – no, Emily, you're too far forward. Everybody take a step back.'

Suddenly Darrell surfaced, thrashing the water with her arms. 'Help!' she panted. 'I've got a cramp!'

Mary-Lou stared at Darrell in horror and disbelief. But she did not move.

'Quick, Mary-Lou, the lifebelt!' Darrell yelled, sinking below the surface for a few seconds before re-emerging, gulping and spluttering. Yet Mary-Lou still remained rooted to the spot, panic in her eyes.

At the other end of the pool the lifeguard was distracted by Alicia's antics.

'Actually, let's do two races, according to ability,' Alicia chattered brightly on. 'Or it's not fair, right,

Barbara?' As the girls busily rearranged themselves Alicia stole a look down the pool at Darrell pretending to struggle in the water and Mary-Lou watching her helplessly. Alicia shook her head – she'd known this would happen!

'HELP!' Darrell shouted again. And then there was a loud SPLASH. Everyone, including Alicia, turned to look.

Mary-Lou had jumped into the water fully clothed and was swimming frantically towards Darrell. 'Hold on to me, Darrell!' Mary-Lou panted. 'I'll save you!'

CHAPTER FORTY-EIGHT

MISS POTTS rushed to meet the girls who were hurrying back from the swimming-pool escorting Mary-Lou wrapped in a towel. 'What happened, Mary-Lou?' asked Miss Potts. 'Did you fall in?'

Mary-Lou was shivering violently, and her teeth were chattering too much to reply.

'She jumped in to save Darrell!' Emily said admiringly.

'Darrell had a cramp and yelled for the lifebelt,' said Katherine.

'But Mary-Lou just leapt straight in!' Jean added, patting Mary-Lou on the back.

'Well, I AM impressed,' Miss Potts said, amazed.

Gwendoline sniffed. *She* wasn't impressed at all by Mary-Lou's behaviour. 'You could have drowned, Mary-Lou,' Gwendoline said coldly. 'I don't see why you didn't just throw in the lifebelt.'

'It isn't th-there,' Mary-Lou stammered. 'It's g-gone to be mended. Didn't you know?'

Surprised, Darrell and Alicia glanced at each other. They hadn't noticed the lifebelt was missing.

'Then you saved Darrell's life!' Emily announced. The girls crowded around Mary-Lou, congratulating her. Only Gwendoline hung back resentfully.

Thrilled, Darrell turned to Alicia. 'Sally will be so pleased. If she ever gets out of the san ...'

'Don't you worry,' Alicia said with a wicked grin. 'I've got that covered ...'

A couple of hours later Alicia washed and put away the science equipment she'd been using. Looking rather pleased with herself, she held up a test tube filled with liquid, then uncorked it. She sniffed it warily, gagged and replaced the cork. Then she sneaked out of the classroom to the san.

Peering warily through the half-open door, Alicia could see Matron tidying up inside. She'd hoped Sally wouldn't accidentally give her away, but there was a screen placed round Sally's bed, Alicia was relieved to note.

Alicia waited until Matron had gone into her room. Then, quick as a flash, she slipped inside the san, tying her school scarf across her nose and mouth. Taking the test tube from her pocket, she uncorked it once more and poured the contents on the floor. Then Alicia beat a hasty retreat.

Matron returned with a cup of tea and her book. Sinking into an armchair with a sigh of relief, she prepared to relax and kicked off her shoes.

Immediately a foul stench filled the whole room. Matron gagged and coughed. Grabbing her shoes, she stared at them in disgust, tossed them into the cupboard and fled the san.

Meanwhile, Alicia had returned to the common room to find the other girls in an excited huddle. 'Nobody's going to be staying in the san NOW!' Alicia announced triumphantly. 'I got Sally out. Just like I said.'

The crowd of girls parted to reveal Sally in the middle of them. 'But I'm *already* out,' said Sally.

'How?' Alicia gasped.

'Darrell asked her father to send a local doctor to check on me,' Sally explained.

'And once he gave Sally the all-clear Matron *had* to let her out,' Darrell finished up.

The door flew open and Matron and Miss Potts sprinted in. 'Girls!' Miss Potts called. 'Please stay calm. I'm afraid we must evacuate!'

'Why?' Katherine asked, alarmed. 'What's happened?'

'We have a suspected chemical spillage in the san,' Matron said gravely. 'And from the unholy stench it may be highly toxic.'

Some of the girls gasped and clapped their hands to their mouths, shocked. Alicia cast a worried glance at Darrell and Sally.

'Personally I suspect foul play,' Matron added.

'We'll know more when the police finish their full investigation,' said Miss Potts.

'The *police*?' Alicia repeated in a panicky voice.

'Fear not, girls,' Matron said calmly. 'I'm sure they'll have the culprit before the night is out.'

By now Alicia was more than a little frightened. 'It was just a prank!' she burst out. 'It's not toxic – please don't tell the police!'

Miss Potts caught Matron's eye, and they grinned at each other.

'Do you really think you're the first girl to let off a stink bomb at Malory Towers?' Matron asked tartly.

Alicia glanced uncertainly from Matron to Miss Potts. 'So the police *aren't* coming?'

'No need.' Miss Potts shrugged, still smiling. 'We've already caught the offender, and she's made a full confession.'

'You pranked ME!' Alicia said furiously.

'Indeed we did, Miss Johns.' Matron looked smug. 'Now, please walk this way . . .'

Later that afternoon, after lessons, Gwendoline was in the changing room preparing for a game of tennis with Mary-Lou.

'Hurry up, Mary-Lou!' Gwendoline called impatiently as she tied the laces of her plimsolls. 'Or we won't have time for this game.'

Mary-Lou came out of the games cupboard looking very distressed, tennis racquet in hand. 'The strings are broken!' she said, showing the racquet to Gwendoline.

'You mean, *cut*!' Gwendoline pointed out. 'Deliberately!'

'But who would do such a thing?' Mary-Lou asked miserably.

'Could have been any one of them,' Gwendoline replied, 'but my money's on—'

'*Not* Darrell!' May-Lou interrupted, guessing what Gwendoline was about to say. 'She wouldn't.'

'Think how humiliating it must be for a show-off like Darrell to be saved by the school's cowardy-custard,' Gwendoline said maliciously.

For a moment Mary-Lou looked as if she was going to burst into tears but then she rallied. 'You can call me what you like, Gwen,' Mary-Lou said in a trembling voice, 'but I won't listen to Darrell and the other girls being put down.' She thrust the racquet into Gwendoline's hand. 'Find yourself another partner, for tennis and for everything else!' And Mary-Lou strode confidently out of the changing room, leaving an astonished Gwendoline behind . . .

Darrell and the other girls had decided they wanted to reward Mary-Lou for her courage in the pool that day, so they'd collected some money together and bought her a gift. They gathered in the dorm that evening to wait for her, Darrell holding a gift box. Katherine was passing round a card and all the girls were signing it.

Gwendoline stomped into the dorm, still in a mood.

'Have you a shilling?' Katherine asked her. 'We've all chipped in to buy Mary-Lou a gift.'

'How lovely,' Gwendoline said grudgingly. She reluctantly handed over a coin from her pocket just as Mary-Lou came in. All the girls applauded, and Mary-Lou looked stunned.

Darrell stepped forward. 'This is to remind you of today,' she said, presenting Mary-Lou with the gift box, 'so you'll never forget how brave you really are.'

Beaming, Mary-Lou opened the box. Inside was an elegant silver fountain pen. 'It's beautiful,' she whispered, overcome with emotion.

'*I* would have chosen a necklace,' Gwendoline said, unable to resist getting a dig in. 'But a pen's *practical*, I suppose.'

'Thank you,' Mary-Lou said joyfully. 'I'll cherish it always.'

Hugely irritated, Gwendoline sighed and turned to leave, but Jean stopped her and held out a small box. 'Ron left this for you,' Jean said, handing Gwendoline the box and a note.

Sorry about the other day, Ron had written. *Thought this might make it up to you.* Gwendoline smiled proudly. 'A present!' she exclaimed. 'Mary-Lou's not the only one with friends . . .' And she sat on her bed to open the box.

'I've never seen Mary-Lou so bucked,' Sally whispered to Darrell. 'You did the right thing.'

'*You* suggested it,' Darrell said gratefully.

Sally grinned at her. 'The pair of us make a pretty good team.'

A blood-curdling scream echoed around the dorm, and all the girls whipped round in surprise to see Gwendoline standing shivering and shaking on her bed. On the blanket lay the open box, and a gigantic spider was crawling lazily out of it.

Mary-Lou paled, but almost immediately took a hold of herself. 'Don't worry, Gwen,' she cried. 'It's only a spider. I'll – I'll save you!' She grabbed an empty glass from a nearby locker and placed it gingerly but bravely over the spider, trapping it underneath.

Darrell and Sally smiled proudly at each other.

CHAPTER FORTY-NINE

IT WAS the dead of night, and the wind was whistling round the towers of the school building. In the dorm Mary-Lou was lying fidgeting in bed, eyes open. 'Darrell? Alicia?' she whispered. 'Is anyone else awake?'

'I am *now*!' Gwendoline muttered, her tone sleepy and cross.

'I need the lavatory,' Mary-Lou said nervously. 'I'd rather not go alone. In the dark . . .'

Gwendoline sat up. 'Mary-Lou, you've just been given a special pen for courage. So be brave. Go by yourself.'

Gathering her courage, clutching the fountain pen to her chest, Mary-Lou did as Gwendoline said and tiptoed into the bathroom alone. After using the lavatory she stood at the sink washing her hands. Then, in the mirror on the wall, Mary-Lou saw the reflection of a hooded figure gliding swiftly past the door.

Mary-Lou shrieked in utter terror. A moment later Emily rushed in, followed by Darrell, then Gwendoline.

'The ghost!' Mary-Lou gasped, clutching her chest. She was hyperventilating and couldn't catch her breath.

Then suddenly she fainted dead away. Darrell caught her before she hit the floor.

'Gwen, fetch Matron!' Darrell cried.

'Why do *I* have to be the one to—' Gwendoline began grumpily.

'NOW!' Darrell yelled.

Mary-Lou was still unconscious when Matron and Margaret carried her to the san and laid her on a bed. Darrell, Emily and Gwendoline hovered around anxiously, watching as Matron shook Mary-Lou, trying to wake her. Gwendoline was being unnecessarily dramatic, forcing tears to her eyes.

'Is she all right?' asked Darrell.

'She just fainted,' Matron said briskly. 'Mary-Lou! Wake up, child.'

Margaret was at the sink, dipping a folded cloth in water, and Matron turned on her sharply. 'Where's that cold compress? Step on it, Margaret, please!'

Emily glanced over at Margaret uncomfortably. Then, as Matron laid the cold compress on Mary-Lou's forehead, her eyes fluttered open.

'You're safe in the san,' Darrell assured her as Mary-Lou looked confused.

Gwendoline threw her arms round Mary-Lou, startling her. 'Oh, thank goodness!' Gwendoline exclaimed fervently. 'My *best* friend . . .'

'That's quite enough.' Matron rolled her eyes.

'Everybody out!'

'Please can a friend stay with me, Matron?' Mary-Lou asked weakly.

'I'm here, Margaret's here,' Matron snapped. 'How many more friends do you need?'

'Just until she falls asleep, Matron?' Margaret suggested quickly.

Matron shot her a grumpy look. '*One* girl may stay for *ten* minutes,' she decreed.

Gwendoline smiled.

'Darrell, would you mind?' Mary-Lou murmured.

Darrell shook her head, sat on the bed and put her arms round Mary-Lou.

Fuming quietly, Gwendoline left, Emily behind her.

'Why does she have it in for me?' Mary-Lou whispered to Darrell, distraught.

'Matron?'

'No, Lady Jane!' Mary-Lou's breath quickened again. 'The wet clothes, the racquet strings. I know it was her!'

'Ghosts aren't real,' Darrell assured her.

'Then who's wandering around in a hooded cloak?'

'I don't know,' Darrell said thoughtfully. 'But I promise you I *will* find out.'

The following morning, the girls were hurrying to class, discussing excitedly what had happened the night before. As they walked down the corridor Emily noticed

Gwendoline fiddling with her fraying hair ribbon.

'I can fix that for you, if you like,' Emily offered.

Gwendoline looked suspicious. 'Why?'

'What do you mean, why?' Emily asked, puzzled.

Gwendoline hesitated, then removed the ribbon and handed it to Emily. 'Fine,' Gwendoline muttered a little ungraciously. 'Now I suppose I owe you one.'

Emily shrugged as the girls filed into the classroom. They had to wait for a few minutes before Miss Potts arrived.

'Girls!' Miss Potts clapped her hands. 'I'm delighted to inform you that our fearless leader has returned just in time for the end of term.'

Miss Grayling stepped into the room, and the girls broke into spontaneous cheers.

'Welcome back, Miss Grayling!' they chorused.

'What an unexpected welcome,' Miss Grayling said, visibly moved. 'Thank you, girls. I wouldn't miss your hobby presentations for anything.'

'This project was Miss Grayling's own idea,' Miss Potts explained.

The headmistress nodded. 'Exams are important, but so is your passion for the things you love to do. I very much look forward to seeing your presentations.'

'Presentations begin tomorrow and continue all week,' Miss Potts said as Miss Grayling left. 'I thought today you might like a study period to prepare?' There were excited murmurs of agreement, and Miss Potts held up a hand. '*If* you use the time wisely . . .'

The girls all nodded in solemn agreement, but the moment Miss Potts went out Irene turned to the others. 'Poor Mary-Lou!' she exclaimed. 'If I saw a ghost, I'd never sleep again!'

'It was probably just a nightmare after all the excitement at the pool,' said Katherine.

While the others continued speculating about the ghost, Sally grabbed a piece of paper and began sketching. Darrell wondered what she was doing. 'Emily you saw the ghost on the back stairs, right?' Sally asked.

Emily nodded.

'And Mary-Lou?' Sally went on.

'Outside the lavatory,' Darrell said.

Sally bent over the paper and continued scribbling. 'And I saw her in the san,' she murmured.

'Oh, *please*.' Gwendoline rolled her eyes heavenwards. 'We all know it's Darrell and Alicia up to their old tricks again.'

'We'd never scare Mary-Lou to the point of fainting,' Alicia said coolly.

'So, the ghost has to be someone with access to the san,' Sally said, still sketching.

Emily sighed. 'Can we please stop this nonsense and get on with our hobby presentations?'

* * *

Mary-Lou was dozing peacefully in the san when Darrell crept in. Darrell smiled and left the orange she'd brought for her on the table.

As Darrell turned to leave her attention was caught by a laundry cart of dirty washing on the other side of the room. There was an enormous heap of games kit on top, but what was that black velvet sticking out from underneath? Darrell's heart skipped a beat. It looked like the ghost's hooded cloak ...

Darrell ran over and began digging through the laundry, trying to pull out the cloak.

'I wouldn't do that, if I was you.' Margaret bustled into the room. 'Senior lacrosse uniforms from the final match yesterday.' She wrinkled her nose. 'Very smelly!' She noticed Darrell eyeing the black material. 'And a few of Matron's personal items.'

Darrell didn't know what to make of this.

'Here comes Matron,' Margaret said as footsteps sounded outside in the corridor. 'You should be getting back to class.'

Matron appeared, humming 'Greensleeves' again. She scowled at Darrell. 'What are *you* doing here?'

Darrell scuttled out, her brain going into overdrive. No! It wasn't possible. Was it? As she rounded the corner, eager to escape from Matron, she bumped into Sally hurrying in the opposite direction. Sally dropped the sketch she'd been drawing in the classroom, and, curious, Darrell picked it up.

'It's a map!' Darrell said eagerly. 'And you've marked the places where the ghost was seen with a red X – the corridor outside the bathroom, the stairs and the san.'

Sally nodded, joining the three X's with a red pen. 'Now we know the path she takes . . .'

'We can follow her!' Darrell's eyes glittered with excitement. 'Ghost watch – tonight!'

CHAPTER FIFTY

IT WAS 2 a.m., and Sally was wide awake. She was wondering if the 'ghost' would make an appearance that night. But all was quiet . . . until Sally gradually became aware of an eerie whispering drifting across from the other side of the dorm.

'The perpendicular dropped from the vertex . . .' the voice announced spookily.

Sally swung herself out of bed and padded across the room. The whispering was coming from Irene's bed, but Irene herself was obviously fast asleep. '. . . of the right angle upon the hypotenuse, divides it into . . .' Irene muttered.

Sally shook her head. Irene was solving maths equations on her sleep! She stifled a giggle.

But then Sally heard a very different sound. A creak behind her, followed by footsteps. Sally whirled round, pressing herself into the shadows, heart thundering loudly. She saw the dorm door close as a figure in a hooded cloak slipped out. The *ghost*!

Sally rushed over and shook Darrell awake, careful to cover Darrell's mouth with her hand to stop her crying out. Darrell took one look at Sally's excited face and immediately grasped what was happening. 'Follow me,' Sally mouthed, grabbing the map.

Darrell nodded, and together the two girls crept out.

The figure was ahead of them down the corridor, and Darrell and Sally followed at a safe distance. The figure showed no sign of having seen them and began to hum a familiar song as she glided along.

'Where've I heard that song before?' Darrell whispered to Sally.

The figure turned down a corridor, and Sally frowned, studying the map. 'According to this, she should be taking the back stairs,' she murmured. 'She's going the wrong way.'

Next the figure had unlocked the entrance door and was leading them outside. Nervously Darrell and Sally followed.

'We'll be in ever so much trouble,' Sally groaned as they tracked the figure round to the back of the school.

'Only if we get caught!' Darrell replied.

At that moment she crunched a twig underfoot. The noise sounded as loud as an explosion in the still night air.

The figure turned, face shadowed by the hood. Swiftly Darrell and Sally ducked down out of sight behind a nearby hedge.

'Matron!' Darrell whispered as they crouched down

out of sight. 'I just remembered – she was humming that tune this morning. Could *she* be our ghost? She's spiteful enough to do it.'

'She does have access to the san,' Sally admitted.

Darrell peeked over the hedge. 'Wait, where is she?' she cried, disappointed. The figure had completely vanished.

Sally sighed. 'We lost her.'

'We'll try again tomorrow,' Darrell said, determined to solve the mystery.

Gwendoline was in the middle of her hobby presentation to the girls, Miss Potts and Miss Grayling. The presentation was titled 'Hairstyles Through the Ages', and Mary-Lou was her reluctant model.

'And then, in 1944, the bouffant style reached new heights,' Gwendoline declared, vigorously back-combing Mary-Lou's hair. Mary-Lou winced slightly. 'And so did the hair itself!'

The teachers chuckled as Gwendoline neatly arranged the front of Mary-Lou's hair into a high rounded shape. Most of the audience were enjoying Gwendoline's presentation, but at the back of the classroom Darrell and Sally were distracted. Gwendoline noticed them whispering, heads together, and scowled at them.

'Do you *really* think it's Matron?' Sally said, perplexed. 'She's frightened of ghosts.'

'A cover story?' Darrell suggested.

'But *why* would she do it?'

'Shhh!' Emily muttered.

Gwendoline glanced at her gratefully. 'Twirl, Mary-Lou!' she said under her breath. Dutifully Mary-Lou turned slowly round so that everyone could see her elaborate bouffant hairstyle.

'And that concludes my presentation!' Gwendoline announced. She curtsied, and everyone clapped.

'Lovely work, Gwendoline,' Miss Grayling said approvingly as Mary-Lou fiddled awkwardly with her huge hair.

'Perhaps you should liberate Mary-Lou from her bouffant,' Miss Potts said, much amused.

Gwendoline caught Mary-Lou's hand and pulled her towards the door, passing Darrell and Sally on the way. 'What were you whispering about me?' Gwendoline said accusingly. 'You almost ruined my presentation.'

'Sorry,' Darrell apologised. 'But not *everything's* about you, Gwen.'

'Fine,' Gwendoline snapped. 'Have your little secret. But I'm watching you!' And she hustled Mary-Lou out . . .

That night, when Gwendoline woke up just after 2 a.m., the dorm was silent, except for Irene muttering in her sleep. Gwendoline yawned and then sat bolt upright as she realised that Darrell's and Sally's beds were empty. Where were they?

Gwendoline hurried to the window, looked out and gave a gasp. 'Unbelievable!' she muttered.

Mary-Lou half woke up. 'Is it Lady Jane?' she asked groggily.

'Oh, hush!' Gwendoline said scornfully. 'There is no Lady Jane. But I just saw *Darrell* crossing the lawn. I knew she was the ghost!'

'Are you sure?' But Mary-Lou's eyes were already closing, and, seconds later, she was fast asleep again.

Gwendoline was now on a mission. She ran downstairs in her dressing gown and slippers and out of the unlocked door. To her intense surprise she saw that Darrell and Sally were following a figure in a hooded cloak round the side of the school. Gwendoline stole after them, keeping her distance.

The figure slipped through a side door, and, after a moment, Darrell and Sally cautiously followed. They found themselves back in the lobby, but, to their frustration, the figure had once again vanished.

'There must be another route to the san,' Darrell decided. 'One we don't know about.'

As Darrell and Sally searched around Gwendoline sidled in and hid among the shadows, listening and watching.

'That's strange,' Sally remarked. 'Look at that,

Darrell.' She pointed at a sock lying on the floor. But only half of it was visible, sticking out from underneath the wall next to the wooden fireplace carved with flowers and birds. Darrell attempted to pull the sock out, but it wouldn't budge.

'This can't be a *real* wall!' Darrell exclaimed. 'There must be a gap behind it. Could it be a secret panel?'

'If it is, there must be a way to open it,' said Sally. But when Darrell pushed eagerly at the wall, nothing moved.

'Hang on.' Sally leant towards the fireplace and pressed the carved flower closest to the wall. The panel swung silently open. Gwendoline, concealed in the shadows, let out a squeak, then clapped her hand over her mouth.

Darrell and Sally gazed at each other in excitement. 'A secret passage!' Darrell whispered, peering through the door into the darkness.

'I can hear footsteps,' Sally said. 'Quick, before we lose her!'

Gwendoline watched as the two girls disappeared through the open panel. Then she approached the secret door herself, peering fearfully into the darkness beyond. But when Gwendoline put her hand through, she shrieked and leapt backwards. *Cobwebs!*

No way was Gwendoline she going in there. Gwendoline turned to leave, but didn't notice the panel swinging gently back into place . . .

Darrell and Sally hurried along the secret passage. It was dark, damp, full of cobwebs and eerily silent, except for the sound of soft footsteps ahead of them. Then the two girls heard a loud click. Someone was unlocking a door at the end of the passage.

Sally and Darrell rushed towards the sound. There was a creak as the door was opened, and a sliver of light flooded the passage, silhouetting the figure in the cloak. She turned, lowering her hood.

'*Emily?*' Darrell gasped, stunned.

CHAPTER FIFTY-ONE

GWENDOLINE WAS knocking frantically at the door of the san. She kept knocking until Matron emerged in a fury, dressed up and ready to head out for the evening. 'I know it's late, but some of the girls are out of their beds!' Gwendoline gasped.

Matron eyed her ferociously. 'And they're not the only ones! Dorm! Now!'

'You have to come!' Gwendoline babbled. 'They've found a secret passage!'

'A likely story!' Matron sniffed. 'Where?'

'Beside the fireplace in the lobby,' Gwendoline replied, grabbing Matron's arm. 'Come on, I'll show you . . .'

Meanwhile, Darrell and Sally followed Emily through the door she'd unlocked and into the san.

'You!' Darrell gasped, still unable to believe her own eyes. '*You're* the ghost!'

'You shouldn't have followed me,' Emily said miserably.

'But why on earth have you been sneaking around?' asked Sally.

Emily looked agitated. 'You couldn't *possibly* understand.'

'Then perhaps we should explain it to them,' said a calm voice behind them.

They all turned to see Margaret standing in the doorway of Matron's room.

'All right, Mother,' Emily replied.

Darrell and Sally exchanged shocked glances. *Mother?*

Gwendoline was hurrying Matron down to the lobby, talking the whole time without ceasing. 'I told them it was a joke. I told them Darrell was the ghost! But no one would listen to me...' Triumphantly she led Matron over to the fireplace. 'The passage is right here by the—'

Gwendoline stopped dead, her face perplexed. She hadn't noticed the panel had shut behind her when she left. Now it looked like part of the wall. 'It's gone!' Gwendoline wailed.

Matron scowled. 'This is a merry wild goose chase you've led me on!'

'It *was* here, I promise you.' Gwendoline began tapping on the wall in frustration. She hadn't seen exactly how Sally had opened it from her hiding place in the shadows. 'I saw them go into it!'

'Enough of this nonsense!' Matron snarled. 'I'll be late for the pictures.' Frowning, she patted her pockets.

'And now I've gone and forgotten my keys.' She stared coldly at Gwendoline. '*Dorm!*' And Matron rushed back to the san, leaving a bewildered Gwendoline wondering if she'd been hallucinating . . .

'Why didn't you tell us Margaret was your *mother?*' Darrell asked Emily.

'You girls are different from us.' Margaret answered for her daughter. 'Your families have money. Your mothers don't work. I didn't want to bring Emily down.'

'But I'm *proud* of what you do,' Emily told her mother.

Margaret smiled. 'I made tea for Emily.' She headed towards the table. 'Let's all have some . . .' She picked up the milk jug but lost her grip on the handle. Emily jumped forward and caught the jug before it hit the table. 'Butterfingers,' Margaret said with an attempt at humour, but Darrell noticed that she was wincing and massaging her right hand with her left.

'Is something the matter?' asked Darrell.

'She's fine.' Emily sounded annoyed as she went over to the cupboard, took out a sewing-box and then picked up a heap of sheets. Glancing around the room, Sally noticed piles of folded darning.

'You've been coming here at night to help your mother with the mending,' Sally guessed.

'So that's why you're always tired!' Darrell said.

'Is she?' Margaret looked worried. 'I should have noticed. I'm sorry.'

'I never meant to scare anyone.' Emily bit her lip as she threaded her needle. 'I only wore the cloak to hide my face.'

'How come you and Matron were humming the same tune?' asked Sally.

'"Greensleeves"?' Emily shrugged, beginning to repair a jagged tear in one of the sheets. 'Matron hears it all the time because Mother hums it too.'

The door of the san opened, and Matron dashed in. She stopped short when she saw Margaret with the girls. And her eyebrows almost flew off the top of her head when she noticed Emily darning the sheet.

'I've been helping Mother with her chores, that's all!' Emily said defensively.

Matron rounded on Margaret. 'I knew you were lazy, but getting children to do your work?' she sneered. 'Have you no shame? You girls, back to bed immediately.' She stared sternly at Margaret. 'I'll deal with you in the morning.'

Emily put down her darning and rushed out of the san, distraught. Darrell and Sally hurried after her.

'Emily, wait!' Darrell called.

'You just couldn't mind your own business, could you?' Emily said tearfully. 'If Mother's fired, I don't know *what* we'll do. I have a free place at Malory

Towers because Mother works here. But if she loses her job . . .' Emily's voice wavered as she stumbled unhappily into the dorm.

'I didn't know,' Darrell said anxiously. 'I'll make it right.'

'You can't fix this!' Emily snapped. 'No one can.' She climbed into bed, pulling the covers over her head.

The others were all asleep, but Sally couldn't help noticing a pair of very dirty slippers by Gwendoline's bed. She pointed them out to Darrell. 'Do you think Gwendoline followed us and told Matron?' she whispered.

'No,' Darrell replied. 'Not even Gwendoline could do something so underhanded.' But secretly she wondered if Sally was right. 'We have to help Margaret,' Darrell went on as she took off her dressing gown. 'I promised Emily.'

'How?' asked Sally.

'I don't know,' Darrell said, 'but I'll think of something . . .'

As the sun peeked over the horizon the following morning Darrell woke up before everyone else. Feeling anxious, she headed straight for the san.

Margaret opened the door to her and smiled.

'Is Matron here?' Darrell whispered nervously.

'Not yet.' Margaret opened the door wider to let

Darrell in. 'Why?'

'I just wanted to explain to her why I was out of my bed last night,' Darrell replied. 'Then maybe Matron won't blame you.'

Margaret picked up the sheet she'd been folding. 'That's kind, Darrell. But if Matron doesn't believe I can do my job, why would she keep me on?'

Darrell noticed that Margaret's hands were stiff and swollen and she was struggling to fold the sheet. Darrell sprang forward to help. 'Is it arthritis?' she asked, taking one end of the sheet. 'My mother has it in her hips.'

Margaret looked surprised. 'You're quite the detective.'

'It gets me into trouble sometimes.' Darrell shrugged. 'No, *all* the time. Does Matron know?'

'No,' Margaret replied, 'and she mustn't. If I lose this job, I can't afford the doctor.'

'Surely a doctor wouldn't refuse to treat you if you couldn't pay,' Darrell argued.

'One day, I hope that's the case. Until then –' Margaret sighed – 'we soldier on.'

'If you just *told* Matron about your condition,' Darrell suggested, 'if you just *spoke* to her . . .'

'What "condition" is that?'

Matron had arrived and was standing in the doorway. Darrell could have bitten her tongue out. She stood there, reddening, as Matron stared at her enquiringly.

'Rheumatoid arthritis,' Margaret said quietly. 'In my hands.'

'You see?' Darrell burst out. 'Margaret *isn't* lazy! She just needs help.'

'I'm sorry about your illness.' Darrell was relieved to see that Matron appeared genuine. 'But what good is an assistant who can't use her hands?'

'Matron, please,' Margaret began.

'Your daughter can't take on your job, can she?' Matron pointed out reasonably. 'It's tiring the poor girl out.'

Margaret bit her lip.

'It's just as well term ends tomorrow,' Matron continued. 'I suggest you start packing. You will not be returning to Malory Towers next year.'

CHAPTER FIFTY-TWO

THE FOLLOWING day, all the girls except Gwendoline were sitting on the lawn, gathered round Emily and listening, riveted, to her tales of being the 'ghost'.

'You left the dorm *every* night,' Alicia said, impressed. 'You're my hero.'

'Practically a superhero,' Irene added.

'Why didn't you use the secret passage all along?' asked Darrell.

'On the main corridor?' Emily smiled. 'Anyone could have come along and seen me. I was always terrified when I went that way. But I chopped and changed my route to avoid discovery.'

'Who did you see on the stairs then, that night you hurt your ankle?' Jean wanted to know.

'No one.' Emily looked rather ashamed. 'I lied so I wouldn't get caught. I'm *so* sorry for frightening you, Mary-Lou.'

Mary-Lou grinned. 'I'm just glad Lady Jane's not real.'

'Can I borrow your cloak next year to scare the new girls?' Alicia chuckled. The others laughed.

Darrell had spotted Gwendoline in the distance, fussing with her hair ribbon, the frayed one that Emily had darned for her. Darrell scooted over to her. 'We could use your help, Gwen,' she said earnestly. 'We're trying to save Emily's mother.'

'I don't even know Emily's mother,' Gwendoline snapped.

'It's Margaret,' Darrell explained. 'Matron's fired her!'

'How awful!' Gwendoline said.

'Then you'll help?'

Gwendoline shrugged. 'Having a mother who works in the school, I meant,' she said snobbishly.

Darrell stared at her, trying to contain her disgust. 'Come to Miss Grayling with us and tell her how beastly Matron's been? Please, Gwen? After all, you played a part in all this . . .'

Gwendoline sniffed, secretly wondering how much Darrell knew about last night.

'If not for me, do it for Emily,' Darrell went on.

Gwendoline finished tying her ribbon and made no reply, but she cast a thoughtful glance at Emily . . .

Darrell knocked at Miss Grayling's door. Emily, Sally and Gwendoline were right behind her, although Gwendoline still looked rather reluctant.

Miss Grayling opened the door and looked out.

'May we speak to you, Miss Grayling?' Darrell asked.

But then, as the headmistress opened the door a little wider, Darrell saw Matron sitting in one of the armchairs. 'Alone?' Darrell added hastily.

'Without *me*, she means,' Matron snapped. 'The impertinence of this creature!'

'Every story has two sides.' Miss Grayling beckoned the girls into the study. 'Or four, as the case may be. Now,' she continued wearily, 'I'd like to keep this short. It's been a difficult day.'

'That's what we need to talk about,' Sally said.

'Margaret shouldn't have been fired!' Darrell blurted out loyally.

Matron snorted with disdain. 'I suppose now you're an expert on running a boarding school!'

Bravely Emily stepped forward. 'She's trying to fire my mother for having stiff and sore hands,' she explained.

'I didn't know your mother was sick.' Miss Grayling sounded surprised.

'Neither did I,' Matron chimed in.

'She's got rheumatoid arthritis,' Darrell pointed out.

Miss Grayling swung round to stare at Matron. 'You never noticed?'

'She's slippery, that one,' Matron said grumpily. 'And no doubt she was hiding it from me.'

'Because she thought you'd fire her!' Emily cried.

'And she was right,' Darrell added.

Miss Grayling massaged her temples. She appeared rather stressed. 'Your mother should have come to me, Emily,' she said. 'It was wrong of her to ask for your help.'

'She didn't ask,' Emily replied. 'I *insisted*.'

'I fired Margaret because she's unprofessional,' Matron said frostily.

'*You're* unprofessional!' Darrell couldn't stop the words flying to her lips.

'It's true,' Sally assured Miss Grayling earnestly. 'Matron didn't take my illness seriously until it was nearly too late.'

'And she gives Mother all her personal mending,' Emily said with an indignant expression. 'That's why she can't keep up.'

'Stuff and nonsense!' Matron blustered, cringing at the concerned look on Miss Grayling's face. 'Gwendoline will set this straight. Won't you, Gwendoline?'

Gwendoline hesitated. Then she shrugged eloquently and stayed silent.

'Emily, please go and fetch your mother,' Miss Grayling said. 'Matron,' she continued grimly, 'we need to talk.'

Half an hour later Emily was pacing nervously up and down outside Miss Grayling's study. Darrell was there too to give her some support.

Suddenly the door flew open, and Matron stomped out, obviously fuming. She was followed by Margaret. Emily gazed anxiously at her mother, and Darrell crossed her fingers.

'We're staying!' Margaret said happily.

'Oh, Mother!' Emily ran joyfully into her mother's arms while Darrell looked on, smiling and relieved . . .

Darrell and Emily couldn't wait to give the others the good news. That evening, after games, still wearing their kit, they all gathered in the dining hall for dinner, and Emily told them everything in detail. 'And, best of all, Miss Grayling's promoted Margaret to Matron of South Tower!' Emily finished proudly.

'You *can* call her "Mother" now,' Alicia said with a grin.

Emily beamed. 'Mother will have her own assistant too. Miss Grayling says they value her too much for her to leave.'

'Is Matron staying?' asked Sally.

'Yes, but she has to do everything *herself* now.' Emily pointed to Matron who was scrubbing rubbish bins in the corner.

'Darrell saved the day,' Mary-Lou said admiringly.

'We all did,' Darrell said, 'even Gwen.'

Gwendoline pulled a face. 'What do you mean, "even"?'

'Well, you didn't do much, Gwen, but we heard

you shrugged your shoulders,' Mary-Lou said, trying to be encouraging.

The others cracked up.

'How does that saying go?' Alicia mused. '"The shrug is mightier than the sword"?'

'Do you mean "the pen is mightier than the sword"?' Irene said.

Alicia rolled her eyes.

Gwendoline had had enough. She stood up and stormed out. Why were they always making fun of her? It was so unfair!

CHAPTER FIFTY-THREE

IT WAS the last day of term. Malory Towers was filled with the sound of joyful laughter and chatter as the girls looked forward to the holidays and to going home.

'Please!' Miss Potts yelled, weaving her way down the corridor between groups of giggling girls, her arms full of books. 'There might be no lessons today, but it's not a day off! Gather your things together and pack your trunks.'

Obediently Mary-Lou skipped into the first-form classroom. '*Malory Towers, Malory Towers, your cliff-top days and golden hours,*' she sang as she opened her desk to clear it. The first thing Mary-Lou noticed, however, was that her special pen was missing. She glanced around the room and let out a shocked cry. '*NO!*'

The other girls dashed in. They saw Mary-Lou kneeling on the floor, staring tearfully at the broken pieces of her pen surrounded by a pool of violet ink.

'But that's your courage pen!' Darrell gasped. 'Did you step on it?'

'N-no –' Mary-Lou gulped – 'I remember putting it in my desk yesterday after class.'

'Someone must have come in between then and now and smashed it,' Darrell said soberly.

'What a mean trick!' Emily said.

Alicia nodded. 'A nice bit of spite for you.'

Gwendoline was walking along the corridor and caught a snippet of the conversation. She paused outside the door.

'It can't have been deliberate,' Mary-Lou murmured, distressed.

'I'm afraid it was.' Katherine pointed to a footprint in violet ink next to the pen. 'See that pattern? Someone was wearing their games plimsolls when they stamped on the pen!'

'Who would do that?' Mary-Lou cried.

'It could have been anyone,' Jean pointed out. 'We'll never find out for sure.'

'Oh, yes, we will,' Alicia said firmly.

Gwendoline, listening in, moved a little closer, but kept out of sight.

'The culprit will have violet ink on their games plimsolls,' Alicia pointed out. Gwendoline's face was a picture of horror.

'You're right!' said Katherine. 'Quick, find the others and tell everyone to meet in the changing room so we can get to the bottom of this.'

Gwendoline fled. She hurtled into the changing room, grabbed her plimsolls from her locker and stared at the soles. They were covered in violet ink. In a panic Gwendoline thought frantically for a few moments and then her face cleared. *Yes!*

Stuffing the plimsolls into her kitbag, Gwendoline slung it over her shoulder and headed for the stationery cupboard. No one was around to see her select a bottle of violet ink and slip it into her pocket.

Next, Gwendoline rushed outside into the grounds. She rounded the corner and crashed straight into Ron who was trundling a wheelbarrow along. With a shriek of surprise Gwendoline lost her hold on the kitbag. It tumbled to the ground, her plimsolls peeping out. But when Ron helpfully tried to pick it up Gwendoline shoved him aside.

'Nosy parker!' Gwendoline said rudely and raced off.

The others were already gathering in the changing room. The mood was solemn, and no one was smiling.

'How to cast a cloud on the last day of term,' Alicia muttered.

'Until all this I didn't even *want* to go home,' Darrell said.

'At least you can.' Alicia heaved a sigh. 'Betty's people can't have me this time, so I'm stuck with Matron all summer!'

'Come and stay,' Darrell said impulsively. 'Mother said I could invite a special friend.' She didn't notice

Sally hear this and turn away, disappointed.

Alicia grinned. 'That'd be ace!'

Gwendoline arrived, out of breath. 'What's up?' she asked innocently, then gasped as she saw the shattered pen. Katherine had laid the pieces on a sheet of paper. 'Mary-Lou, isn't that your courage pen?'

Mary-Lou nodded miserably.

'Someone stamped on it,' Sally explained.

'What a beastly thing to do!' Gwendoline said with false sympathy.

'We're going to examine everyone's shoes,' said Katherine.

Gwendoline sat down on the bench. 'Check mine first, if you like.'

'Thanks, but it's your plimsolls we need.' Katherine indicated Gwendoline's locker. Gwendoline jumped up obligingly. As she opened her locker Gwendoline suddenly noticed a smudge of violet ink on her hand. Quickly she shoved the offending hand behind her back.

Katherine took out the plimsolls and studied them. They looked clean enough. 'You're clear, Gwen.' Katherine replaced the plimsolls while Gwendoline smiled smugly.

Katherine moved along, checking the lockers – Emily's, Sally's and then Darrell's. With a sharp intake of breath Katherine drew out a pair of plimsolls. One of them had a bright violet stain on the sole.

Horrified, the girls turned to Darrell. She was speechless.

'I don't believe it!' Sally said loyally.

Alicia bounded over and grabbed the plimsoll from Katherine to read the name inside. '*Darrell Rivers*,' Alicia said, raising her eyebrows.

'Well, well,' Gwendoline said, trying to hide her glee, 'who would have guessed?'

'But it wasn't me!' Darrell burst out.

The door was flung open.

'Honestly, girls!' Miss Potts was thoroughly exasperated. 'Matron's waiting in the dorm – your trunks should be packed by now. What are you doing in here?'

Subdued, the girls began filing out, Mary-Lou casting a hurt glance at Darrell. Only Sally and Darrell remained behind.

'Alicia!' Darrell called. But Alicia ignored her and followed the others out.

'Why did she walk away?' Distressed, Darrell turned to Sally. 'She's meant to be my friend!'

Sally shrugged. 'Then she'll stand by you.' She slid her arm round Darrell. 'I know you'd never do this. Someone's framed you. And we're going to find out who!'

CHAPTER FIFTY-FOUR

THE GIRLS were in the dorm, packing their trunks in strained silence under Matron's supervision. No one felt like talking much until Mary-Lou turned to Gwendoline.

'Gwen, is that a *cobweb* in your hair?' she asked.

Gwendoline shrieked, ignoring Matron's glare, and began frantically clawing at her hair. 'Is it gone?' she squealed.

Mary-Lou nodded. 'Poor Gwen,' she said sympathetically.

Miss Potts came in. 'I'll take over, Matron, while you fetch the girls' confiscated tuck.'

Alicia's face fell as Matron marched out. 'My hamper!' she groaned. 'We stole all that tuck back for the midnight feast. Matron'll make my summer hell!'

Darrell and Sally came into the dorm together. Gwendoline was utterly delighted to see how miserable Darrell looked.

'We've decided we'll hold a class court at lunchtime,' Katherine told Darrell. 'Then we can hear your side of the story and decide how to proceed.'

The bell in the corridor rang.

'Music!' Irene gasped. 'I forgot – we're supposed to be practising for final assembly!'

Irene raced off, and the others scrambled to follow her. In the melee Darrell caught Mary-Lou's arm.

'Mary-Lou, please believe me,' Darrell said earnestly. 'I would *never* do this to you.'

'Stop bullying Mary-Lou!' Gwendoline said sternly. She put her arm round Mary-Lou's shoulders and ushered her away.

Frustrated and hurt, Darrell followed the others to the common room, Sally quietly at her side.

Irene was already seated at the piano, Mary-Lou beside her. 'Mary-Lou, your solo!' she was saying when Darrell and Sally arrived. 'One, two, three!'

Mary-Lou opened her mouth, but no sound came out. She cleared her throat and tried again. Nothing happened. 'I can't sing when I'm upset,' Mary-Lou said tearfully. 'I think Emily should sing the solo.'

Immediately Emily shook her head, coughed loudly and pointed at her throat.

Irene frowned at her, puzzled.

'We can't let this pen business take away her new-found courage!' Emily whispered to Irene.

Irene nodded understandingly. 'Emily can't sing, Mary-Lou,' she said firmly. 'She's lost her voice. We NEED you!'

'Come on, Mary-Lou,' Darrell encouraged her. 'You know you can do it!'

Mary-Lou took a breath, but before she could sing a note Gwendoline leapt in. 'You're *such* a bully, Darrell Rivers!' she said accusingly. 'Piling pressure on Mary-Lou! She's clearly not up to it.'

Mary-Lou's face crumpled. She dashed from the room, and, frustrated, Irene played a loud, clashing chord. 'Thanks, Gwen!' she said sarcastically.

Emily hurried after Mary-Lou, and the others followed, but Sally caught Darrell's hand and held her back.

'You know, whoever smashed that pen didn't want to hurt Mary-Lou,' Sally pointed out. 'They wanted to hurt *you*.'

'But who?' asked Darrell.

'Gwen's had it in for you all term,' Sally said quietly. 'And she's the one doing all the blaming.'

'Yes, but it's just my word against hers,' Darrell said. 'And my plimsolls ARE covered in ink.'

'But we know you didn't smash that pen. So the shoes that smashed it must be *somewhere*. Let's at least *try* to find them!' Sally suggested. 'I'll search the changing room. You stay and look around here.'

Once in the changing room Sally went straight to Gwendoline's locker. She took out the clean plimsolls Katherine had checked and examined them more closely.

What was the name inside? Sally squinted at the small label, and her face broke into a beaming smile. *Yes!*

The girls gathered in the dorm for the class court, perching on their trunks. The beds had been stripped and their possessions packed away.

'Quiet, please!' Katherine said. She had the evidence, Darrell's ink-stained plimsoll, in front of her. 'We have an hour until final assembly.'

Eagerly Sally held up the plimsolls she'd found in Gwendoline's locker. 'The shoes in Gwen's locker weren't hers!' she said. 'Look!'

Gwendoline raised her eyebrows. She wasn't worried. She had everything worked out.

Katherine read out the name inside the plimsolls. '*Josie Lucas.*'

'Ooh, I know her—' Emily began. Irene jabbed her in the ribs and nodded at Mary-Lou. Emily pretended to cough. 'She's a third year!' she whispered as the girls passed the shoes around, examining the soles.

'I lost my plimsolls weeks ago and borrowed these from lost property,' Gwendoline said coolly. 'We've all done it.'

'I'm afraid these don't prove anything,' Katherine said apologetically to Sally.

Disappointed, Sally mouthed *sorry* at Darrell who gave her a sad but grateful smile.

'Who's speaking first?' Katherine asked. Darrell stood up, but Gwendoline got in first.

'*I* will,' Gwendoline said bossily. 'Mary-Lou's too scared – and I don't blame her.'

'Scared of what?' Darrell asked.

'You and your beastly temper!' Gwendoline retorted. 'We all know what you're like – you pushed a teacher down the stairs. *And* you *slapped* me in the pool. You should be in a remedial school, not just a class!'

Darrell clenched her fists in utter frustration. 'That's not true!' she cried.

'See?' Gwendoline said complacently. 'The Rivers temper strikes again! True colours revealed!'

Desperate to be believed, Darrell stared around at the girls she thought were her friends. But everyone except Sally was watching her warily.

CHAPTER FIFTY-FIVE

'OH, MY stars!' Matron exclaimed. She was in the san collecting the confiscated property together, and she'd just brought down Alicia's hamper. It felt strangely light, and, opening it, Matron understood why. It was empty!

'What happened to all that tuck, Matron?' asked Miss Potts, coming into the san.

'Gone!' Matron said dramatically.

Miss Potts chuckled. 'Mice?'

'Girls,' Matron said grimly. 'Alicia Johns in particular.'

'Isn't she staying here all summer?' said Miss Potts. 'Poor Alicia . . .'

In the dorm Gwendoline was enjoying herself hugely. Tossing back her hair, she pointed an accusing finger at Darrell. 'This pen-smashing is part of a campaign that Darrell's been waging for some time,' she announced.

'Of course it isn't,' Darrell said.

'Campaign?' Alicia repeated.

'The spider in Mary-Lou's desk.' Gwendoline ticked

the items off on her fingers. 'Her tennis racquet strings – cut. Her games kit left in a puddle of water.' She turned on Darrell. 'You hated it when Mary-Lou rescued you from drowning. It made you look a fool. This is your revenge!'

'Darrell's not the sort to take revenge,' Jean said uncertainly.

'No,' Alicia agreed. 'But she *is* a hothead.'

'She's fiery, but not scheming,' Irene said. 'Isn't she?' Suddenly her tone was doubtful.

'The truth is, I'm scared of you too, Darrell Rivers,' Gwendoline said maliciously. 'I don't feel safe in a school with you in it.'

Looking at the expressions on the other girls' faces, Darrell suddenly felt very lost and alone. She went over to her bed and sat down. Sally followed her while the other girls huddled together, talking in low voices.

'We can prove what Gwen's saying isn't true,' Sally whispered. 'Explain that the swimming-pool rescue was just to give Mary-Lou confidence. Alicia will back you up.'

Darrell shook her head. 'No, I can't do that to Mary-Lou. It'll destroy her confidence more than ever.'

'Come on, where's your temper when you need it most?' Sally urged her. 'Keep fighting!'

But Darrell's shoulders slumped even lower. She had

no fight left in her. Quietly she got to her feet and walked out of the dorm.

Outside Darrell leant against the gardener's potting-shed, looking up at the beautiful view of Malory Towers in front of her. She'd been so happy here, but now her heart was aching.

'Smile,' said a familiar voice. 'It might never happen.'

'I think it already has.' Darrell attempted to smile at Ron who'd arrived with his wheelbarrow. 'I messed up. My parents will be so disappointed.'

Ron looked bewildered.

'I think I'm about to be *asked to leave*,' Darrell added with a heavy sigh.

'Why? What've you done?'

'Nothing.' Darrell shrugged. 'But I can't prove it. And nearly all the people I thought were my friends believe the other girl, not me.'

'Which girl's pointing the finger at you?' Ron asked curiously.

'Gwen,' Darrell replied. 'Blonde, pretty, hates sport and water and—'

'Spiders!' said Ron.

'*What?*'

'She made me catch a spider for her,' Ron explained, 'couple of weeks back . . .'

'Ron, thank you!' Darrell gasped, eyes suddenly

shining with relief. 'That's more helpful than you'll ever know!'

Re-energised, Darrell rushed back to the dorm and burst in.

'*There* you are!' Katherine said sternly. 'We were waiting. Final assembly is in ten minutes.'

'I didn't do any of those things Gwen's accused me of,' Darrell panted, 'but I know who did. *Gwendoline herself!*'

'Me?' Gwendoline drew herself up, highly affronted. 'I'm Mary-Lou's best friend!'

'Then why put a spider in her desk?' Darrell shot back.

'That was *you!*' Gwendoline glared at her. 'Revenge for smashing your picture frame.'

'Don't lie!' Darrell said. 'Ron told me – he caught that spider for you!'

The other girls began whispering to each other.

'Mary-Lou, you know how much I hate spiders,' Gwendoline said earnestly. 'You know I can't even bear a cobweb in my hair. I could never have put a spider *anywhere*. Tell them!'

Mary-Lou stared at Gwendoline, confused.

'It's nearly three,' Katherine said, glancing at the clock. 'Time to vote. Mary-Lou, stand here next to me.' She looked round in surprise. 'Where *is* Mary-Lou?'

Mary-Lou had slipped away without being noticed. She ran outside and along the shadowy garden paths calling 'Ron! *Ron!*'

Ron popped out unexpectedly from behind a bush, almost frightening Mary-Lou to death. 'I thought you *wanted* to see me!' he said, bemused, when she let out a frightened little yelp.

'I do,' a flustered Mary-Lou replied. 'Gwen, the girl who was catching spiders – was she out here this morning?'

'Yes,' Ron replied, 'She and her kitbag sent me flying!'

'Kitbag?' Mary-Lou repeated, eyes wide. Then she gulped. 'Could you *possibly* show me where she found that spider, Ron?'

In the dorm the vote had begun.

'Those who think Darrell's guilty, stand on my left, please,' Katherine said gravely. 'Those who think she's innocent, stand with Darrell on my right.'

Sally immediately joined Darrell as Gwendoline, nose in the air, went to Katherine's left. Jean hesitated, then walked towards Gwendoline. Irene looked from one group to the other and then moved towards Darrell. Emily followed her.

'Three for us, two for Gwen,' Sally whispered hopefully to Darrell. But then her face fell as Katherine cast her vote with Gwendoline and Jean. Now it was even.

'Alicia?' said Katherine.

338

Alicia waited a moment. Then, shrugging, she turned towards Gwendoline.

'How could you?' Darrell cried, feeling betrayed. 'I thought you were my friend!'

'The evidence is there,' Alicia replied coolly. 'And I think you're capable of anything in a fury.'

'Three for Darrell and four against,' Katherine announced. 'Everyone – down to assembly, please. And, Darrell –' Katherine's tone was solemn – 'please come with me to Miss Grayling.'

Darrell nodded mutely. She was shivering with shock as she followed Katherine across the dorm.

'Do you think she'll be expelled?' Jean asked, aghast.

'I hope so!' Gwendoline said spitefully, thrilled with the astounding success of her plan. 'Anyone with a temper like that doesn't deserve to be at Malory Towers.'

'You know what?' Darrell turned in the doorway with a flash of her old spirit. 'If you all think I'm as mean as that, I'd rather leave anyway . . .'

Ron threw open the door of the potting-shed, and Mary-Lou hesitated, peering into the cobwebby darkness.

'Spiders galore!' Ron grinned. 'What size do you want?'

'About size thirteen,' Mary-Lou replied.

Ron shot her a confused look. 'I'll be in trouble if I don't get on,' he muttered.

'It's all right,' Mary-Lou said. 'You go.'

After Ron left Mary-Lou summoned up the courage to enter the potting-shed. It was quite dark inside, but Mary-Lou was sure she could see something poking from underneath the pot Ron had pointed out to her. Taking a deep breath, she flipped the pot over and let out an ear-splitting shriek . . .

Inside school, Katherine was knocking on Miss Grayling's door. Gwendoline stood triumphantly next to her, and behind them was Darrell, pale and trembling.

'Sorry, Miss Grayling,' Katherine said, opening the door, 'but we need an urgent word before assembly.'

'One moment, please, Katherine,' Miss Grayling said, continuing to write at her desk.

The other girls were heading to assembly when an excited Mary-Lou raced up to them.

'Look what I found!' Mary-Lou squealed. She waved a plimsoll, the sole covered in violet ink. 'It's Gwen's!'

Sally understood immediately. 'She hid her shoes and borrowed Josie's to cover up!' She glanced down at Darrell's inky plimsoll clutched in her hand. Sally had grabbed it before leaving the dorm.

'Gwen's the pen-smasher!' Irene said, round-eyed.

Alicia frowned. 'Is she, though? We just have *two* pairs of shoes and *two* possible culprits.'

'Hang on,' Emily said, holding her hands out for the shoes. 'Give me those.'

Mary-Lou gaped at her. 'I thought you'd lost your voice?'

'Yes, and I'll lose it again after this!' Emily replied. She turned both plimsolls over. 'Someone has *poured* ink over Darrell's. Look, the drips run *up*. That couldn't happen if you stamped on something. Now, this other shoe *did* stamp on the pen. Look at the ink splashes.'

They all peered at the name inside the shoe.

Gwendoline Mary Lacey.

CHAPTER FIFTY-SIX

SALLY AND the others immediately rushed to Miss Grayling's study where Katherine, Gwendoline and Darrell were still waiting outside.

'Katherine!' Sally gasped, holding out Gwendoline's shoe. Gwendoline turned pale when she saw it. 'We've uncovered new evidence!'

'It's a bit late for that,' Katherine began.

'But this changes everything!' Mary-Lou said breathlessly. 'The pen-smasher *isn't* Darrell!'

'It's *Gwendoline*!' Sally announced.

'It is not!' Gwendoline wailed as Darrell's knees shook uncontrollably with relief.

'Really?' Emily said sternly. She thrust the shoe at Gwendoline, pointing at the name inside.

'The only person who should be expelled is *you*!' Irene said.

Gwendoline collapsed in floods of tears, just as Miss Grayling's door opened.

'Goodness!' the headmistress exclaimed, surprised. 'What's happened? Gwendoline?'

'I'm so sorry, Miss Grayling,' Katherine said, 'we've

had a rather unfortunate end-of-term drama—'

'And we thought we might need your help, but we've managed to sort it out ourselves,' Darrell interrupted quickly. The others gazed at her in amazement, and Gwendoline's tears dried up as if by magic. 'Sorry to bother you, Miss Grayling.'

The headmistress eyed them all keenly for a moment, then shut the door again.

'Gwendoline!' Katherine was stern. 'How *can* you have been so deceitful?'

Gwendoline gulped and began crying again.

'Sorry, Darrell,' Jean said fervently.

'Me too,' Katherine said.

Alicia couldn't meet Darrell's eye. 'And me.'

'That's all right,' Darrell said generously. 'I suppose the evidence *did* look suspicious.'

Irene glanced at Gwendoline who was still sobbing. 'Why did you let her off the hook?'

'Everyone deserves a second chance,' Darrell replied. 'Malory Towers gave me one! But, Gwen, somehow you have to make it up to Mary-Lou . . .'

'You do the solo for me,' Mary-Lou told Emily as the girls gathered onstage for final assembly. 'You don't have to fake a sore throat!'

'I don't want to sing,' Emily replied firmly. 'You have a *much* better voice.'

'No, I don't,' Mary-Lou began.

'Yes, you DO!' Emily and Irene chorused.

Alicia left Betty and crossed the stage to Darrell, who was standing with Sally. 'Sorry about earlier,' Alicia said sheepishly. 'No hard feelings?'

Darrell smiled. 'The invitation to visit is still open,' she said. 'If you'd like . . . ?'

Alicia broke into a huge grin. 'Would I!' She held out her hand. 'Come and stand with me and Betty?'

'Actually, I'm in a three with Sally and Mary-Lou now,' Darrell replied, and Alicia looked taken aback.

There were only a few moments left to the start of the assembly when Darrell noticed that Gwendoline was missing from the stage. Slipping away, Darrell went to search for her. Finally she found Gwendoline, eyes red-rimmed, sitting outside, trying and failing to plait her hair.

'Potty will have a fit if you miss final assembly,' Darrell warned her.

Gwendoline sniffed. 'I can't face them all.'

'You can!' Darrell said encouragingly, beginning to plait Gwendoline's hair. 'We're giving each other second chances. You just have to work out why you do mean things . . .'

'All I want is a best friend,' Gwendoline muttered. 'But Mary-Lou adores *you*!'

'But I don't WANT to be adored!' Darrell said, tying

Gwen's ribbons. 'Friends are people who know you and can speak honestly. You're not a bad sort – you just let vanity get in the way.'

The bell sounded inside school.

'Quick!' Darrell hauled Gwendoline to her feet. 'We'll be late!'

The two girls just made it on to the stage before Irene struck up the first chords on the piano. The hall was now packed with an audience of girls and teachers.

Irene glanced at Mary-Lou. 'Ready?'

Mary-Lou nodded nervously. As Irene played the introduction, Darrell and Sally held Mary-Lou's hands as she launched into her solo:

> *'Four tall towers,*
> *The train blasts steam*
> *Oh, that cliff corner view*
> *Of the school of our dreams!'*

The other girls joined in.

> *'Four tall towers*
> *That teach us how to strive,*
> *To be women the world can lean on,*
> *Women who will thrive . . .*
> *Malory Towers, Malory Towers!'*

After final assembly the girls spilled out on to the drive, lugging their trunks down the steps. Cars were already parked, and parents were searching for their daughters. The coach had also arrived to ferry those who were going home by train to the railway station. Everyone was in high spirits, yelling goodbyes to each other, and Miss Grayling stood on the steps, waving them off.

'Young lady!' Matron nodded at Alicia when they met in the lobby. 'I need a word.'

Alicia gulped. Matron was carrying her birthday hamper. 'Open it!' Matron instructed, dumping the hamper on a table.

Quaking, Alicia did as she was told. Her eyes almost fell out of her head with shock. The hamper was crammed to the brim with delicious tuck – cake, biscuits, sweets and other goodies.

'I don't understand!' Alicia gasped, bewildered.

Matron smiled. 'You and I have a *long* summer together. Happy belated birthday, Alicia.'

'Thank you, Matron.' And Alicia gave her the most enormous hug.

'Get on with you now!' Matron said, trying to hide her pleasure. Alicia opened a box of sweets and offered her a lemon sherbet. Matron took it, and they smiled at each other.

Meanwhile, Gwendoline was searching for Mary-Lou. She was outside on the steps, saying goodbye to Darrell.

'Mary-Lou, this is yours now,' Gwendoline said solemnly, presenting Mary-Lou with her prized hairbrush.

'But – it's your special brush!' Mary-Lou began.

'It's not a pen, but a hundred strokes a night might give you courage,' said Gwendoline.

Mary-Lou was touched. 'Thank you.'

Darrell smiled. 'Next term, let's put all this behind us, Gwen, and start afresh,' she said warmly, holding out her hand. 'Pax?'

Gwendoline shook Darrell's hand. 'Pax!' she agreed.

However, Darrell had no idea that Gwendoline had the fingers of her other hand crossed behind her back . . .

Darrell raced off, jumped down the last few steps and dashed over to Sally. She was waiting on the drive with her trunk.

'Aren't you coming on the coach?' asked Darrell.

'Mother's bringing the car,' Sally replied, 'because of my operation.'

'Oh, no!' Darrell's face fell. 'I hoped we could talk.'

'We'll write,' Sally assured her.

'Write?' Darrell repeated. 'You have to *visit*!'

Sally glowed with happiness. 'Really? I heard you ask Alicia—'

'Alicia's great fun,' Darrell broke in, 'but *you're* the one I can count on.' She blushed, suddenly shy. 'You're the best!'

'You too!'

The two girls hugged each other warmly, then Darrell hopped on to the steps of the coach.

Suddenly a strong breeze whisked her straw boater from her head and whirled it away. It got caught in the lower branches of one of the trees, and Sally ran to retrieve it. 'No torn dresses today!' Sally teased, and Darrell grinned, remembering their very first day.

As soon as Darrell had seated herself next to Mary-Lou, the coach moved off. Lacrosse sticks and boaters were waved from the open windows, and there were shouts of 'Goodbye! See you next term!'

Darrell spotted Ron waving at her and gave him a thumbs up as the coach pulled away. Joining enthusiastically in the school song, Darrell turned and watched the four towers surrounded by the glittering sea and the towering cliffs until they were completely out of sight.

It had been a tumultuous first year, that was for sure. But she'd come through it all, Darrell reminded herself joyfully. And although she was looking forward immensely to the summer holidays, she knew that Malory Towers would be waiting for her to return next term.

'Goodbye, Malory Towers!' Darrell whispered. 'See you again very soon . . .'